AF557796

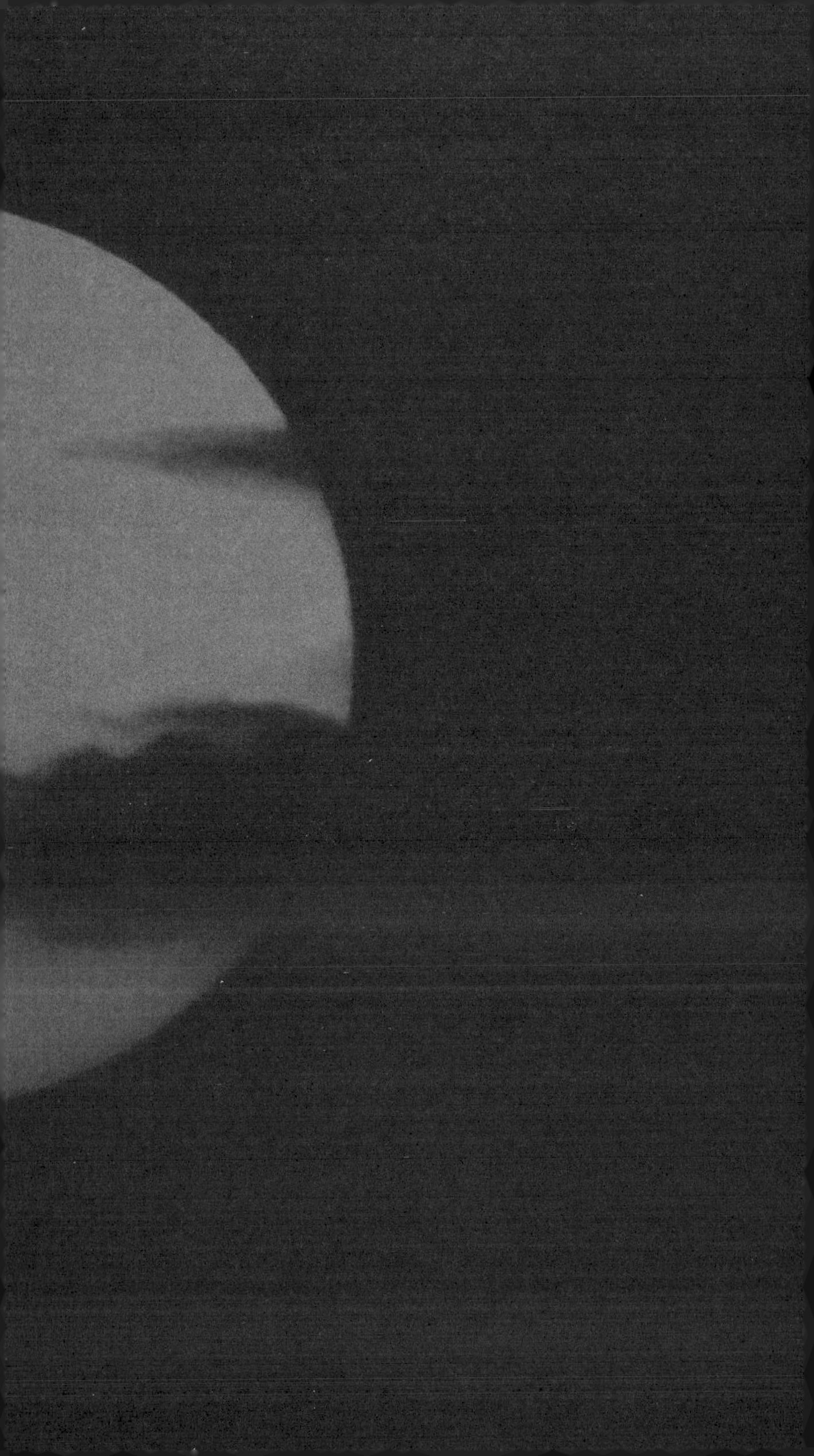

FALLEN CITY

Other Books by Sudeep Chakravarti

HISTORY, CULTURE, GOVERNANCE, CONFLICT

The Eastern Gate: War and Peace in Nagaland, Manipur and India's Far East (2022)

Plassey: The Battle that Changed the Course of Indian History (2020)

The Bengalis: A Portrait of a Community (2017)

Clear.Hold.Build: Hard Lessons of Business and Human Rights in India (2014)

Highway 39: Journeys through a Fractured Land (2012)

Red Sun: Travels in Naxalite Country (2008)

NOVELS

The Baptism of Tony Calangute (2018)

The Avenue of Kings (2010)

Tin Fish (2005)

ANTHOLOGY

The Other India (ed.) (2000)

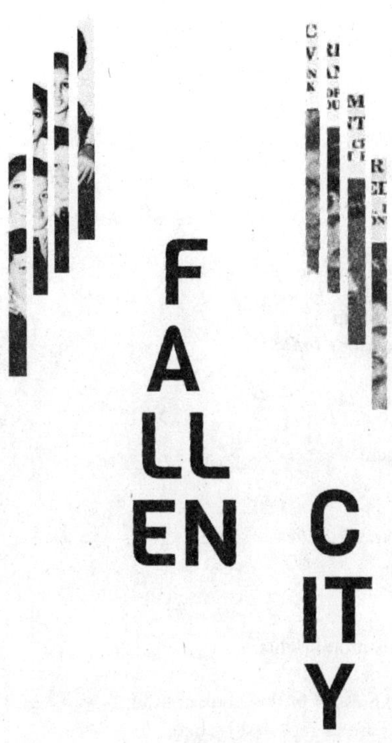

FALLEN CITY

A DOUBLE MURDER, POLITICAL INSANITY, AND DELHI'S DESCENT FROM GRACE

SUDEEP CHAKRAVARTI

ALEPH

ALEPH BOOK COMPANY
An independent publishing firm
promoted by ***Rupa Publications India***

First published in India in 2024
by Aleph Book Company
7/16 Ansari Road, Daryaganj
New Delhi 110 002

ISBN: 978-81-19635-17-7

1 3 5 7 9 10 8 6 4 2

Printed in India.

For Aruna and George

CONTENTS

A NOTE ON READING *FALLEN CITY*

A crime often has several versions as news of it breaks. Back in the 1970s the versions sometimes took several weeks, even months, to streamline or reconcile into a credible whole from media reports, speculation by both official sources and media, and court papers.

While this book draws on all such sources to present as real-time a feel as possible, for contentious matters it relies on judgements of various courts that present evidence as a part of both judicial arguments and as annexures.

Spellings of cities reflect the older, Anglicized versions. For instance, Bombay, Madras, Calcutta, and so on, marking a time before they were renamed Mumbai, Chennai, and Kolkata.

Readers of my books will know that I sometimes inject a personal element in my writing: as reportage, and also as elements drawn from experience. Journey with me.

S. C.

PROLOGUE

When Geeta and Sanjay Chopra were killed on a Saturday in late August 1978, I was a student of Class 10.

My relatively sheltered existence at a boarding school in Ajmer was a world away from New Delhi. In that bubble of privilege on some days it seemed like a world away from India.

As an unabashed bookworm and 'general knowledge' junkie, I was among a tribe that thronged the school's well-stocked library. It remained open on all days except Sunday. On Saturdays we had more library time.

Saturdays were special in this residential school as in several similar schools. It usually brought a lighter load of classes, a special dinner, and movie night. After the screening on a 16 mm projector, we would return in the dark to our dormitories and rooms by torchlight. Our torches were usually Eveready—it was 'the best your money can buy', as advertisements reminded us—powered by Eveready batteries; or the homegrown Geep brand. We critiqued the plot of the movie or spoke in awe or dismissal of the 'heroes', 'heroines', and 'vamps' and 'villains'. Most of us walked to the movie screening and back. Some of us rode prized BSA, Avon, or Hero cycles.

In the throes of the somewhat anti-transnational policymaking by the Janata Party government in power at the time, some of us would look forward to special permission on weekends to visit 'town', beyond the boundaries of school, to walk about, eat non-school food, and to consume soft drinks that were born after the Coca-Cola Company chose to leave India instead of carrying on with the Janata government's mandated dilution of foreign majority ownership in local businesses, and risk leaking its 'secret' formula as a result. So, instead of Coke and Fanta we now had homegrown Campa Cola along with Campa's orange and lemon flavours that stood in competition to Parle's Thums Up, Gold Spot, and Limca; and Double Seven, a trying government-owned concoction in celebration of the Janata's electoral victory in 1977.

That Saturday, 26 August, had been special for another reason. News had arrived in the morning that the Indian cricket team would visit Pakistan later in the year for a test series; news relayed by small 'transistor' radios and radios in en vogue 2-in-1s—part cassette recorder, part radio, all mojo. News was passed on by some students who possessed these gadgets and dispensed such 'live' information with the mien of Orwellian overlords.

The cricket madness in us was overshadowed by joy for the success of some of our own. News had also arrived from Delhi of three divers from school—Shivesh Ram, Mahipal Singh, and Mahavir Singh—winning their age-group categories at a national springboard and platform diving championship. We would read of it in the library two days later the following Monday, on account of the time Delhi papers took to arrive by train, and the intervening holiday on Sunday.

To our Anglicized middle-class minds on the make, airline advertisements were a favourite. Even with all the world's airlines enticing us to be a part of the jet set, we were proud of our own chariot in the skies—Air India—and its grand offers. After all, it seemed stylish if, on our way to America on some fantastic trip, we could drop in to several European cities, one on the way, and a different one on the way back. The visual of a portly Maharaja in pinstripes descending on Europe with his landing made soft with an unfurled umbrella was compelling. As was the offer of five 'fascinating and swinging' cities to pick from—London, Paris, Geneva, Rome, or Frankfurt, arrayed like destinations on a bottle of forbidden perfume.

However, before a week had passed, my friends and I—indeed, the entire school—would discuss little else besides the brutal deaths in Delhi of Geeta and Sanjay, two siblings not much older than us.

In some ways we were primed with unease. Jaipur, Rajasthan's capital and the biggest city near us that we occasionally visited for its museums, forts, and restaurant treats along its landmark M.I. Road (Mirza Ismail Road) had its own ghastly moment earlier in the year. A local businessman's son had been abducted from the Adarsh Nagar neighbourhood, not far from the lavish Rambagh Palace Hotel. The boy was later found murdered. The case, a part of our ghoulish fascination with someone like us, remained unsolved.

Now Geeta and Sanjay's deaths had brought back that darkness.

■

We weren't exactly strangers to violence. In some ways we were even inured to it, meanwhile reciting Mohandas Gandhi's creed of non-violence as a prayer at Assembly each morning, as if that would keep at bay a land awash in institutionalized indignities of caste, poverty, and religion, and the blood of engineered enemies.

India and its capital so often seemed cloaked in a darkness that appeared determined to derail the fantasy of a country so dramatically broken free of the colonial yoke to chart its own version of a brave new world. Caste-related crimes were horrific, daily news. Uttar Pradesh had yet again topped the national charts for atrocities against Dalits. The Partition and its horrors were three decades in the past, but the poisoned chalice of our forebears was still an easy sip away. For so many of us from India, in a swathe from Kashmir and Punjab to the northwest all the way east to Uttar Pradesh, Bihar, Bengal, and even Assam, the scripted, unbridled hatred between Hindu and Muslim, the anger and despair over lived and dramatized tales of lost homes and lost lives were regurgitated at family gatherings as both litany and holy writ for worshipping brutalized lives and, courtesy of some relatives, for continuing hatred against the religious other who were blamed for brutalizing such lives.

Within days of Geeta and Sanjay's death, religious violence would flame on in southern India, and we worried if the fires would spread elsewhere via this apocalyptic weather system. The southern metropolis of Hyderabad, the uneasy capital of Andhra Pradesh which several school friends called home, hadn't been the same since that March when Muslim–Hindu rioting broke out. Trouble would flare up again on 3 September, and another stretch of curfew—the third already in the year—would blanket large parts of the old city.

The year 1978 was beginning to resemble 1948, when Hyderabad had witnessed widespread violence as the government of India took over the city and the territory of a nizam reluctant to join the post-Partition Indian union. It had got so bad that India's president, Neelam Sanjiva Reddy, remarked on it. 'It is my hope,' Reddy would tell media, 'that all sane people will help in restoration of normalcy.'

■

Violence did not always need the concocted hatred of caste and religion. It also came with political ideology, and its ideas of supremacy and inferiority.

As a child I had seen raw, runaway left-wing violence in Kolkata in the 1970s and the equally raw, unfettered state counter. My sibling and I saw blood on the streets. People we knew disappeared, or were disappeared. The cries of the tortured from a police station across the street from our home, in a genteel neighbourhood near Jadavpur University, reverberated in our young-old minds.

With the imposition of the Emergency in 1975, we had seen the cowing of India by Indira Gandhi, seen how newspapers in our school's library changed their look and tone as if by Orwellian magic (yes, the library also contained *1984*). Only the comics pages and children's supplements remained the same—a polite façade, like conversations with our parents and families when we went home on vacation; or when some teachers hushed us if we asked awkward questions about the occasional blank sections in newspapers—as we learnt, left blank in potent protest against government censors. We were witness to a democracy in meltdown. Some of us wondered about what was in store for us in a country that so prided itself for breaking away from the depredations and repression of the British and for demanding freedom and freedom of expression as birth rights—indeed, such sentiment was de rigueur in school curricula in books of history and 'civics'. And yet, here we were, with the entire country deprived of freedoms to save one leader, her family, and her party.

In 1976, more than a year into the Emergency, famously iron-fisted Indira visited my school for its centenary celebrations. Like several hundred students I too was made to line up along freshly tarred and gravel-lined roads on campus to welcome the prime minister as she alighted from an Indian Air Force helicopter onto one of our cricket fields. She was then driven in an open-topped limousine of a former maharaja, an alum, to the venue where the function would take place—Bikaner Pavilion. It was named after the benefactor, an erstwhile 'princely state'. There, she made a speech and gave away prizes in front of enthralled or uneasy schoolchildren, their parents, staff, and alumni.

That grandeur ended less than a year later when Indira presumptively did away with the Emergency, thinking she would win the elections after India led two years of its life in rigorously imposed undertone.

Then we saw anger against an empress, anger against all the horrors of the Emergency imposed by her, and enforced by Sanjay, her younger son and heir apparent.

One day in that spring of 1977, I saw Indira Gandhi riding a donkey. Some friends and I had been on the roof of our dormitory—'dorm'—just chatting in the brief lull in the 'timetable' between lunch and sports—'games'—idly feeding on jungle jalebi (sweet-sour fruit from a species of acacia). The boundary of our 'house' was in this case also the boundary of school. A narrow road lay across the wall.

We heard a knot of people. They were moving in our direction. When they came close, women, men, girls, and boys, we saw they had rigged up a framed photo of Indira on a ragtag saddle, on a donkey. That day she wore a necklace of old and broken sandals and shoes. They were hurling invectives at her likeness, they were laughing, singing songs with bawdy lyrics.

'Indira Gandhi hai-hai,' they jeered.

One lanky boy spat on her photo.

Indira on a donkey was a memory so firmly etched, and of such transformative force, that it decanted into a scene in my first book, *Tin Fish*, a bildungsroman, alongside other examples of long-suppressed surprise, shock, and a seemingly infinite catharsis from a time of the crass, the corrosive, the confounding and, sometimes, the comical.

Here was Indira—some likenesses even portrayed her as a goddess in Durga Puja celebrations in the year following India's massive victory in the war with Pakistan in 1971—brought to earth by her subjects.

That day we learned about the rise and fall of empires.

There would soon be more such lessons right in our neighbourhood. Zulfikar Bhutto, a co-architect of Pakistan's genocide against East Pakistan in 1971, and co-signee of a peace treaty with India and Indira, was swept from power in a military coup, and hanged. Mohammad Reza Pahlavi, the lavish and brutal Shah of Iran, was swept from power by bands of rampant Islamists who quickly demonstrated they were far from angels of mercy. Next door, in brand new Bangladesh, the iconic Sheikh Mujibur Rahman, the country's first prime minister, had been assassinated along with most of his family in a military coup, less than two months after the imposition of the Emergency in India.

There was great churn and brutality everywhere one turned. In Delhi, across India, over in the immediate neighbourhood. The shadows over our young lives had grown more pronounced.

▪

Indira would soon lose the elections in a landslide to a coalition led by the Janata Party. That storm system, for a time the primary one among so many competing storm systems that beset the capital and country, had brewed for a while, and found life force in the oppressive heat of the Emergency and the upheaval in the summer of 1977 that saw Indira, her rampant younger son, Sanjay, and their cohorts unceremoniously swept from power.

But after the near-shambolic Janata government's suicidal politics, blunders, and its eventual implosion, Indira came back ever more imperious in 1980. Her younger son was back too, now elected as a member of parliament, a heavy-handed princeling with his own court and equally heavy-handed courtiers who had run riot for two years as the bleeding edge of the Emergency. All the exposed villains of the Emergency arrived with them, energized, ironically, by an electorate jaded into hitting the reset button, perhaps hoping that lessons learnt from being dethroned would teach India's political first family about being careful of what they now did to retain power.

And so, we learned of the fall and rise of empires.

■

The Middle-earth that Geeta and Sanjay inhabited away from this visceral ebb and flow, the world of the middle- to upper-middle classes, was closer home. They were schoolchildren like us, aspirational, bright-eyed, with the sense of a productive future within reach. Their death stunned us, ripped away the shroud of relative safety and assiduous institution.

In some weeks, two young men accused of killing them—Billa and Ranga—would be caught. They would shortly be convicted. In some years, these convicts would die at the hands of what was described as a justice system—and, in the process of so doing, become dubious media stars and even set judicial precedence, and trigger judicial upheaval and a constitutional crisis of sorts when their appeals for clemency threatened to bring the judiciary and the executive to a collision.

Short years later, Indira too would be gone, taken by the bullets of assassins incensed at her ordering an attack on the Golden Temple in Amritsar in June 1984 and the consequent desecration of Sikhism's holiest shrine. It was a loop that began with her party encouraging a ruthless self-professed saint for political leverage, who later turned rogue and took up residence in the Golden Temple complex as a rampant warlord, leading a heavily armed band of followers. To oust him, Indira sent in India's army.

Soon after, two of her Sikh bodyguards desperately angry at that act of desecration shot and killed her on 31 October. Then hate flowed like all the life-giving rivers of Hindustan turned toxic, with the maiming, raping, burning, killing of thousands of Sikhs for the price of killing of an empress by two of their kind—a hate I witnessed during my final years at university in Delhi. It would set the template and ideological justification and what in the future would come to be called 'whataboutery' for more rivers of hate which continue to flow, unfettered, undammed.

▪

Geeta and Sanjay wouldn't see all that. We of their generation did. We, who so easily could have been them.

On the day the Chopra children lived and died, in a way Delhi—and India—lived and died with them.

That day Delhi would create a new sordid layer in its history of slippage, of dystopia, for its future generations, as it boisterously—even elegantly in great part—carried its thousand years and more through its nine serial cities of capital ambition; from mythical Indraprastha to the mythic 'New' Delhi in the waning years of the British Indian empire, Delhi had displayed epic histories of trials, triumphs and tragedies and acted out dramas of light and dark, love and hate, beauty and beastliness. That day Delhi, as it had done in its past, once again resembled a fallen city, as if whatever passed for its soul had been ripped out anew for a new generation, as the dark arc that began with the Emergency had several more years to run till the seismic violence of 1984, and beyond that to 1992, and....

The story of siblings suddenly adrift, and the shocking end of their lives remains a story of our times. The intertwining of two children, a capital, and a country.

THE UNSETTLING

During the winter months in the mid-1970s, Delhi's sprawling parks, the peerless Lodi Garden with its grand ruins amidst manicured lawns and walkways, Nehru Park in Chanakyapuri, Roshanara Bagh to the north, the numerous parks in residential areas across the capital, and even the borders of ubiquitous roundabouts in Lutyens' Delhi—still associated with the eponymous Raj architect who co-created the new capital district for a waning British empire—came alive with flowers and grooming.

In summer, glorious blood-red and deep orange flowers set alight gulmohar trees. Delhi's other signature ornamental trees, the amaltas or Indian laburnum—'golden shower' to the more dramatic—and jacaranda with their glorious weight of blue-and-purple flowers, spread a sense of joy that persisted through burning hot summers.

The city's less colourful but equally welcome trees, the ubiquitous neem and jamun, lent shade and shelter—rain or shine, riot or shame.

This veneer of gentility was reinforced by New Delhi's charming, quiet enclaves peopled by the rich and powerful—some scions had already become adept at the capital's emerging go-to threat of the entitled, 'Do you know who my father is?' for obtaining a range of services from jumping all manner of queues to finessing traffic violations in their bedecked, air-conditioned Ambassadors and Fiats, or for the lucky few who could afford the numbing import duties, 'Mercs' and Chevrolets.

Address was everything.

To waft through the residential neighbourhoods around and near the quaint and understated Khan Market with a few bookstores, groceries, a handful of modest eateries, barbershops, stationers, and butchers was to soak in the quiet of elegant privilege. Golf Links, Jor Bagh, Amrita Shergill Marg, even the stately government bungalows of leafy Lodi Estate that were second-tier to the top-tier government bungalows and the handful of private residences of nearby Aurangzeb Road, Tughlaq Road, and Teen Murti Road were a part of the collective, the updated power centre created for the 'new' Delhi of the British Indian empire in the twentieth century. These neighbourhoods supplanted the 'old' of the still-charming pre-Lutyens Civil Lines neighbourhood of early empire that had usurped power from a crumbling Shahjahanabad of the Mughals; here, only the Red Fort and Jama Masjid stood tall amidst memories of grandeur.

At the edge of Lutyens' Delhi lay quiet, plush Sunder Nagar with its vast houses. Further south, newer enclaves like Defence Colony and Nizamuddin East claimed primacy over the busier, more crowded, noisier Nizamuddin West and its adjacent warrens of Nizamuddin Basti. Relatively new South Delhi neighbourhoods in an arc further to the south, Maharani Bagh, Greater Kailash, South Extension Part I, and emergent Green Park, and Hauz Khas took the upscale and Partition-refugee overspill from Old Delhi—or, perhaps more precisely, older Delhi.

Even public housing projects appeared to cater to the status-conscious. Whatever the names of the neighbourhoods, in the books of the Delhi Development Authority they were classified into HIG, MIG, and LIG—high-income group, middle-income group, and low-income group.

The colonial club culture had become post-colonial by welcoming the newly superior and browner skins but changing little else. Those away from this pale had found luxe refuge in destinations such as the dining and meeting rooms of the Oberoi Intercontinental Hotel overlooking the Delhi Golf Club. The Oberoi enticed the capital's expatriates, the wealthy, and the upwardly mobile to come by the Tabela nightclub for a dinner and dance over the weekend, visit Café Chinois for a Chinese meal, or simply combine a lazy day by the pool with the delights at the poolside coffee shop. (Those more economy-minded could instead visit the nearby Lodhi Hotel. It was state-run and reasonably priced and seemed to always have a discount sale on. Most weekends would host sales, a typical example being a Friday-to-Sunday all-day 'Export Sale by Nitya: New York, Paris, London, Montreal' who presented their 'surplus stock at slashed prices': dresses for 20 to 30 rupees, skirts for 15-20 and the same for trousers, and blouses for between 10-15 rupees....)

There was, of course, more luxe. More than a decade after the Oberoi opened in 1965, the Maurya Sheraton took wing in 1977, in the so-called Diplomatic Enclave of Chanakyapuri, another emergent power centre of modern bungalows and modernist—and some 'Brutalist'—embassy and government buildings and shopping complexes. Just to the north of Khan Market, edified by being named after Khan Abdul Jabbar Khan—brother of Independence-era political and peace icon Abdul Ghaffar Khan—the Taj Mahal Hotel on Mansingh Road was preparing to open in October 1978.

These hotels served a purpose in the growing, increasingly ambitious metropolis. The grand edifice of the government-run Ashoka Hotel, Delhi's first five-star property set across 16 acres of prime land in the heart of New Delhi, which opened in 1956—urban legend had India's first prime minister, Jawaharlal Nehru, making monthly visits to see how construction of this showcase was coming along—had by the seventies begun its descent into public sector sloth and corruption.

Alongside swish Delhi, the young and restless in a crossover crowd—upper-middle class, middle-class, students and young professionals, homegrown and drawn from across India—had taken to their own version of the Vietnam-era draw of narcotics, music, film noir, and modern relationships in the shadow of urgent discussions over the course and future of the Naxalite movement, the ultra-Left rebellion that took its name from the area around the North Bengal village of Naxalbari where sharecroppers had gone head-to-head with landlords and the police in 1967; the ensuing and explosively violent political movement that called for 'annihilation' of 'class enemies' had also rapidly drawn in students and urban intellectuals across India. In Delhi and India's ever-present irony, some could die practising a romanticized revolution while others could freely speak of it as theory.

Many of the city's artsy crowd and young professionals lived in barsatis—rooftop one or two-room apartments—or shared SQs or servants' quarters, made fashionable in nouveau-Delhi slang. Fashion statements in wintry and blazing Delhi alike had men and women in jeans and pants with flares wide enough to propel a sailboat, and shirts with collars that appeared to be designed to stabilize a small plane. Their music: rock and roll. Their discos—Tabela at the Oberoi for the moneyed; the less so and the students and young professionals hung about Cellar in Connaught Place—CP—and Sensations at Oberoi Maidens in Civil Lines that also drew in packs of youngsters from the nearby clutch of colleges in Delhi University—naturally, DU.

'That was my life,' the photojournalist Pablo Bartholomew, a perceptive and organic chronicler of the times would later speak of 1970s Delhi counterculture. 'I was in it.'

Even with this urbane churn it altogether gave the impression that several layers of Delhi had begun to settle; that the city long buffeted by Partition had embraced a new normal.

■

The Emergency destroyed that, and began a dark arc that would last a decade.

The project to save Indira's seat as MP and, consequently, her position as prime minister from judicial review triggered the imposition of emergency measures accorded by India's Constitution. A threat to Indira was interpreted as a threat to India, and acquiesced to by a rubber-stamp president. It made abnormality the new normal. Overnight, on 25 June 1975, freedom of speech and expression and civil liberties were suspended.

What followed was the lawlessness of law. It was led by the prime minister's cohort, and a parallel cohort of a younger breed of Congress-men and women led by her younger son, Sanjay.

Opposition politicians and journalists alike were hounded, and several jailed. Information czars censored the media—a move that began on the eve of Emergency with the government disrupting the electricity supply to what was sometimes referred to as Delhi's Fleet

Street—Bahadur Shah Zafar Marg. It housed the offices and printing presses of several major newspapers. In New Delhi and elsewhere, editions of *The Statesman* and *Indian Express* pushed back by exposing this censorship in a way that became an instant classic of protest—they ran censored articles and editorials as blank spaces that spoke eloquently of the situation.

Several decades later, Soli Sorabjee, among India's best-known jurists, and among a handful who defended those victimized by the Emergency, would process those years—which he called 'a real watershed in my life'—in a freewheeling conversation. While the effects of the Emergency were felt countrywide, they were felt most in the Capital. 'It wasn't in Bombay so much,' Sorabjee would exclaim, 'but in Delhi!...'

He articulated those times in Delhi as '*such* an atmosphere'. To battle the government through a deliberately wrecked system of judicial redress was essentially a case of 'inconvenient briefs'—several of the country's best and brightest provided 'good excuses to avoid such battles'. There was a reason, Sorabjee explained. 'You'd be a marked man.'

The Emergency years were in many ways an atrocity exhibition of hammer-fist and overkill as Delhi soaked in its dark side.

One such manifestation had to do with family planning. A World Bank report suggested an urgent need for India to control its population growth for socio-economic well-being. A graded government-led programme of 'family planning' that began in the early 1970s gradually escalated to include coercive sterilisation of males, a practice massively ramped up during the Emergency. It even spawned a quota system that led to forced vasectomies of hundreds of thousands of men in Delhi and across India.

This uptick began after Indira announced her development-oriented 20-point Programme just days after the Emergency was imposed. Sanjay added to this push his own 4-point Programme that had family planning a pillar.

'Emphasis was placed on sterilization of males, larger goals were established, and for the first-time incentives verging on strong-arm measures were possible,' American scholar Carolyn Henning Brown wrote in a paper for which she conducted onsite research in 1980. Cash payments of several hundred rupees to men led to 7 million sterilizations in 1976. But Emergency-era strong-arming also became a practice. 'Civil servants were told if they produced a fourth child after September 1977 they would lose their jobs,' Brown noted. 'In places incentives gave way to compulsion, and protest was met with police violence, as in Muzzaffarnagar, where several dozen protesters were killed by police.'

Sanjay's shadow loomed over an urban renewal and project in Delhi's Turkman Gate area, in the borderlands between Old and New Delhi. In April 1976, bulldozers were used to clear slums and evict residents. Paramilitaries shot dead several of those evicted who returned to protest such a final solution instead of judicious resettlement and rehabilitation. The government claimed ten had died. Foreign media—the muzzled Indian media were prevented from reporting it—estimated several hundred were killed.

FORTUNATE SON

The template of brash entitlement that had come to mark Sanjay Gandhi as it marked Delhi and India through the Emergency years would outlive him and crisp the soul of this politically supercharged city, in a manner not unlike the despondency that gripped many as the horror of the crimes of Billa and Ranga sank in.

Where his mother wielded the carrot and stick, silk and steel, Sanjay was often just jackhammer. He made his position clear to those he deemed too obtuse to recognize it. There's this story from the dying days of the Emergency.

On 14 March 1977, two days before parliamentary elections began, and a week before the Emergency officially expired, Sanjay, who was thirty at the time, had a bizarre exchange with *India Today* magazine's Sunil Sethi and Mandira Purie in what was designated his pocket borough, the backwater constituency of Amethi, in Uttar Pradesh. Sanjay had decided to stand for elections to be a MP, an attempt to transform from a backroom enforcer of the Congress's youth wing and the Emergency to a frontline enforcer of a diminished democracy.

'Temperamental, brusque and openly evasive,' the magazine described him, and cattily added: '...(the) milk-faced, pink-lipped, balding younger son of former Prime Minister Indira Gandhi known variously as the maker of the Maruti, a Five-Pointer prodigy, self-styled Youth Congress dynamo, and lately the prima donna of Indian politics....'

Sanjay was full prima, as Sethi and Purie saw when they were ushered into a room at a government guest house by Sanjay's wife, Maneka. Earlier, two old ladies from a nearby village had been dismissed for presuming free food and clothes were being distributed to the needy. Sanjay was at the desk with his back to the door, signing the reports of polling agents.

'Out, out, you there...you get out,' he snapped at Purie the moment he turned around and saw the photographer.

'Why?' she asked.

'I can't concentrate.'

Surely a few clicks of the camera would not....

'No, it irritates me.'

Sanjay continued to sign papers, his back turned to the journalists. Undeterred, Sethi asked his questions. It made for quite a sampling.

What are the needs of the people of Amethi?

'Improved irrigation, roads, electricity, and a regular water supply.'

What has the Opposition to offer?

'Nothing.'

What cause does your opponent advocate?

'Dacoity, mostly.'

People are upset about sterilization.

Here he looked up sharply. 'I have advocated family planning. But I have never stood for any forcible sterilizations.'

But you do admit to excess?

'There might be instances of overzealous officials and pradhans....'

By the end of that interview a few more descriptors would be added about Sanjay: '...curt and cryptic', and 'rude and crude'—this last alluded to by his elegant grand-aunt, Vijaya Lakshmi Pandit, sister to Jawaharlal Nehru, aunt to Indira.

Pandit, a suave diplomat, had taken a critical knife to her niece after the Emergency was imposed. Now, with elections announced, Pandit actively campaigned against her, urging India's electorate to elect the Congress's opponents, to collectively punish years of imperious, unfettered rule and runaway misrule.

Sanjay lost the election. A year-and-a-half after that summary ejection, as Delhi reeled from the aftershocks of Geeta and Sanjay's killings, a monsoon of mayhem, and cracks within the Janata government now signalling the imminent return of the dictatorial team India's voters had summarily ejected, the same publication would write of Sanjay's dramatics whenever summoned to court for a range of issues from allegations of financial misappropriation to merely furnishing sureties through his lawyers. His supporters would accompany him in large numbers during court appearances. During one such in Lucknow, his supporters entered the courtroom to rail at a judge.

'Sanjay Gandhi, errant son of the former prime minister, has a remarkable talent for conjuring up militant support at the drop of a sterilization scalpel,' *India Today* wrote. 'He also displays a remarkable allergy to law courts.'

At any rate the knives were out—had been out ever since it was announced that the Emergency would end. Journalists and writers were churning out what the editor Vinod Mehta once described as 'quickies' against both Sanjay and Indira—he published a book too, in 1978, *The Sanjay Story*. Mehta would share much later that Sanjay had 'refused to cooperate in the writing of the biography, insisting on copy-approval', which Mehta declined. The biographer Katherine Frank would note in *The Life of Indira Gandhi* that such books ran the gamut from barely literate narratives filled with innuendo and gossip to polished intellectual assaults. 'Indira (and Sanjay) bashing,' as Mehta observed in *Sanjay*, 'was not only safe but also intellectually fashionable.'

He was for many such a dark force that, according to some accounts, his elder brother—and future prime minister—Rajiv Gandhi was discomfited by Sanjay's attitude and behaviour. Mehta discussed it bluntly in his book, relating a second-hand telling: 'Even in the opinion of his elder brother, Sanjay had much to answer for. "I will never forgive Sanjay for having brought Mummy to this position,"' in his book Mehta quoted Rajiv as sharing his angst with 'family friend' Pupul Jayakar, a confidante of Indira's. At the time there wasn't evidently much love lost between the brothers; and Sanjay took out his legendary temper even on Sonia, Rajiv's wife; family scuttlebutt spoke of an incident when, in the presence of Indira, Sanjay, her political heir, flung a plate of eggs Sonia had cooked across the room because it wasn't to his liking. According to Mehta's recording of this alleged incident in *The Sanjay Story*, Indira remained quiet in her desperation to maintain familial balance.

Lewis M. Simons, who was the *Washington Post* correspondent in Delhi during the Emergency years, would write at the time of a more severe tantrum—also mentioned by the journalist Coomi Kapoor in her book on the Emergency Years, *The Emergency: A Personal History*.

Simons, who recounted the tantrum, his article, and the outcome in detail several decades later in a conversation with the journalist Ajaz Ashraf, wrote about an incident just before the Emergency where, at a private dinner party, Sanjay was said to have slapped his mother several times—six times, as Simons wrote. Kapoor doubted the veracity of the incident as Simons hadn't named sources in his article for the *Post*, but Simons told Ashraf in 2015 that he had two independent sources confirm it to him. Both had been present at the dinner, and their 'reliability was, and remains, impeccable'.

Simons wrote the article right after he had been ejected from India after the *Post* published an article by him which featured remarks by some Indian Army officers, who had told him 'of their distaste for the imposition of the Emergency and of Mrs Gandhi's behaviour leading up to it'. Simons was arrested by armed police, taken to the immigration office, and, five hours later, driven to Delhi airport and put on a flight to Bangkok.

'An Indian customs or immigration officer (I do not recall which) confiscated a dozen or so of my notebooks,' Simons told Ashraf. 'They were returned to me many months later, with every name meticulously underlined in red. Many of those people, I subsequently learned, had been jailed. This experience taught me never to name names when covering a sensitive story.'

Simons says he met Indira after the Emergency, when she had ceased to be prime minister. During that visit to Delhi, he told Ashraf, he also met Rajiv and his wife, Sonia, at a private dinner at which a dozen other guests were present.

'During the course of the evening, someone at the table stated to all present that I was the journalist who had written about the slapping incident. Rajiv nodded his head and smiled.

'"Well?" I asked him across the table. He nodded his head and smiled again. He said nothing. Sonia looked furious. She, too, said nothing. I never met Sanjay.'

This, then, was Sanjay, actual or apocryphal, anointed heir to Indira. The one who was to rule Delhi, rule India, after she was done.

■

On the day Geeta and Sanjay Chopra died, deliberations of the Justice J. C. Shah Commission probing the excesses of the Emergency arrived in the public domain. A final report of this government-led execration of Indira Gandhi, nearly a thousand pages, had reached the desks of government on 7 August and it was expected that the report would likely be tabled in Parliament at the end of the month or early September.

There was also the government-led execration of Sanjay. A sometime trainee at Rolls-Royce, he also had a pet and stuttering car project—Maruti. His time at Rolls-Royce had for some years been presented as evidence of his expertise in the automobile industry.

Now, news about Sanjay's stint at Rolls-Royce came via a leak through United News of India (UNI) of a letter purportedly written by a blandly-named official of Rolls-Royce, John D. Smith, to Justice A. C. Gupta. The judge, retired like his colleague, Justice Shah, was overseeing a commission—Commission of Inquiry on Maruti Affairs—a transparent attempt to investigate Sanjay as being unsuitable at best and fraudulent at worst—and to cross-check the submission in 1972 by Maruti executives to the Government of India that Sanjay was an accomplished engineer.

According to the letter, as conveyed by UNI, Sanjay Gandhi apprenticed with the firm from mid-1964 to mid-1967, but the quality of his work deteriorated after the first year. It had been so unsatisfactory, UNI quoted sources as saying, that Rolls-Royce officials, presumably aware of the young man's political pedigree and his enormously powerful mother, approached the Indian High Commission in the UK to amicably end Sanjay's four-year apprenticeship a year earlier.

'In 1967, representatives of the company visited the High Commissioner for India at India House, Aldwych,' read the letter, 'and during the ensuing discussion suggested that any further time spent by Mr Sanjay Gandhi with the company would be mutually unprofitable.'

Maruti was named after the god of wind in Hindu mythology. The operation to build an indigenous car had been exposed as an empty shell, although several investors had been roped in. Few would deny the princeling. But there was no pressure to invest in Maruti, Sita Ram Singhania, a prominent entrepreneur, told the commission of inquiry into Maruti's alleged and proven fiddles. Singhania, president of J. K. Synthetics, deposed before Justice Gupta insisting that the nearly three million rupees his firm invested in Maruti was not made 'under pressure'—and was evidently a sound investment in a worthy cause.

Within days another businessman with Maruti links, Raunaq Singh, would feature in a clarification in Parliament. Foreign Minister Atal Behari Vajpayee of the Bharatiya Jana Sangh—a hard-line Hindu party in the Janata coalition—would clarify that the businessman's passport, which had been confiscated to ensure he cooperated in the investigations for his alleged roles in Sanjay Gandhi's Maruti project, had not actually been restored on the say-so of a former home minister. It was restored for the businessman to travel abroad with permission granted—in bureaucratese—'on a case-by-case basis'.

In the daily game of skeletons in cupboards, word arrived that the commission of inquiry headed by Justice P. Jaganmohan Reddy had told the government that it was unable to give any 'conclusion' about the Defence Ministry's order for two Boeing jets for VIP use during the tenure of Bansi Lal as defence minister in the ousted Congress administration. But he had moved far along in his investigations and conclusions to hold the Indira-and-Sanjay loyalist responsible for clearing the purchase of fifty heavy recovery vehicles from MAN, a West German company, 'with a view to helping Sanjay Gandhi'.

There was evidently no end to such alleged, suspected, and proven shenanigans. This Gandhi scion's near-daily outing by the government which portrayed him as entitled and heedless of the law was duly broadcast by a media gleefully handing out the news as if was a payback to being muzzled and hounded for two years during the Emergency. On 26 August 1978 there was more about Sanjay's obsession with the tin-can operation that was Maruti. P. R. Sasidharan, an accounts officer with Maruti Ltd until September 1977 told a government inquiry panel that Sanjay remained the hub that transferred cash amounts ranging from petty to substantial, for self-help, as it were.

The former employee sang to the committee that Sanjay's bank accounts 'showed' transfers of a tiny—and surprising—amount of 25,000 rupees to his mother between April 1974 and January 1977. A meatier allegation was that Maruti Technical Services, a subsidiary in which Sanjay owned nearly all the shares, transferred 300,000 rupees to Sanjay's own account in January 1973. This subsidiary had received 500,000 rupees from its parent Maruti Ltd in August 1972 for providing 'technical know-how'. In any case, Maruti Ltd paid a monthly salary of 4,000 rupees to Sanjay as managing director.

Whatever the ongoing games of hide-and-seek and the various witch hunts and, in turn, exculpatory petitions, the prime minister, Morarji Desai, appeared to have made up his mind about his predecessor. At least it appeared that way during an interaction with journalists from the United States and United Kingdom in New Delhi on 26 August.

Some among the crowd compared Indira Gandhi's position being akin to that of Richard Nixon, the disgraced American president burned by the so-called Watergate scandal barely five years earlier. Nixon had been controversially pardoned by his successor, Gerald Ford, barely months after Nixon's resignation and Ford's appointment. Desai dismissed the idea of 'any national pardon' for Indira.

Indeed, with typical terseness he pushed back, saying that 'personally' he felt Nixon's pardon wasn't 'a good thing'. Indira would be prosecuted, not persecuted, to the full extent of the law. And if that resulted in 'some punishment' it would be a deterrent for anyone who 'wished to subvert the Constitution in future'.

There couldn't be any national cohesion or democracy, Desai insisted, 'if you murder truth'.

The object of his ire was meanwhile on her way from Delhi to Trivandrum. She was in transit at Madras airport when media persons barged into the 'VIP Lounge'. She was asked about the future of Desai's Janata Party and its coalition which included both leftists and the hard-line Hindu right.

'I am not an astrologer,' Indira was at her cryptic best. 'I do not want to become an astrologer.'

But she couldn't resist a final dig at her opposition. 'I do not want to join the line of astrologers who are predicting the future. There are already too many of them.'

It was a subtle foreshadowing of the future.

ABSURDISM

Alongside, there was a proliferating absurdism that only seemed to add to the sense of a confused and dysfunctional nation instead of one that was in the process of renewing and reinvigorating itself.

On the day Geeta and Sanjay died, the *Hindustan Times* ran a story, sourcing it to information that was 'reliably learnt', about how intelligence operatives had reported to the government that 'enemy agents' might have set off explosives to block the Bhagirathi River in the lower Himalaya. The river had caused widespread devastation through floods and snapped communications in early August. Indian investigators had based their analysis on the discovery of several deep conical pits in the hillsides along the river, nearby trees with 'cut marks' as if made by sharp weapons. The slippage might have been sabotage because the local people 'said the pits were made' a day before the incident. There had been no clouds, so 'no question of lightning or cloudburst' or 'no sound of thunder....'

The Central Intelligence Agency of the United States was the whipping horse. A member of parliament from the Soviet-friendly Communist Party of India (Marxist), Jyotirmoy Basu, flatly accused the government of failing to prevent espionage and 'subversive activities' of foreigners. Indeed, he insisted such operatives were about in greater numbers and their evil on the rise in India. Basu reserved his fire and brimstone for America's overseas intelligence arm. He criticized the government for failing to name and shame those operatives 'belonging' to the CIA which he accused of sabotaging the course of the Bhagirathi River.

There was also this matter of the hilarious Nagarwala episode that added layers to India's appearance of being a banana republic—and an indication of how much of a password 'Indira' had become for all manner of leverage in Delhi, the belly of the beast.

New Delhi residents were offered a particularly comic turn a scant day after the Chopra siblings were taken, with the revelation that day of the full text of the confession of Rustam Sohrab Nagarwala, who had conned the State Bank of India of 6 million rupees in May 1971—well after the genocide in East Pakistan had begun—pretending to be speaking on behalf of Prime Minister Indira Gandhi.

Nagarwala's artfulness and high chutzpah had aided the con which carried the eminently plausible logic of India needing to do something to aid the 'Bangladeshis', but not yet overtly. The hapless victim was V. P. Malhotra, chief cashier with the SBI at the bank's Parliament Street branch.

'I told him that the PM's secretary, P. N. Haksar, would like to speak to him,' Nagarwala confessed.

In his confession to a judicial magistrate, Nagarwala detailed how he pretended to be Haksar and the prime minister in turn:

Myself (as Mr Haksar): Mr Malhotra, I am speaking on behalf of the prime minister. A matter of great national importance has come up.... A sum of Rs 60 lakh has to be made ready for the relief of Bangladesh almost immediately. Can you do it?

Mr Malhotra answered: Please wait a minute.... (Then there was a pause of two minutes.) Yes, sir, I will have the money ready within twenty minutes.

Myself (as Mr Haksar): Good, now listen carefully to instructions. After I have finished speaking, the PM will also talk to you personally.

The bank manager was to hand over the cash to a courier waiting nearby, upon utterance of the same code words the PM would imminently share.

Here, evidently, the chief cashier's good sense kicked in, albeit briefly. He couldn't take the money out of the bank without a receipt, he protested. Even though it was highly irregular, he would be willing to bring the cash to the PM's residence and have her sign for it.

Absolutely not, Nagarwala-as-Haksar replied. It's much too hush-hush for all that. He would be seen by others and that couldn't be permitted. Then Nagarwala-as-Haksar played his trump card:

'However, I am now putting you through to the prime minister herself: please speak to her.'

(Pause of five seconds)

Then I spoke in the voice of the prime minister: Mr Malhotra this is the PM Mrs Indira Gandhi speaking.

Mr Malhotra answered: Namaste Mataji. I am an old soldier and I am prepared to do as you order.

Then I spoke as PM: Very good, Mr Malhotra. When you meet him, he will ask you Aap kis desh ka, Babuji, and you will reply Bharat ka (From which country are you, sir? India.) The courier will in turn say Main Bangladesh ka Babuji (I'm from Bangladesh). Once this identification is complete you will follow the instructions of the courier.... After you have handed the money to the courier, please report to me at my residence.

Nagarwala nearly pulled it off, even with that bizarre conversation and bizarre code. After the cashier headed off to the prime minister's residence Nagarwala flagged down a taxi. But he permitted the taxi driver to see him transfer the stacks of cash from a tin trunk in which the cashier had delivered it to a suitcase and bag Nagarwala carried. More lows followed. He led the taxi to the Parsi Dharamshala where he was rooming. Sure enough, by the evening the police, now looking for the con artist and tipped off by the cabbie, showed up.

While this comic scam stretched incredulity even in Delhi's hyper-real, politics-driven cesspool, stumbling criminals, some with a preternaturally vicious streak, like Billa and Ranga and their fellow travellers in inflicting trauma, would soon be all the rage.

▪

Meanwhile, the Janata government had begun to implode from conspiracy, jealousy, and ineptitude.

The stench of failure was already in the air. In 1977, the Janata Party had promised a 'Gandhian alternative' of 'both bread and liberty' as opposed to the Indira-Gandhian diet of roti and repression, as they put it.

A year in, key coalition leaders had quit, some in disgrace.

Governance was largely shambolic. The defence minister Jagjivan Ram's son was embroiled in an alleged sex scandal with photos of his dalliance with a young lady and sordid details splashed across Congress-friendly media.

Another controversy was the continuation of those with affiliations to the ultra-right Rashtriya Swayamsevak Sangh in the government—the result of the Jana Sangh forging common cause with the Janata as an anti-Indira, anti-Congress, anti-Emergency platform. There were occasional reminders of this unholy alliance, as it were. A delegation of a group calling itself the Anti-RSS Front presented a memorandum to senior government ministers and officials at the Parliament Annexe, asking them to stop the 'infiltration' of the RSS in government. Indira wasn't the 'only force of fascism', the petition read. The RSS's role had proved to be 'equally nefarious'.

The RSS pushed back with the clout of a partner in government. A significant template appeared to be set, to be refined and reapplied by this most patient of supremacists whose run began in pre-Partition India, and who never really managed to shake off, despite all the legal finessing, association with the assassin of Mohandas Gandhi.

In the middle of this saffron-wash, the ever-acerbic Piloo Mody, who had a tendency to call a spade a hydraulic excavator, had on the very day that Geeta and Sanjay were killed, castigated a cabal of his own Janata Party coalition as 'Alibaba and all the forty thieves'.

Political defections were the order of the day. In the arena of total-politics, who could say who would stay loyal, who would emerge as turncoat? Mody was essentially counting the days to the government's staggered but inevitable downfall.

And, in the ongoing unease about the continuing dislocation of law and order, and rising unemploymemt, it appeared that the absence of a third political alternative could well trigger the return of Indira and her son Sanjay. It was a surreal, hyper-real, even disturbing likelihood at a time of anarchic politics.

The least Indira could have done, M. V. Kamath, editor of the *Illustrated Weekly of India*, would suggest before the year was out, is to have offered 'the right kind of prayaschitta' for transgressions during the Emergency. 'She has done nothing of the kind. She sounds unrepentant.' Her fall-back argument about having offered firm leadership hardly softened a tyrannical overreach.

'Even those who might be willing to accept her explanation are chary about her because of their fears that, if she ever comes to power, she will be bringing along her son Sanjay with her.' Kamath was blunt about the prospects: 'Too many promises have been broken by her in the past for them to accept her word that Sanjay Gandhi has given up politics.'

Indira Gandhi and her younger son waited. They licked their wounds without retracting their claws, bided their time, and pounced. Indira had proven her grit several times since her spectacular fightback in 1966, from being written off as 'gungi gudiya' by some in the Congress's old guard, to being this 'dumb doll' who soon steamrolled them and emerged as empress of what she surveyed.

Indira would, of course, win again three years later with the eventual and total implosion of the chaotic Janata coalition that had replaced her and the coterie. She would have back her fabled kursi—the chair of the power-players.

With Indira's Congress back, with Indira and Sanjay Gandhi back, there would no longer be need for pretence. Political self-absolution was at hand.

But that was in the future. Delhi's dark arc, bookended, as it were, by the Emergency and the butchering of Sikhs, still had some years to run. In the interim there was the abomination of the deaths of Geeta and Sanjay Chopra, an atrocity that wounded the capital so deeply that even the Congress, which had wilfully destroyed nearly every vestige of democracy for close to two years by exposing law and order to be so seamlessly Janus-faced, would discover moral gumption to accuse the Janata government of being unable to deal with lawlessness.

26 AUGUST

It was warm and humid when the day began.

The previous day's rain, a little over 7 millimetres, and the lowered temperatures the rain brought, were already a memory to all except record-keepers at New Delhi's met office, not far from the grand tomb of Safdar Jang, a Mughal-era noble from that empire's waning years.

On 26 August 1978, the minimum temperature would not travel below 28 °C, the peak would step off the pedal only at 36 degrees. Overcast skies made it a humid cauldron. History has shown it since the time such history began to be recorded: Hard mid-monsoon rains earlier in the month had slowed to a relative trickle, dispensed every couple of days; the air remained as a thick curtain. It would stay that way until the month's end, the heat hovering in the air moist enough to quieten a dragonfly's wings or slow a determined fly—and the maggot-carriers of Delhi are hardy and practised. This city of cities had witnessed bloodletting, spectacular and commonplace, of people and cultures from a vast arc of Asia, for over a thousand years.

The bubble that contains the self-important oxygen of any capital (and, after more than a millennium of assiduous practice, Delhi was an adept at self-importance) carried on in its elliptical orbit, making and breaking the futures of nearly 670 million people of India it governed or misgoverned with acts small and grand.

■

There were criminals about, big and small, and from time to time, a macabre justice visited them.

What happened to Shashi Rasam in Bombay seemed straight out a Bollywood pot-boiler. Just a day earlier, newspapers reported, Rasam, the leader of the city's 'Cobra gang' was found dead at Bombay Central Station. This son of a policeman had stab wounds all over his body. And, of course, a cobra tattooed on his left arm—the same as all his gang members who, the police said, were involved in illegal betting, running brothels, and peddling black-market cinema tickets.

Another legendary criminal's amazing run of murderous luck appeared to have run out. Only a week or so earlier, Charles Gurmukh Sobhraj, who had caused grief to unwary travellers across Asia, and was now resident in Delhi's Tihar jail, was convicted by a lower court judge of attempting to 'administer intoxicating drugs' to some French tourists in an established modus operandi of lull-trap-rob-kill.

All that remained for Additional Sessions Judge D. R. Khanna to pass a sentence was to hear final arguments for and against the French national called 'The Serpent' by some.

As some big fish were caught or cancelled, in some ways it became easier to be inured to petty crimes across the country—or its capital. There were several such daily occurrences in the past week alone.

Like the case of Prabhu Dayal, a visitor from Haryana, who was knifed in his palm as he resisted robbers who managed to take over 300 rupees from him one night on Qutub Road in South Delhi. A nearby police constable had caught one of the two robbers upon hearing Dayal's call for help, but not before sustaining a knife wound himself. Two associates, Om Pal of Varanasi and Sudhir Shah from Ahmedabad, collectively lost over a thousand rupees and their watches to a group of robbers. It happened in broad daylight on Nicholson Road as the two rode a rickshaw towards the nearby Inter-State Bus Terminus. In Shahdara across the Yamuna in East Delhi—often dismissively regarded as a social universe away by those on the west bank of the river—a lady had her gold chain snatched. Another lady, Nirmala, was luckier. She was robbed of two gold chains as she waited for a bus in Tilak Nagar, a West Delhi neighbourhood. She screamed for help. A police constable, Raj Singh, who was on his way home from the police station in that very neighbourhood heard her, and jumped off a moving bus to give chase. The thief, identified as Pushp Kumar Chatterjee from Howrah way to the country's east, escaped. But after an all-points alert about his description, he was later arrested near the Supreme Court in Central Delhi.

The law, and its keepers, appeared to be on the ball.

It was all a composite of yesterday, today, tomorrow. Just a day in the life of dogged Delhi, the seemingly eternal pivot of the subcontinent. As ever, here the underbelly was the belly. Open, upfront, parallel. Every universe, all at once.

▪

And on that evening of that day, 26 August, as aspirational Delhi homes settled in to dream about purchasing a new air-conditioned Ambassador car with a 'high horse power engine'; as travellers planned vacations to beautiful Gulmarg in Kashmir, or enticing Kathmandu with its casinos and timeout at exotic-sounding new hotels like Yak & Yeti; or as other hopeful homes considered the 'Fabulous' chance, upon the purchase of an Avon bicycle, of winning a first prize of either a Vijay or Allwyn scooter, the second prize of a Racold brand cooler, a third prize of a blender—'mixie'—of either the Rallis or Sumeet brands; as policy pundits discussed news of the United States resuming aid to India for the first time since the bilaterally frigid Nixon–Kissinger years (Indeed, in New Delhi, American ambassador Robert Goheen and Manmohan Singh, India's finance secretary, had only just signed an agreement for US$60 million in development assistance for on-again India); or as some music aficionados listened to rock and roll or Ravi Shankar on their HMV Stereo 3131 Supertrack sets that showed off a '0.5 mil spherical diamond stylus that is housed in a stereo magnetic cartridge,'; or watched on their Dyanora or Texla solid-state televisions a series of programmes by the state-run television station (a health programme at 6.30 p.m. followed by a missing-persons bulletin, followed by a play followed by news in Hindi followed by an obscure Czech film, *Diver of the Risky Category*, followed by the news in English followed by a global recap, *Around the World*); or decided instead to catch the evening or night show of *Duchess and the Dirtwater Fox* at plush Archana theatre, or *The Exorcist* at Sheila near New Delhi station, or go Bollywood with the love-triangle romcom *Pati, Patni aur Woh* at Chanakya, the minimalist architectural showpiece of the shopping, hotel, and entertainment hub of Yashwant Place, or at the less fashionable but no less popular Liberty or Nataraj in West Delhi; as Lido Restaurant in a grimy corner of Connaught Place's Outer Circle ('Daily Cabarets at 3.30, 7.45 & 10 p.m. by four beautiful girls') prepared for its peak weekend crowd which would fork out a ten-rupee cover charge per person to gain entry; as, a couple of blocks away, the brightly lit and always busy Nirula's welcomed teenagers and families alike to wolf down the house speciality of Big Boy Burger, cheese-sausage-capsicum pizza and shakes by the dozens; as the College of Guitar prepared to present its 'Young Ones Nite' at IMA Hall near Vikas Minar; as actors of the Dhrishtantar theatre group prepared for their 7 p.m. show of Kuldip Gosain's play *Naya Kotwal* at Sapru House; as the Delhi 'A' radio station wound itself up for its health and music programmes on 370.4 Megahertz; and, as some listeners of the sister channel Delhi 'B', on 294.1, were looking forward to the station transitioning from a programme of earthy folk songs to the slicker grooves of 'Dance Time' to light up their Saturday night, Geeta and Sanjay Chopra met their fates.

MISSING

Delhi continued to swelter in its late-August avatar. The 27th and 28th of August were cut in much the same mould as the 26th. Maximum temperature at around 35 °C, some rain, oppressively humid outside and in, the nights mercifully cooler at around 27 degrees. 'Generally cloudy with likelihood of one or two showers or thundershowers' was the placid met outlook for the metropolis.

Neighbourhoods counted their blessings by gauging how far they were from the rampaging Yamuna that daily threatened the north and east of the city. It was keeping to the capital's character. Segueing between imperiousness and being imperilled had remained Delhi's signature on-again off-again cycle for well over a millennium.

Tucked away on page three of *Hindustan Times* on 28 August, surrounded by news about graffiti on walls and buses for the 'varsity poll war', Delhi University's often-violent elections that had begun to mirror the increasing thuggery in India's electoral politics from Bengal to Bombay and from Delhi to the Deccan and beyond; 'What's On in Delhi'—news of how the president of India's assent to Police Bill that was expected to trigger reforms; and how spurs by the Yamuna had deflected floodwaters and saved large areas of eastern Delhi from doom, was this tiny article.

CHILDREN MISSING
Hindustan Times Correspondent

New Delhi, Aug. 27 – A search is on for Geeta, 17, and Sanjay, 15—children of Captain M.M. Chopra of Service Officers Enclave, Dhaula Kuan—who have been missing since last evening.

The children had left home around 6.30 p.m. for AIR station on Parliament Street to participate in a Yuva Vani programme.

But subsequent inquiries there showed they did not reach AIR.

The police who have registered a case of kidnapping, have sent parties to Haryana on receipt of some information.

The children, it is believed, might have hitched a ride in some passing car, whose occupants might have whisked them away.

Not far was an advertisement for the cover story in the latest issue of *New Delhi* magazine. The article asked a premonitory question: 'How young did your God die?'

STORM WARNING

Monday rolled to Tuesday—was rolled tightly into Tuesday with strings of jute or rubber bands recycled from the inner tubes of tyres. Newspapers arrived as they did, heavy with humidity, the newsprint soaking up moisture as it did the inks of news and advertisements, landing with a soft thunk outside the doors, or onto balconies arrayed one on top of the other. Occasionally—an amateur delivery boy perhaps, days or weeks from becoming an adept at accuracy as he threw papers with the flick of a wrist, or by masterfully chambering and releasing an elbow, even as he held on with the free hand to the handlebar of his bicycle—some newspapers would be delivered onto parapets and the odd cornice, some retrievable, some irretrievably lost to the ages or a crow or kite that took a fancy to it for padding a nest; at any rate setting off a frenzy of activity to grab the papers before the August wet of the ground or the balcony floor ruined the read.

The day would be hotter than the previous day, the night a little cooler, but only just. Humidity would cling like irritating news. Partial showers would make the sense of damp even worse.

General discomfort was added to general unease.

■

On Page 3 of *Hindustan Times* there was a follow-up to that slim blink-and-you-lose-it item from a day earlier. On this day, 29 August, it merited more space: across three columns. It was sandwiched between 'What's On', news of various concerts, and how an embankment saved some villages from the fury of the Yamuna.

The news item carried a photo of a dignified, solemn young girl, identified as Geeta Chopra. Alongside her was the image of a smiling young boy, exuberant and innocent. He was identified as Sanjay Chopra.

KIDNAPPED TEENAGERS UNTRACED

Hindustan Times Correspondent

ND, Aug. 28: Police today were looking for a 17-year-old girl Geeta Chopra and her 15-yer-old brother, Sanjay Chopra, who were allegedly kidnapped on Saturday evening while on their way to All India Radio.

The two had left their Dhaula Kuan Service Officers Enclave house for the Radio Station to record a programme there. But they never reached AIR and have been missing since.

Police Commissioner J.N. Chaturvedi today announced an award of Rs 2,000 for giving information being helpful in finding these two teenagers.

The police suspect that a yellow or light orange coloured Fiat car was used to kidnap the two. Some passersby are said to have seen the car near the Gole Dakhana [Sic] and Willingdon Hospital. They heard someone crying for help.

A police party went to Panipat following a report that the kidnap car had been found abandoned there.

The Delhi police denied that the car used in the Dhaula Kuan abduction had been traced.

PREMONITION

There was frenetic activity away from media glare as the missing children's parents searched desperately for them.

The way Captain Madan Mohan Chopra and his wife Roma recalled it, Geeta and Sanjay left their apartment in Dhaula Kuan officers' enclave around 6.15 in the evening for All India Radio on Parliament Street—Sansad Marg—in the heart of New Delhi. Geeta, a keen music enthusiast, had a turn as DJ and host for 'In the Groove', a pop Western programme at the generally stolid government-run radio station.

Sanjay accompanied her. The strapping fifteen-year-old was at 5-foot-10 as much a chaperone as a sibling proud of his big sister, ready to be witness as she spread her wings doing something she loved—being with music, recording 'In the Groove'. This would be her second time as host—compère, to use a term of the times. The naval captain would collect his children at around 9 p.m. from the radio station.

He arrived punctually but didn't find his children at the pre-arranged spot outside AIR, the popular acronym for All India Radio. The captain parked the car and walked inside to ask about their whereabouts. He was told Geeta hadn't turned up to record the show.

After the missed rendezvous with his children at AIR, a frantic yet methodical Captain Chopra didn't waste time. He rushed back to Dhaula Kuan where Roma told him their children hadn't arrived back home either.

The captain then did two things. He reached out to his colleagues in the navy. And he registered a missing persons' report for Geeta and Sanjay at Dhaula Kuan police station. The police record—the First Information Report—showed Captain Chopra called the Central Control Room of Delhi Police around 10 p.m. that night.

The police moved quickly—without having a clue that a report about the teenage siblings had meanwhile been filed, and dismissed, at Rajinder Nagar police station. A patrol car reached the Chopra residence in fifteen minutes. Together with the police team the captain scoured the capital's hospitals and restaurants in the central district, the homes of friends, even some outlying, relatively underpopulated areas that lay on Delhi's west bank, as it were—west of the Yamuna.

Nothing.

As Captain Chopra and police personnel engaged in a frenzied, fruitless search, there was a suggestion by the captain that they go looking for Geeta and Sanjay in the Ridge—a forested finger of hardy trees and rocky land that formed the northern extension of the denuded, ancient and still grand Aravalli Range. A section of the Ridge ran through Dhaula Kuan in a north-easterly direction and, after a small gap, ended in the vicinity of Delhi University's North Campus.

'I suspect the kids have been killed and thrown on the Ridge,' he told an accompanying police officer.

It was an explosion of despair and desperation. And logic. The desolate Ridge was a short drive from their home, and among the more desolate places in the capital.

The captain's remarks were relayed to the commissioner of police for South Delhi, K. K. Paul, who had by then taken charge of the operation to find the children. The police on this search now numbered nearly 150, with several dozen patrol cars in play—thirty according to one account. Naval police personnel too had pitched in.

A search team began to comb the ridge. A *India Today* article from a fortnight later would tautly recall those tense hours, and some snafus:

> *The darkness, the incessant rain, and the dense nature of the undergrowth seriously hampered the operations. To combat the darkness, Paul radioed for Very Pistols to be sent to the Ridge. The cartridges, however, refused to fire. By this time, it was almost 2.30 a.m. and the search was called off till the following day.*

Three days into the frantic search, with an all-points alerts for the 'yellow or orange' Fiat in the neighbouring states of Haryana, Punjab, Uttar Pradesh, and Rajasthan, and to highway patrols in an expanding radius, there was still no sign of Geeta and Sanjay.

TWILIGHT

A group of herder-milkmen had moved with their cattle to the uplands of the Ridge to escape the Yamuna's lowland deluge. A little past midnight on 28 August, on a relatively cool yet muggy early morning of the 29th, they were moving with their animals along the Upper Ridge Road. They ambled along the periphery of the forest that made up the Buddha Jayanti Park and other unnamed and untamed patches. Some of the periphery was walled, some fenced with barbed wire.

The dairymen encountered a stench towards the northern end. It smelled of putrefaction. They ventured into the bushes not far from the carriageway and came upon two bodies.

One was of a girl. She was face down in a small pit.

About 50 metres to her north lay a young boy, his face to the skies.

That was enough for the horrified party to rush back to the road in search of the police. They found Head Constable Rohtas Singh of the Mandir Marg police station, situated several hundred metres to the northeast of the spot, on patrol nearby. Singh relayed the message to the police control room, which in turn got in touch with police stations in the area, including the Rajinder Nagar police station to the west of the location.

Police arrived to find the girl lying in a large grassy patch which looked to be darkened with her blood. Other darkened patches and long hair would be found nearby as the uneasy night lightened to horrified day.

The boy looked as if he had been hacked to death.

N. K. Shinghal, an assistant police commissioner, soon arrived at the spot along with a team from crime branch and a dog squad of Delhi Police. The crime scene provided no clues beyond the blood and the mangled, putrefying bodies.

A police team quickly reached the residence of Geeta and Sanjay Chopra. Their bodies had to be formally identified. Their parents would need to do it.

■

The deluge of shock and grief arrived for Delhi and the country with the papers on 30 August.

But for Captain Chopra and his wife Roma their nightmares had escalated to devastation a day earlier, around 3 a.m. That's when a police team arrived to tell them of the discovery of the bodies of a boy and a girl answering to the description of Sanjay and Geeta.

Captain Chopra left immediately. The location on the Ridge was just minutes from their residence in Dhaula Kuan.

It didn't take time for him to identify the bodies even with the mutilation and advanced state of putrefaction.

Geeta was wearing a printed kurta and a pair of black trousers on the day she had disappeared. She had worn a silver ring. Sanjay had mimicked his sister with the choice of black trousers. He had on a blue T-shirt.

The clothing matched that on the bodies.

Madan Chopra sank to the ground, speechless. Life as he knew it had ended.

It was 3.30 a.m. on 29 August.

As the bodies of his children were taken to a nearby morgue for a post-mortem examination, the broken parent returned to his wife and their emptied nest.

■

Captain Chopra was inconsolable. He cried. He sobbed. He unreservedly reached out to his colleagues who came by to console him, hugged members of the family. The jovial yet dignified officer who headed the Judge Advocate General's (JAG) office of the Indian Navy in Bombay, and had arrived in Delhi in February 1977 to take up another assignment, had no time or inclination for a public face of stoic grief. His children had been brutally taken from him. Nothing else mattered.

He beseeched the family doctor. 'Please give me some injection.... What is there left in life for us?'

Then he broke down again. 'Everyone has to die someday. But not in this way.'

He sobbed: 'Why were they murdered?'

Usually more expressive, his wife had become grief-mute, turned to stone since returning home after seeing her children in their tortured death at the morgue. She had stopped speaking.

That broke the captain's heart thrice over.

'Roma, you must cry. I beg you with folded hands, please cry. Otherwise, you will die too and I will be alone.'

He begged the doctor: 'You must make her cry.'

But Roma Chopra wouldn't cry. Not yet. There would be a lifetime for tears.

That deluge would arrive just days later. For now, she sat on a bed in the children's room, hands folded on her knees, her right hand occasionally gripping the wrist of her left, and sometimes the other way around, in support. She set her eyes to infinity, a statue of dignity in grief as friends and family gathered around her, hugged her, cried for her as they cried for themselves as the world outside, her world, the captain's world, Geeta's world that was Jesus and Mary College—'JMC' to all—and 'Modern', the world of Sanjay at Modern School, went into collective grief. And, in short order, anger.

Why were they murdered?

'She was such a bright, attractive, likeable girl,' grieved Sister Agatha McLoughlin. 'Very active too.'

The principal of JMC held a wreath. She visibly struggled to hold back her tears. With her, waiting outside the apartment and in the neighbourhood were several hundred students and faculty of JMC. College was closed for the day; to do anything else would have been unthinkable. They were here to pay homage to their friend, colleague, student; best in her class in commerce in her freshman year. A teacher recalled how Geeta had spoken to her excitedly about her father having agreed to sponsor an MBA if she did well at JMC.

A swimmer, she was to also have taken the trials for a championship event just the day earlier. That day had died.

Now they all waited for Geeta and Sanjay to arrive. But they would not. They were too mutilated and decomposed to be placed in public.

'But I want to *see* Geeta,' wailed Sujata Malhotra, a dear friend.

An aunt spoke of Sanjay's 'blue eyes'. 'He was *so* good looking,' she marvelled.

Rumours and suppositions floated about like motes of rising anger riding on deep distress.

The police knew of the children being kidnapped just minutes after they had been bundled into a mustard-coloured Fiat. They had slipped up massively by waiting for the parents to file a missing persons report. The bodies of Geeta and Sanjay were actually discovered a day earlier, on the 28th, at about six in the evening. The police waited several hours to tell the parents. Why?

Why were they murdered?

Captain Chopra played back the scenarios in his mind. Was it something he had done during his time in Bombay in the Judge Advocate General's office? Had someone at the wrong end of naval justice decided to take revenge? He dismissed it as unlikely. After all, he reasoned, he hadn't directly sentenced anyone, just offered legal advice to court martial juries as they went about acquitting or convicting alleged offenders.

Waves of grief threatened to drag him under. His pride and joy Geeta, he was convinced, had died protecting her 'honour'. And Sanjay—'my poor, little, small baby'—died protecting his sister. His tears flowed freely.

A slice of cake still lay on the children's study table, partly eaten.

Geeta had baked it.

She had eaten a bit and then rushed off to record her programme, evidently with a mind to finish the dessert upon her return.

Like the shared study table piled with books, a couple of pairs of her shoes, their schoolbags, the neatly made beds, the exuberant oddity of the piece of cake was touched by wrenching memory.

The stale cake had become a fresh shrine.

POST-MORTEM

Roma and Madan Chopra were denied their request to bring the children home.

Besides the decomposition of the bodies, much still needed to be done by way of investigation. They were assured by the police and the government that the bodies of Geeta and Sanjay would reach Nigambodh Ghat in time for their cremation at 3 p.m. on 29 August.

As the shocked parents and a shocked city waited, the brutalized siblings were forensically examined. It told the story of the chilling madness of those desperate few hours between their abduction and death.

The post-mortem examination was conducted on 29 August by a police surgeon, Bharat Singh; he would later be listed as Public Witness 30 by the prosecution seeking justice for the killing of Geeta and Sanjay.

Dr Singh began his examination of Geeta at 11 a.m.

Delhi's greenhouse monsoon weather had speeded decay.

'In a state of advance decomposition with bluish discolouration of face which was also partially destroyed by maggots,' Dr Singh observed. 'There was distention of abdomen, superficial skin from nearly all over the body. Skull hair was falling on its own due to decomposition. Eye-balls were decomposed and liquified. Mouth was open. Soft issues of lips were decomposed. Tongue was decomposed. Soft tissues of nose were partially destroyed by maggots. Both ears were intact. Nails were pale.'

Dr Singh routinely investigated for evidence of sexual molestation but the decomposed state of the body, according to him, prevented a 'definite opinion'.

'No injury to perineum,' the pathologist noted. 'Vaginal swab was collected and sealed for chemical analysis....'

After other observations related to the state of traumatic death and quick decay of organs from the brain to genitalia, he went on to describe the mayhem inflicted on Geeta as she resisted, evidently turning from one side to another, flailing, attempting to fend off with her arms all the slashing and hacking, a blade finding her head, face, neck, arms, hands, fingers.

Dr Singh first noted the massive injuries to her skull and neck. A bone-deep near-horizontal cut on the right side of the head, over the 'right frontal parietal', just behind the frontal lobe. A 4 x11 inch bone-deep slash on the right side of neck reached the jaw: 'All the major blood vessels of neck on the right side were cut in one line. Lower jaw was partially cut and then fractured completely in two pieces.'

An inch-and-half cut on her right wrist went to the bone. A massive 10-inch slash cut to the ulna, the slimmer of the two bones in the forearm—the one that extends to the elbow in line with the little finger. The slash cut into the bone. There were also bone-deep cuts on her right index and middle finger. Dr Singh noted a large wound over the 'left forearm near the wrist joint placed horizontally'. It cut deep into the bone and 'all the major blood vessels and nerves were cut....' There was a deep wound on the mound of muscle on the left palm below the little finger.

Geeta's skull cavity and insides of her torso showed advanced decomposition: the brain, heart, trachea, lungs, liver, kidneys, and stomach—now distended. Her ribs were intact, showing how the attack was concentrated on her head and neck—precisely the areas she appeared to have defended with her arms.

'There was no blood in the body cavity,' Dr Singh observed, noting a chilling evidence that explained the 'darkened green' of the spot where she was found. 'Hence the same was not preserved.' Geeta had bled out.

'Hair from the skull, vaginal swab, were preserved and sealed and handed over to the police. Injuries were ante-mortem possible by sharp cutting object. Injury to the neck was sufficient to cause death in ordinary course of nature. Death was due to haemorrhage and shock resulting from injuries. Time since death was about 54 to 60 hours.'

■

On the same day, an hour and half after he began a quite rapid post-mortem on Geeta, Dr Singh began his examination of Sanjay.

Sanjay's face, mouth, eyes, and head showed decomposition in more or less the same manner as that of his sister. The decomposition of his internal organs and spaces showed a similar trajectory as that of Geeta.

His remains, like his sister's, showed the physical extent of the horror. It was evident that a special brutality was reserved for this boy who appeared to have fought for his sister's life even as he fought for his own.

Sanjay's scalp had nearly a foot-long cut that went into the bone on the left side of his head—the left parietal area. There was a smaller gash below it, on the left temporal. Another big slash, 11.5 inches long behind the left ear, had devastated the mastoid area; in one area, an inch long, the slash had broken through the bone. Dr Singh found 'brain material' oozing out of that wound.

There was a cut on the front of the head. A gash on the upper left portion of Sanjay's neck.

Then came the torso and the arms.

A deep wound below the right clavicle, slicing an inch into the right upper lobe of the lung.

And a wound about 10 inches below his left armpit. There was another cut nearby.

An 11-inch-plus slash to his upper right arm near the elbow. A deep wound of similar length, to the bone, across that elbow joint. A 5-inch gash on the lower part of his right forearm, midway between the elbow and wrist.

Item 12 of the 21 'items' specifically addressing cuts to Sanjay read: 'Four incised wounds over the right palm placed vertically oblique 1/4" apart, size of each wound was 4" x ½" bone deep. Bones of the hand were also cut underneath the wound. Blood vessels and nerves were cut in one line.'

There was a 11" x 4" bone-deep gash on Sanjay's left shoulder. And a 6" slash to the left upper arm.

A series of cuts around the left elbow region highlighted a 5" x 1" bone-deep cut to the front of the elbow joint. 'All the major blood vessels were cut in one line,' Dr Singh noted.

A slash to the left forearm. A cut through the web by the left thumb and on the index finger. A bone-deep cut on that thumb.

From the wounds it was also clear his attacker had moved around Sanjay, trying to literally get in edgeways. Indeed, any which way that would end this stubborn, fighting boy the same as his sister's attacker had determinedly, demonically, ended her. At some point in his fight to protect himself—the slashing and hacking on his arms signs of his desperate attempt to shield his head, his face, his torso—Sanjay appeared to have turned over, flailed with his legs as he did with his arms.

That fetched him a deep horizontal cut on the back of his left thigh. 'Major blood vessels on the back of the thigh were completely cut,' Dr Singh observed.

There was a smaller cut on the side of that thigh. A slash went bone-deep into the front of the left knee joint.

Dr Singh described four of Sanjay's injuries, to the back of his ear, to his chest that punctured his right lung, to his arm and thigh both of which cut through the veins and arteries, as being 'sufficient to cause death in ordinary course of nature'.

He added: 'Some of the injuries were caused by heavy cutting weapon and some were possible by light sharp object such as knife.'

The pathologist held that all of the injuries on Geeta could be possible with a kirpan. For Sanjay, besides a kirpan and possibly a sword used—at any rate 'a heavy cutting implement'.

He admitted there could he a variation of five to six hours in his estimation of the time of their death.

Several decades later, I took the post-mortem report for a second opinion to Ambarish Satwik, a well-known vascular surgeon at Sir

Ganga Ram Hospital in Rajinder Nagar, just a few short turns of the road from the Ridge and the spot where Geeta and Sanjay's bodies were found. Satwik is also a fine writer, and I wished for him to clarify the post-mortem report and also sought his opinion as to how the murders might have played out—as observed from the record of the injuries.

In the medical evidence of mayhem, one recorded in 1978, and the other through expert interpretation offered more than forty years later, one thing remained abundantly, achingly clear.

Until the time life left them in the quiet forest on the Ridge, Geeta and Sanjay had fought and fought and fought.

On another day, it was as if India had reached out to the Chopras. Defence minister Jagjivan Ram visited the Chopra residence accompanied by his wife, Indrani Devi, and S. Banerjee, the defence secretary. That was expected; Captain Chopra was after all a serving naval officer.

Indira Gandhi spent about forty-five minutes with the captain and Roma. The president of Congress, Indira, learned little from the parents except what remained speculation at the time; the post-mortem report was not yet widely available. Their children had probably resisted 'goondas', they told her as they had told themselves and others countless times. Prime Minister Morarji Desai too visited the Chopras. He made the time even though he had matters of state to deal with and a funeral to attend. On the evening of 30 August, he would leave for Bombay on an Indian Air Force aircraft and then connect with the regular Air India flight to Nairobi. Kenya's iconic first president, Jomo Kenyatta, had died eight days earlier and his funeral was scheduled for 31 August. Desai's visit was being pitched by the foreign ministry as a special gesture to Kenya in particular and to Africa in general. It was intended to step up India's Africa outreach from tepid to transformative.

▪

Sanjay's school friends had no time for such business of state that mixed studied amity with studied grief. Shocked and outraged, grieving for Sanjay and for Geeta, more than 600 students of Modern School took out a procession of protest and remembrance on Barakhamba Road, an artery that branched out east from Connaught Place and on which their school was located.

Then, clad in their sky-blue summer cottons marked with the

crest that symbolized the circle of eternity—it was designed by the turn-of-the-century artist Sarada Ukil who had also been an arts teacher at Modern—the students of classes 10, 11, and 12, girls and boys alike, marched off, raising slogans, to the Rashtrapati Bhavan about 3.5 kilometres away.

They didn't ask their school for permission. They just did it, as much for Sanjay and Geeta as themselves. They wanted to take their anguish to Neelam Sanjiva Reddy, the president of India, nestled in the lavish former palace of British colonial viceroys, off an avenue that still bore its imperial arrogance: Rajpath, the avenue of kings.

At about a quarter past one in the afternoon, they reached the lawns of India Gate, about halfway from their school to Rashtrapati Bhavan. The police stopped them. As angry and distraught students milled about, police officials told them there was already a protest in play further down Rajpath, by the Boat Club. There were still protesting farmers about; they had parked their rally in the area across from the grand expanse of Rashtrapati Bhavan. To permit a rally of agitated students to merge with a gathering of agitated farmers could snowball into a law-and-order snarl.

The students were far from convinced by what appeared to be a gambit to downplay an embarrassing photo-op at the gates of the palace of the head of state, but they finally agreed to send a delegation of five students to the president rather than descending on him en masse. They didn't meet the president but a special assistant to the president, to whom they presented a hand-written memorandum.

The students wrote that they were 'shocked at the gruesome and sadistic butchering of one of us', and that the murder of 'the innocent children because of the apathy shown by the authorities has destroyed our already crumbling faith in the police'.

The students begged that every effort be made to apprehend the killers of Sanjay and Geeta.

'We hope this plea will not go unheeded,' the memorandum urged.

The special assistant to the president of India asked the students to meet the lieutenant governor of Delhi.

They were smoothly fobbed off down the administrative chain, but the students were determined to meet the ranking boss of Delhi's administration as well as the capital's police chief. They would, of course, visit their classmate's residence in Dhaula Kuan, but that wouldn't assuage their hurt or stop them from visiting every significant administrative address in Delhi, they said.

The outrage had begun to spiral outwards. Students of Shivaji College, situated several kilometres northwest of the spot where the bodies of Geeta and Sanjay were found, walked to the Dhaula Kuan police station to register their anger, their horror.

▪

The days were a blur to Roma Chopra.

She seemed to wake briefly from her grief to register the gesture of a voluntary organization. Save a Tree in Your Area—SATYA—arrived to give her two saplings. An arjuna in the memory of Sanjay because *Terminalia Arjuna* usually grows into a 20-25-metre-high sprawl of canopy—sheltering, protective, as Sanjay was towards his sister. A harshringar—parijat or 'night jasmine'—for Geeta; its blossoms are fragrant, cherished, loved, and, ironically, of the season of floral charm that brought death to Geeta.

The saplings would be planted where the children were found.

Roma Chopra was moved. She offered to plant the saplings herself. But she had a question, similar to the one she had asked ceaselessly of herself since the death of her children.

'Who will protect them?'

SAMARITAN

Inderjeet Singh Noato had tried.

On the evening of 26 August, the twenty-three-year-old junior engineer with the Delhi Development Authority was on his way back from a project site in Patparganj, across the Yamuna in eastern Delhi, right by the border with Uttar Pradesh. He had stopped briefly in Connaught Place on the way to his home in West Delhi.

He had gone past Gole Dak Khana and had passed the Emergency section of Willingdon Hospital—as most in Delhi referred to the hospital named after the wife of a viceroy of India, ignoring its renaming after the socialist politician Ram Manohar Lohia—to his right. He was driving sedately that day, unlike his usual rapid transit.

A Fiat drove past him at speed. As it did, Inderjeet heard a girl scream. The scream was muffled by thick automobile window glass, but enough for him to realize all wasn't well. He was jolted into alertness, and speeded up.

He then saw two men in the front seat of the Fiat, and a boy and a girl at the back. The boy was being 'beaten', he saw, and that made him realize something was seriously amiss.

He caught up with the car at the next roundabout, by the southern perimeter of the hospital.

'Kyon bhai, kya ho raha hai?' he yelled.

Inderjeet wasn't certain if the men in the front seat heard his shouted query—'What's going on'—but evidently the boy did. He turned to press his face to the rear left window and kept pointing to his bloodied T-shirt. The boy was fair-skinned, Inderjeet noted, fair enough to be taken for a 'foreigner'.

The girl had her back to him. He noticed she had styled hair—the journalist Prabha Dutt would later articulate it for him as 'feather cut'. In stereotypical northern Indian fashion, he recorded her complexion as 'wheatish', a lighter palette of dusky. The girl was pulling the driver's hair. The driver had his right hand on the wheel. With his left he slapped at her.

Then the car was past the roundabout and on to a straight stretch. It jumped a red light.

Inderjeet toyed with the idea of jumping the light too, but held back. He thought he would shout for help, but remained frozen. 'No words came out of my throat.'

When the signal turned green, he again gave chase.

He saw the car slow down near a bus stop because of traffic. He hoped something would give the children would make a break for it.

'I thought maybe the children will try to jump out or shout for help but nothing happened.'

The car sped away.

Inderjeet followed but couldn't keep up. His scooter was acting up; as it would turn out, at issue was a problematic piston. He last saw the car as it reached the crossing of Mandir Marg and Park Street. The Ridge and the road along the Ridge that rode its southern spine all the way to Dhaula Kuan were just a couple of turns from there.

And he saw the hands of the children. ('...small hands waving as if in a final goodbye', a major newspaper would later dramatize the moment. Another report would record: '...he had seen a boy and a girl, sitting in the rear seat of a car, making gesticulations.')

Inderjeet's mind now kicked into detail mode. He processed the colour of the car and the number. He recorded a dent in the front bumper. It was the result of crashing into a cyclist near Gole Dak Khana—the detail that would subsequently be stitched to the overall abduction narrative and police investigation.

(The police version tallied Inderjeet's account with other eyewitness accounts. After knocking down a cyclist the driver of the Fiat had stopped the car for a while. A crowd had gathered as it usually did for events both small and big, and this crash was significant. From police enquiries a version would emerge: crowded in and heckled, an occupant of the car pulled out a knife and attacked one among the crowd before driving off.)

Inderjeet drove on towards the Ridge, hoping to find a police patrol. He saw them nearly every day, especially around the Shankar Road crossing. On 26 August, there were none, at the crossing or near the Ridge. He decided to head on to the police station in Rajinder Nagar, nearest to his location. It took him five minutes to find it. In all, Inderjeet estimated that it took him about ten minutes from the time he lost sight of the car to the time he reached the police station.

It was then 6.45 p.m.

The officers of duty took another ten minutes or so, Inderjeet estimated, to note down the details he provided them. The SHO, or station house officer, asked the young engineer to write down his report, but Inderjeet declined, insisting he was passing on the information as a concerned citizen—on 'humanitarian grounds'. Inderjeet began his observation with the time he saw the struggling children, to his giving chase, to the time he lost sight of the car.

'Probably some relationship problem,' Inderjeet recalled the officer blowing off his concern.

The officers then remarked to his colleague—Inderjeet recalled—that the precise area of Inderjeet first noticing something was amiss was out of their jurisdiction. It lay within Mandir Marg police station's ambit and they ought to be informed. So, they informed the Police Control Room which in turn passed it all on to Mandir Marg police station.

It was 7.40 p.m.

This chronology was later confirmed—on 29 August, after news of the killings had fire stormed across the capital and the country—by Avinash Chander, an assistant commissioner of police. He claimed that the number of the car as provided by Inderjeet as HRK 8930; and, that police patrol cars and motorcycle patrols were sent to look for the car for over an hour but failed to turn up anything.

■

On 27 August, a Sunday, Inderjeet was summoned to the Dhaula Kuan police station. There, Deputy Commissioner K. K. Paul showed him photographs of the children.

'I told him I had not got a very clear view of the girl,' Inderjeet recounted. 'But the boy was unmistakable. I even told him it was his picture when he was younger. The big eyes, the nose that had been pressed to the glass all the time as if trying to communicate through the barrier of glass, was distinctive.'

On his way back home from work on the 28th, his eye caught the photos of Geeta and Sanjay in an evening newspaper. He stopped his scooter to purchase a copy, expecting that it would feature a story of them having been found. The article was instead about the missing children.

'I was so upset.'

The mood and the disquiet followed him home. He couldn't eat anything that evening. His ageing mother fretted too.

▪

Inderjeet would speak of his experience to Dutt within days of the incident. She began her story in *Hindustan Times* with this most dramatic image of the children, translating and amping up Inderjeet's memory recall and emotion:

> His hand folded in a plea for help, pointing from time to time to his bleeding shoulder, his face pressed to the rear glass of the speeding car; the girl next to him pulling fiercely at the hair of the car driver sitting immediately in her front even as he slapped her mercilessly again and again—this was the last glimpse that Inderjeet...had of...the brother and sister found brutally murdered on the Ridge yesterday.

POLITICS

The siblings were rapidly transformed into political ammunition. When it met on Wednesday, the 30th of August, a day and a half after the discovery of the bodies of Geeta and Sanjay, Parliament was in an uproar. It was all Ravindra Varma, the parliamentary affairs minister, could do to assure legislators in the Lok Sabha that government would do everything to apprehend the killers and see that justice was done.

MPs from adversarial parties, the in-power but fractured and fighting Janata Party, the Congress, electorally banished but adamant and ever-watchful for an opportunity to hit back at their nemesis of 1977, and the Marxists—plump with a huge victory in elections to West Bengal's Assembly the previous year and loud with a slew of doomsday conspiracy theories that spelled CIA in red neon—clamoured to present their distress at the killing of Geeta and Sanjay. Congress MP Vasant Sathe termed it 'too shocking'. Deputy speaker of the Lower House, his party colleague, Godey Murahari, agreed.

The Rajya Sabha's vice chairman A. G. Kulkarni, also from the Congress, railed against the 'dastardly murder' and termed it a 'matter of shame' for all. He was triggered by party colleague Kalpnath Rai, a persistent voice in the Upper House, who called the episode a 'sad commentary' on law and order in Delhi.

The Congress escalated it to 'deep concern' for 'deteriorating' law and order across India. The coalition in power that had spectacularly dethroned the Congress a little over a year earlier could, according to its political blood-enemies, do nothing right to protect the Chopra children, and, by extension, protect the capital and the country.

A day later, Prime Minister Desai had to intervene to calm the concern in Parliament over the killings, and assured MPs that he would 'certainly dismiss those officers' if any were proven to be negligent in following up on initial information and subsequent investigations. 'It is his'—the police officer's—'business to inform the concerned police station,' acknowledged Desai, who was also the country's home minister, 'and not ask the party to go over to the other police station. I will certainly look into it.'

Ganga Swarup, the station house officer of Rajinder Nagar police station, and the duty officer, Harbhajan Singh, would be suspended that day. An inspector in the Police Control Room was temporarily removed from duty, pending investigations to gauge if there had been a delay in flashing the message about the children in the Fiat. Police Commissioner Jayendra Nath Chaturvedi ordered these actions, but it wasn't clear whether these were pre-emptive disciplinary actions by the police or a result of prime ministerial pressure. Either way, they were clearly designed to show the public that the buck stopped somewhere.

Desai got a dig or two in against the Congress, which didn't waste the opportunity to chip away at the prime minister's credibility—there was even a shouted suggestion that he resign as he was the home minister. Desai pushed back, and suggested the police was the way it was because there was 'laxity' in the past but now 'we are trying to tone up the administration'. That attracted derisive laughter from the Congress benches.

At one stage Congress leader Vasant Sathe even insinuated the prime minister was dismissive about the entire matter. He mentioned a 'high dignitary' had pooh-poohed the killings when a visitor came calling.

'Why are you panicky?' this dignitary is said to have announced. 'A murder in America takes place every two minutes.'

'Who is this dignitary?' demanded Raj Narain, whose case against Indira for electoral malpractice at the Allahadbad High Court—which he won—triggered the Emergency. Narain had also defeated Indira in Rae Bareli by a huge margin in the 1977 elections. Now health minister, the combative Narain was a critic of both Desai and the government of which he was a part.

'Name him,' Narain insisted.

'The prime minister had said this to Mr Radha Raman'—said Sathe, naming a former top official in the capital's administration who had made his concerns known to the PM.

That's not what he meant—an angry Desai responded. His words had been taken out of context and the entire conversation hadn't been reported. He hadn't at all meant to diminish the 'grievousness' of the deaths, he had merely remarked on such occurrences in the United States as a commentary on the kind of society it was. Desai leavened this backpedalling by saying it was easy to beat the government with any stick but it was doing what it could to follow up on the killings. 'The government is responsible, but ultimately it has to be shown that we are negligent about it' for any criticism to stick.

Congress satrap Ambika Soni upped the emotional quotient by providing a generous measure of hyperbole to her more temperate plea that the children be posthumously honoured for their fightback. It was an appropriate gesture, she felt, at a time when the coming year, 1979, was to be marked by United Nations as International Year of the Child.

'Get the Scotland Yard, get Interpol,' Soni wept dramatically, 'but catch the criminals in a week.'

'I don't know how to express my sorrow, especially to the parents of the two children,' the usually snappish Desai softened his delivery in response. 'There can be no greater calamity for them.'

It was as if the dignity of the two minutes of silence with which Parliament began the day's proceedings to honour the memory of Geeta and Sanjay, was diluted by the subsequent discussion Parliament had on the children for a full seventy minutes.

■

Just how significant those seventy minutes were could be measured with other businesses of concern at hand—indeed, a day India's very security seemed to be a threat.

Pakistan remained a strategic concern. It appeared Pakistan's army had indulged in the usual 'unprovoked firing', in the peculiar language of offence and defence along the bizarrely but aptly named

Line of Control that determined its border with India in Jammu & Kashmir.

But more disturbing than that incident in Rajouri which yet again signalled that Pakistan and its security establishment wouldn't remain cowed by its massive defeat in 1971 and a subsequent treaty for an uneasy peace in 1972, was news of negotiations that might bring Pakistan a flock of a hundred Northrop F-5Es 'deep strike' fighter jets from the United States—but they were also appraising the suitability of French Mirage fighters and a fresh-off-the-block US fighter that was the talk of America and its allies and foes alike, the General Dynamics F-16 Falcon. Pakistan was concerned Indian fighters and bombers could within minutes reach its on-the-make nuclear research facility in Kahuta, not far from the military hub of Rawalpindi.

(There was a little good news too, this about India's technological efforts. Parliament was informed that Indian Space Research Organisation was well on its way to launch its Apple satellite. It had nothing to do with the eponymous computer company launched a couple of years earlier by college dropouts, the two Steves, Jobs and Wozniak, but was in fact a shortened form of Ariane Passenger Payload Experiment, India's experimental satellite, to be boosted into geostationary orbit by the European Space Agency's Ariane rocket from faraway Kourou in French Guiana. The launch was planned for May 1980. If all went well with Apple, INSAT-1 would quickly follow in 1981, to enhance meteorology, telecommunications and television services; and India's space age would arrive.)

The urgent matter of electoral reforms was also a point of intense debate in Parliament. H. M. Patel, the Janata government's finance minister, said he wished to ensure the role of 'money power in elections was rooted out, or at least reduced'. The discussions were taking place in the shadow of allegations by the Opposition Congress that Kanti Desai, the prime minister's son, had struck a deal of 5 million rupees with a Calcutta-based businessman to ensure the appointment of an official, I. P. Gupta, as the chairperson of the all-powerful Central Board of Direct Taxes.

None of such cynical or uplifting mechanics of state, though, masked the daily Page One headlines across India expressing distress over the murders of Geeta and Sanjay. In a way all this was structured, the product of teams of journalists and editors packaging news and deciding, in the so-called hierarchy of news selection in newspapers, what went where, how the news of the day was displayed across various combinations of point sizes, photographs, and 'column inches' given to a particular news 'item'. That decided the decibel level of a newspaper article, to use a mixed metaphor, relegating something to a blip, or to a utilitarian purpose, or importance—even sensationalism.

While such presentation was by default largely second-hand, unfiltered anguish was exhibited by readers in Delhi and elsewhere who wrote in to newspapers. It didn't matter if a particular letter writer was habituated to doing so—a species often derided by the 'desk' that selected such letters—or when a random reader was moved deeply by an event to pen an outpouring on a postcard or 'inland letter form'.

'I do not know the Chopra family,' wrote Raksha Balvir, 'but today I mourn with them. Have things come to such a pass that criminals have no fear of the law left in them? Has the life of an innocent citizen become completely insecure in this capital city of Delhi?'

'Sir,' wrote K. K. Razdan. 'The murder of two innocent children puts me into a perpetual state of sorrow.... The tragedy could have been averted....' A. J. Banerjee took a lofty route to outrage, accusation, and damnation: 'A learned judge once mentioned that the police were the most well-organized corrupt group in India. Suffice it to say in this context that if a survey is conducted, perhaps no other city will be able to compete with the capital's police force.' From Srinagar, Syed Abdul Haq suggested terminal measures: 'The murderers responsible for the grisly killing of Sanjay and Geeta should be publicly flogged and hanged when they are caught.'

Some wrote sentiment-soaked verse, like Niti Paul Mehta.

Leaves grow pale
Wither and fall;
But my heart aches
When a green leaf falls!

Meanwhile, there were farmers protesting at the nearby Boat Club, a short walk from Parliament, demanding better prices for their produce. Many of them were arrested.

There was a thread here—anger and despair over Geeta and Sanjay's deaths would soon spill over from media outrage and Letters to the Editor to be manifested at the Boat Club.

SILLY SEASON

Information remained scant and confusing.

Was it a lime green Fiat? Or brown? Or mustard? Who, exactly, were the killers? What was their motive?

Newspapers were full of reports quoting 'reliable reports'.

One such on 31 August asserted what was known, that the 'mustard colour car' seen by Inderjeet Singh with plates reading HRK 8930—the plates had turned out to be fake—was the vehicle of death, as it were. The owner of the Fiat had been traced.

As to the killers, it quoted a 'reliable report': '...the description flashed throughout the country—the one believed to be the "brain"—is a fair-complexioned man with thin moustache and medium height.' Both killers are believed to in their 'early thirties'.

A person answering to the description used to fill petrol at a particular petrol pump, went another 'reliable report'. Thirty-five litres every Monday, like clockwork.

They were 'hardened criminals'.

There was an investigation on in Bombay, another such 'reliable' report maintained, which was attempting to chase down a lead that the killings of Geeta and Sanjay was a 'mafia-like vendetta'. It was, this lead suggested, 'spurred by a petty officer in the navy against whom action had been taken for alleged involvement with a multi-crore smuggling ring.' The inference was that it could have something to do with Captain Chopra's time with the navy's JAG in Bombay.

'The apparent brutality of the murder and the absence of signs of molestation give initial credence to the story,' a newspaper wrote. All this was 'substantiated', the article concluded quoting 'reliable reports' which provided such substantiation, that 'there had been disturbing reports of participation of naval personnel in smuggling activities especially in the India-West Asia sector.' Interpol reports 'suggested' that a branch of Bombay's mafia—the paper spelled it with a capital M, an honour usually reserved for the Cosa Nostra in Italy—ran the operation.

With limited clues and the pressure piling up on the police, government, and media alike to deliver, the silly season on the killers of Geeta and Sanjay was officially open.

TIPPING POINT

By the morning of 31 August, the Boat Club, the capital's gathering place for protests against the all manner of perceived and real government missteps, became a magnet supercharged by the deaths of Geeta and Sanjay.

The outrage gathered like a growing storm, even though it was largely a middle-class storm. Amidst all the atrocities of India, this had a special resonance as two of New India's shining crop from a family of elegant purpose and dignity, about to take wing for a flight to an empowered future free from all the shackles of prejudice and hoary perceptions holding back the 'Indian Dream', had been attacked. This statistic of violation and death had become personal.

Several thousand students from schools and colleges across Delhi poured into the space facing the massive Lutyens-era edifices that flanked Rashtrapati Bhavan—North Block and South Block. It was within view of the Parliament Building a little to the north-east. The Boat Club, where a club hadn't been seen for decades, and couples and families punted in small, flat-bottomed boats in shallow pools in summer and winter alike, drew large crowds in the evenings and over weekends to create a festival atmosphere in a city that largely lived and died by politics. This triangle of structures focused a forceful outrage.

The largest contingent arrived from Lady Shri Ram College, known to generations of students as LSR. Twelve hundred students and ten faculty from the all-female institution marched in silent protest from the college, tucked away between the busy residential neighbourhoods of Lajpat Nagar in south-east Delhi and the quieter and quaintly named East of Kailash, to India Gate, and then down the broad avenue of Rajpath to the Boat Club. It was a trek of more than a dozen kilometres.

They were joined by students from several colleges that represented socio-cultural roots from Anglicized to Indic: Janaki Devi, Satyavati, Mata Sundari, Delhi College of Engineering, Jesus and Mary or JMC—which Geeta attended—Dayal Singh College with its rough-and-tumble reputation....

'The police have become complacent,' the head of LSR's students' union Mayna Singh told the numerous journalists gathered to record this remarkable show of solidarity. 'The law-and-order situation in the Capital has completely broken down.'

The students had reached Boat Club at 10.30 a.m. but were prevented from going further. So, many of them squatted on Rajpath and blocked traffic. The numbers had swelled by noon.

Elsewhere, small groups of students fanned out and laid siege, figuratively and literally, to some of Delhi's lawmakers and law-keepers.

Commissioner of Police Chaturvedi had a group of raucous students from Delhi University show up at his residence and 'gherao' him. It was a word that, thanks to left-wing and labour agitations since the 1960s, had gone rapidly from similar usage in several Indian languages to signify the verb, to surround, in everyday Indian-English. The students demanded accountability for errors in the policing system that at first dismissed, and then delayed, information about two eyewitness accounts that described struggling youngsters in a car.

Commissioner Chaturvedi came out to meet the students.

'Shame-shame,' they shouted, echoing the peculiarly subcontinental chant used for a range of sins from indiscretion and irresponsibility to a crime.

The commissioner didn't duck the situation—he had correctly sensed the mood. He said the only thing he could at the time: 'No effort will be spared in apprehending the culprits.'

Across the city, moving from so-called Lutyens' Delhi to that other bastion of the British Indian empire across town in the Civil Lines area of Old Delhi, students of Modern School were buttonholing the lieutenant governor of Delhi, D. R. Kohli. They hadn't been able to meet him a day earlier, at the suggestion of a factotum of the president of India—first citizen of the country—and they had a petition to present to the city's top-ranked official—the first citizen of Delhi. This petition urged the lieutenant governor to ensure the killers of Sanjay, their 'schoolmate', and his sister, Geeta, were quickly arrested.

Kohli too sensed the mood. Delhi administration is doing everything it can, he assured them.

By the end of the day, representatives of nearly every school and college that had gathered at the Boat Club presented memoranda demanding action to the speaker of the Lok Sabha, and Commissioner Chaturvedi. There wouldn't be any let-up in the pressure for several days. The students of Delhi's numerous schools and colleges, privately-run and publicly funded, would ensure it.

On the following day, 1 September, students of the Convent of Jesus and Mary, a school located across Gole Dak Khana, the post office that would soon assume a notoriety of address that overlaid its genteel history, planned to take out a protest march to honour Geeta and Sanjay and mark their concern at slippage in the capital's law and order. They also planned to present a memorandum to the prime minister.

Modern School, Sanjay's own, remained closed in mourning. Springdales School a few short kilometres north of where Geeta and Sanjay's remains were found, held a condolence meeting.

▪

The mood wasn't always pacific, as the erudite Atal Behari Vajpayee, rarely at a loss for words or smooth public relations, discovered. India's foreign minister, in government because the Hindu-nationalist ultra-right had decided to team up with the Janata Party-led coalition in post-Emergency exuberance, showed up at the Boat Club on 31 August. He was accompanied by a fellow MP, Kanwar Lal Gupta. Vajpayee's was a diplomatic mission to receive memoranda from the agitated students, talk to them, calm them, assure them the process of governance hadn't failed them even if the police seemingly had, India's government was doing all it could to solve the murders. In particular he wanted to assuage the feelings of the students of JMC.

It backfired spectacularly.

'Shame-shame,' a group of students shouted when he and his party approached them on Rajpath.

Go away, suggested a knot of charged Delhi University students, we haven't invited you.

Instead, Vajpayee decided to wade in. A sprightly fifty-three, he attempted to climb onto the bonnet of a police jeep to be able to better speak to the throng; there wasn't another public address system at hand. But the restive public evidently did not wish to be addressed with what they assumed was platitudes. The crowd also contained student leaders from various political parties. It became a bit of a melee. Two stones were hurled at Vajpayee. One hit his forehead and opened an inch-and-half long gash to the bone.

That triggered a charge by bamboo- and cane-wielding police personnel—lathi-charge, to use another Indian Englishism that had firmly taken root alongside other peculiarities such as air dash, the act by a politician or businessperson or bureaucrat to take a flight for urgent consultation or to answer an urgent summons from somewhere in increasingly frenetic India to Delhi, or to wherever there was a man-made or natural crisis, or power play, instead of a journey by train or car. But the police held back. The charge was mild, just to disperse the angry knot of students and to rescue the foreign minister, not the severe beatings India's law keepers routinely administered to impose order, to maintain peace.

Bleeding profusely, Vajpayee went somewhat dramatically to Parliament, accompanied by his colleague, Gupta. Vajpayee took a seat in the back benches, kurta spattered with blood, his head covered in a large, now-bloodied handkerchief.

Gupta interrupted house business to relate what had transpired at the Boat Club and launched a scathing attack on the Congress-I, accusing its cohorts of hijacking the protests and 'known history-sheeters' affiliated to the party for triggering the attack on Vajpayee. Congress leader Vasant Sathe immediately denied it. He was shouted down.

Two students would be arrested on the charge of throwing stones: a first-year Masters student of Punjab University in Chandigarh and a student of DAV College in Delhi. There were two catch-and-release arrests too: Jay Mala, a leader of the Indian Students' Congress, and Bhim Singh, a legislator from Jammu & Kashmir who had steadily gathered street-cred for belligerent protests. After being released from police custody, interrogation done and statement recorded, Mala would show media persons her torn and bloodied sari as a mark of police brutality. She claimed to have actually tried to protect Vajpayee from a group of aggressive young men who had 'suddenly appeared' among the students and started to 'create confusion'. There seemed to be some truth to the triggered violence—whether spontaneous or engineered.

Meanwhile, in Parliament Vajpayee sat through Gupta's rant and the ensuing hullabaloo. He eventually stood up and spoke slowly to offer his version of what had transpired.

'Shame-shame,' shouted his colleagues in the treasury benches.

'But I don't want to blame anybody,' Vajpayee declared. That egged on the treasury benches some more.

He was then taken to Ram Manohar Lohia—Willingdon—hospital to have his wound seen to. A procession of doctors accompanied Vajpayee to an operation theatre. There he received five stitches. The medical superintendent at the hospital, L. R. Pathak, announced that the foreign minister had been sedated and would remain in the hospital for two days under observation. He would not be receiving visitors.

▪

In a few weeks, Vajpayee's visit to Willingdon Hospital and the treating of his cut on the forehead would seem like an eerie foreshadowing to a revelation intimately related to the grisly murders of Geeta and Sanjay.

But that was still in the relatively distant future. The present, and immediate future, was a chaos of suppositions, allegations, suspicions, and shock that followed a tragedy that a city, and a country, appeared to collectively sense.

The horror that had clearly accompanied the children to the last moments of their lives led to a massive upwelling of resentment against the administration in general and Delhi Police in particular—even though the blame for a part of 'DP's' perceived and evident ineptitude lay with how the police force was routinely misused in the capital.

The media began to trot out numbers that until now had been the preserve of bureaucrats, slicing and dicing them every which way. Crime statistics were suddenly the focus of ghoulish chats over tea and astonishment.

Did you know Delhi has the highest number of crimes, at 800 to every lakh compared to other big cities? This comparative crime chart to every hundred-thousand of the population was 600 for Madras. You would think the numbers for Bombay, a den of real and Bollywood villains for decades, would be really high—but it's 550. You know Calcutta to be a city of violence, with the Naxalite movement and labour troubles and political goondas and whatnot, but even there the number is 500.

Yes, but even though our crime rate may be high, the murder rate is low. In Delhi, a murder is *attempted* on an average only once in 30 hours but a murder is actually *committed* once every 44 hours—that's much below the national average of a murder going down every 20 minutes, or 3 murders an hour.

So what? Look at the numbers when stacked against the population. It's just 1.8 murders per lakh in Calcutta, 2.3 in Bombay, 2.5 in Madras, 2.7 in Ahmedabad. It's 3.3 in Delhi.

What else do you expect in this den of vipers? These politicians take everything and give nothing. They live like kings and queens and make us beg for the lives of our children. They say Delhi is the most policed place in India. There are nearly 1,400 police personnel for every 100 square kilometres in Delhi; for India the average is 25. All other major cities in India don't top 800 for every 100 square kilometres.

Bring it down to bodies and it is as stark. Delhi has 40-plus police personnel for every 10,000 people; for Bombay it is 35; Calcutta, 20; Madras, a lowly 17. Delhi Police is better funded than police forces anywhere else in India: per capita expenditure on police personnel in Delhi is 35 rupees—while it is 30 rupees for Bombay and less than 20 rupees for Madras and Calcutta.

Delhi's relatively better numbers are hardly a help. The capital has 22,460 police personnel but more than 40 per cent of them are diverted from maintaining law and order and preventing and investigating crimes to protecting VIPs and guarding embassies. Add a tenth more who are tasked with traffic management and airport security, and more than half the police force are removed daily from the board.

The media continued to churn the conversation mills.

There isn't much money, so there isn't much upkeep either. Did you read?—DP has 75 patrol cars, but 45 are out of action because there's no money to repair them.

And what happens because of all that? Even children die. See what happened to Geeta and Sanjay.

It was as if arrogant commentators had descended to the sobering level of earthy citizenry and citizens had assumed the mantle of all-knowing commentators—the fallout of any crisis from a stunning crime to a stunning cyclone, political and atmospheric.

▪

Some commentary stood out with their sentiment and conclusions that were easy to arrive at in a time of chaos and flux. The signed, front-page comment by Hiranmay Karlekar, editor of *Hindustan Times*, the day after Geeta and Sanjay's corpses were found, was one such. 'Delhi's police is admittedly hampered by high-level interference as well as inadequate manpower, equipment and mobility,' the usually equanimous Karlekar had fumed. 'Protection of very important persons and their escapade-prone children encroaches heavily on time meant for prevention and detection of crime, as do the rallies and demonstrations which are a part of the Capital's ambience.'

But few could doubt, he wrote, that matters could have been 'markedly better' had the police been 'less lethargic' and 'inept'. The capital's police had been accused of theft, robbery, murder, and molestation. They have been known to take the side of the accused.

The Emergency hardly helped, Karlekar continued. Indeed, it worsened the situation. Who could forget the case of Chitra Jagannathan, a twenty-four-year-old college lecturer, who left her home in Sarvodaya Enclave one morning in early February 1977, and remained untraced to this day?

The Emergency wrought 'severe damage', the signed editorial concluded. 'It made a habit of arbitrary, illegal and high-handed action and undermined discipline by encouraging officers to bypass normal channels and report directly to the powers that were.'

Powers that are.

■

Another comment, indeed, one that many would term an instant classic, would feature in an issue of the *Economic and Political Weekly* published in the week after Geeta and Sanjay—sometimes it seemed the suffix of were-killed or found-dead was unnecessary. In *EPW*, as that magazine had fondly come to be known among certain socio-political circles and the media, the editor and public intellectual Romesh Thapar unleashed a salvo against deteriorating law and order and plummeting governance.

He did so in his much-read 'Capital View' column, which in this issue ran alongside a sign of the times: advertisements for the annual results of Metal Box, Indian Hotels Co. and Tata Oil Mills Co—which announced that, at a time of a relatively controlled economy, when a business needed to find any way at all to earn foreign exchange even in an area totally unrelated to its core business, the company had 'secured a license for chartering 25 fishing boats from Thailand for one year and has already started fishing operations with 12 boats from Port Blair in the Andamans' to export the 'entire catch of fresh fish' to Thailand and other Southeast Asian countries.

'One of the first casualties of non-government is law and order,' Thapar wrote, and it is here that political leadership needs to be steadfast in quality application if only to assert itself. 'We have been reminded of these obvious truths by the brutal murder of the Chopra children.'

Thapar saw the public protest in the wake of the killings, 'admittedly in sharp contrast to the casualness over all manner of killings at the deliberately faceless levels of society', as a sign the citizens were jolted out of several years of a dangerous ennui born of hopelessness. Among other things, this had normalized thuggishness. This new normal, as it were, sanitized as commonplace the rule of 'local toughs' given their fiefs by 'indifferent or demoralized police'. Strikes and political clashes were not taken for the warning signals they were. With the onset of the Emergency in June 1975 and during its two-year run, the police force was 'used with a cynicism unparalleled in our history'. The killings triggered again the wakefulness to an all-pervasive fear that Thapar maintained 'prevails in our towns'.

Here Thapar segued to the purpose of his cathartic column: a sign of the times in Delhi—capital rot that was both cause and symptom of a system made rotten. He wrote about assertion of the 'wrong kind of power' by the government of the day that only seemed to perpetuate the wrong kind of power seen during the Emergency, a wrong kind of power that 'created an impression in the police force that only a fool would try to assert the ground rules'.

It mirrored a descent into civic darkness, he maintained, that took in a range of lawlessness from chaos on the roads to the tendency to 'settle scores on the spot' that was fast becoming a Delhi imperative, a lack of norms 'even in the city's more organised areas'—more genteel, gentrified and orderly, less ghetto, less slum. The function of judges, juries, and executioners—lawkeepers—were really at the initiative of local 'goondas....'

It had come to pass that courts were the place for 'the sons and daughters of the nation' to spend 'most of their time'—an Indira, her son Sanjay, so many more.

Delhi's soul was dying, and with it, India's.

Public commentary, whether sincere or sarcastic, Thapar maintained, remained 'unheard' because the inheritors of secret ballot and public wish—politicians—were busy with 'inane' internal jousting. 'The silence' to this request for redressal, Thapar wrote, 'was sickening'.

'The police force has to be geared to coping with a crime wave now headed by educated operators, capable of elaborate organization. Crime is no longer an exclusive resort of the unemployed hoodlum or desperado,' Thapar flagged imminent, millennial chaos. 'We are hopelessly unaware of the ramifications of our enormous urban spreads. It is an aspect that is likely to intensify during the last years of the century when our population approaches 1,000 million.'

The future had to be redressed with a police force engaged with citizens, not isolated from them. To think otherwise would be plain silly, and to consider coping with a growing crime wave without active and willing cooperation of citizens would be 'naïve'. A palatable future would need to take on board such understanding. And if this meant a reorganization of the police force, so be it.

'The old men who rule India today, and their self-satisfied or silent secretariats,' Thapar fumed, 'imagine that they are dealing with "familiar" problems. This accounts for idiotic statements of reassurance about increased police patrolling and what have you.... And, finally, the thought does occur that if this is the depressing situation in the capital, how far behind are the other cities of India?'

Instead of protecting citizens, politicians appeared to be interested only in getting hold of the home ministry 'intelligence files' to protect their cronies and attack critics and enemies.

'If the Janata Party, donkey-like, refuses to stir, maybe then there will be little left (for the committed cadres of the parties who perceive the future!) but to organize from now against a second Emergency. It's a salutary thought.'

■

Thapar's grand sweep would be undercut by cynicism in the very next issue of the magazine. The 16 September issue of *EPW* tore into how directionless and impotent the government had become. So directionless and impotent, suggested the columnist Hemendra Narayan, that the defence minister, Jagjivan Ram, who positioned himself as a messiah of the so-called Scheduled Caste and low-caste folks of India, appeared elitist in some ways. The killings in Pupri showed it.

Pupri was a village in Ram's parliamentary constituency of Sasaram, in northwest Bihar. Two landless workers of the Scheduled Castes were chased down by wealthy local upper-caste farmers with guns, handguns, swords, and staves. One was shot dead, and the second was shot dead when he intervened on behalf of the first victim. It happened on the very day the Chopra children's corpses were discovered.

'Yet, Jagjivan Ram, who had time to visit the Chopras and express his grief over the tragic murder of their children, who also had to fly to Kanpur to address a "special convention" of the Uttar Pradesh branch of the Bharatiya Dalit Varg and call upon the "oppressed masses to unite and rise to fight against the existing social and economic irregularities..." found no time when two members of those very masses were killed by their social oppressors. In fact, Jagjivan Ram has never visited his constituency since before the elections.'

This was in heavy counterpoint to the privileged being entitled even in death—a thing nobody wrote in black and white and nobody of note spoke aloud, but the inference was always present as an uneasy undercurrent. In several ways it was implicit in the people-like-us manner with which mainstream media projected Geeta and Sanjay. Examples were at hand—a major Delhi newspaper began a front-page story on policing slip-ups with this opening sentence: 'Could the two handsome and bright children, Geeta and Sanjay, have been saved from their merciless killers....?'

In any case in the eyes of both well-wishers and critics, it was as if the government could do nothing right.

■

And there was the ever-present anguish of Madan and Roma Chopra.

'These days no mother and father feel secure about their children,' the captain declared in one of his several interactions with the media. 'It is not the question of my children. It is my children today. Tomorrow it can be others.'

UNHITCHING

An immediate outcome of the killings—alongside near-constant waves of outrage and recrimination—was the near-total absence of youngsters hitching rides. Thumbing or waving down a passing scooter or car was standard operating practice for both single or groups of relatively young girls and boys, even young working folk, who supplemented Delhi's deficient and over-burdened public transport system and sometimes aggressive and extortionate taxis and auto-rickshaws—shortened to 'auto'—with their own brand of locomotion. At times, the media sneeringly referred to it as a phenomenon of the relatively elite, the upper crust of DU—Delhi University. One newspaper wrote of the 'familiar sight' of 'groups of young girls standing outside the city's more fashionable colleges with their thumbs raised'.

Jaya Shourie of Lady Irwin College, down the road from Sanjay's Modern School, spoke of how more than half the students of women's institution would thumb lifts. Now, in the two to three days since news of Geeta and Sanjay splashed across their lives, only a handful had the 'courage' to 'travel with a stranger'. She spoke of those students who lived in Delhi and had to regularly commute as well as those who arrived from elsewhere and roomed in Delhi, either at hostels and residences in various colleges or in 'town'—from paying guest accommodation to several students sharing an apartment.

A colleague of hers spoke of how 'everyone is terribly scared after the murder of the Chopras'.

Another colleague, Gina Mehta, voiced the lament of generations of female commuters in Delhi. 'If you travel in a bus you are pushed around and pinched by eve-teasing types,' she said, using the peculiar DU syntax to include a range of male entitlement and aggression from harassment to molestation that formed a hideous, everyday part of being female in Delhi. She added without a trace of irony: 'While hitch-hiking you at least reach your destination in one piece.' Another student spoke of the pointlessness of waiting for a DTC bus after 5 p.m. when the evening rush hour began. 'The bus hardly ever halted and there was never any space.'

Others offered hitch-hiking formulae with an eye to safety. Don't take lifts from people who look 'dubious'. Hitching a ride on a scooter may be safer than one in a car. If you take a lift in a car, ensure the ratio of hitchhikers to occupants is 2:1. Look for drivers who look 'completely safe'.

These were all theoretical mercies in a time of singular and collective trauma. They all agreed there was no such thing as feeling completely safe.

▪

Decades later, Usha Rai, among the doughtiest journalists in Delhi of her generation, recalled the time.

'I've seen so much of cruelty in general and cruelty on women in particular, that sometimes the mind just blanks out,' she pierced me with her trademark look—the sharpest eyes framed with a polite smile. She reeled off a list over and above the daily atrocities and deaths that routinely accompanied—accompany—everyday India employing twisted rationales for horrors using religion, caste, gender bias, racism, income disparity—altogether an endless list.

'The rape of Jain nuns by some guru, Roop Kanwar's committing sati—the crimes kept getting worse.'

As disturbing as the times were, layered with the abominations including the young widow Roop Kanwar's spectacular forced immolation in Sikar, Rajasthan, in 1987, the arc of horror for Rai began in the 1970s. Evil was made glamourous in that decade with the 1975 Bollywood blockbuster *Sholay*, and, in it, iconic evil embodied by the dacoit Gabbar Singh. It made the career of the actor essaying the role, Amjad Khan, and cemented in the public imagination the silkily ruthless character with an arresting rasp and rakish demeanour as the era's bogeyman, chopping the limbs off his arch enemy, blithely killing henchmen who showed fear or failure, destroying the lives of villagers who would stand up to him—and do it all with horrific élan.

'There was a saying,' Rai recalled, 'Gabbar Singh ayega.'

The threat was designed to scare children into doing a chore, or homework and, of course, was a scary chide to sleep. Or else Gabbar would visit.

'Then this happened.'

At the time Geeta and Sanjay were killed, Rai lived in Kaka Nagar, a government housing enclave southeast of India Gate, a short walk from the zoo and the magnificent Purana Qila, still imposing after 600 years, the fort complex easily dwarfing Delhi's high-rises-on-the-make not too far away.

'Buddha Jayanti Park was sought after for picnics and romancing couples,' she said. 'The trend for taking lifts had started.'

'This was a crime that changed the minds of people,' Rai recalled. 'There was more policy and police vigilance, better public transport, more carefulness. And, of course, for a long while people stopped asking for lifts.'

She discussed the killings with another pioneering journalist of the time, Prabha Dutt. Rai described the two as being 'very close', part of a resolute sisterhood in a profession then overwhelmingly male. Among others things, like Dutt, Rai had to balance her career with bringing up her young children.

'We talked about it for days afterwards. There was great disgust, and great concern—in general and certainly for our young children.'

The two colleagues and friends would together journey to the end of the arc of horror, from the killing of Geeta and Sanjay to the execution of their convicted killers. Along the way, Dutt would set legal precedents that sought for journalists the right to perform their jobs better, with more access to prisoners, more freedom to interview death row convicts, even if it seemed that all the world wanted the subject of her queries to be hanged and be done with it.

But that was still some years into the future. Meanwhile, Delhi's soul would be dragged through capital muck. Again. And again.

On 31 August 1978, Day 2 since the discovery of Geeta and Sanjay, the police provided a name.

Billa.

That was an alias of a known thug, Jasbir Singh. 'Billa' now became the name most frequently mentioned in the media as a likely culprit, quoting 'informed' sources among the police who provided 'reasonable information'. He was said to mostly operate in Bombay but had been seen in Delhi.

Investigative activity had begun to crank up since Captain Chopra sounded the alarm on 26 August. Delhi Police and their colleagues in other cities had begun to feverishly beat out tattoos since the discovery of Geeta and Sanjay on 29 August, in part spurred by the subsequent public uproar and consequent embarrassment to the government.

In Parliament, continuing accusations of the murder of democracy since 1975 now ran parallel with discussions of the fait accompli murder of the teenage siblings. The pressure to deliver was intense.

Police in at least two cities—Delhi and Bombay—were now working overtime, pushing their network of informants to the limit to glean even the briefest glimmer of clues.

That is how Billa's name surfaced.

Now Delhi Police declared they would catch Billa soon. So did Bombay Police. Police from other cities, like Chandigarh, chipped in with their theories.

By 31 August, what passed for information came in a torrent.

One police-media scenario had Billa, who had been 'seen' moving about in Delhi with an associate, also working alone for his preferred modus operandi that began with giving his mark a lift. This ran against the eyewitness statement of Inderjeet Singh;

he had mentioned two men in the front seat of a Fiat.

A newspaper reported that Billa and a partner-in-crime from Bombay, 'Banga' was behind the killings. The letter B was suitably away from the letter R on the typewriter—two rows south—for it to be a typesetting error. Perhaps, one of hearing: lost in translation between police briefings and its journey to the 'page'. But most other newspapers had it right:

Ranga.

A report from Chandigarh described Billa as being Punjabi, and ascribed to him six aliases—Bir Singh, Baxi Singh, Ashok Verma, Ashok Khanna, Ashok Mehra, and Prakash Mehra. He was described as being between twenty-four and twenty-five years old, and five-foot-six in height.

Ranga was pegged at a lanky six-foot-three, his age as yet indeterminate

This information, 'officially learnt', came from sources in Delhi which credited it to a person who had made four sets of fake plates for two men of such description.

Another police source described the two men as having visited Chandni Chowk to purchase swords and guptis—daggers—and a couple of toy pistols. After killing the siblings, Billa had wanted to slip away to Pakistan but chose instead to return to Bombay.

Billa sustained head injuries, offered one such police-media thread, based on eyewitness accounts. And he has been seen in Bombay with a handkerchief around his head.

He has cropped his hair.

He has shaved off his thin moustache.

He had done to the Delhi children what he did to countless couples in Bombay—lure them into his stolen taxis and then take the couple to a secluded place to rob them.

He is suspected to have raped at least one of his female victims.

He is a kidnap specialist.

The police got close to catching him once, by keeping him talking on a 'line'—a phone—at a victim's house while the victim's parents and he talked terms for ransom, but he managed to evade the police because when they traced the call to an address, they found it to be a decoy; Billa was elsewhere. The journalist reporting this titbit misspelled 'ingenious' as 'indigenous' and in the free flow of adjectives to pin on the suspects, nobody corrected him.

With such a frenetic circus of whodunit and whydunit, there were layers to what passed for information and contradictions to what citizens, like the civic engineer Inderjeet Singh, had to say. And yet, some of the information filtering in to the public domain through newspapers—the primary vehicle to portray the alleged killers' identikit, the killers' profile to the public—was eerily close to what would, in a few short weeks, emerge as the primary story.

It was easy to ride public anger and dismiss the police as inept. It was also logical to place crossed wires at the hands of the media. In Bombay, the media depended on sources in Bombay Police and the police grapevine to deliver news from Delhi. In turn, Delhi depended on Bombay for updates, especially with the outing of Billa as a suspect. In the pressure of conveying news to an eager and angry audience, for which the media leaned on the police for fresh updates and the police counted on the media to provide an impression that the police in Delhi and elsewhere were on the ball, it wasn't unusual to see quite different versions of the same investigation on the front page of a newspaper.

Confusion reigned.

■

A Premier Padmini—as an ageing Fiat model had been christened by its licensed manufacturers in India—had been found in the Adarsh Nagar neighbourhood of Delhi, in a lane in Majlis Park. The car was yellowish green. It was mustard. It was a shade of green. Lime green.

Nuances of the colour palette aside, it wore the number plate DHD 7034, and was found abandoned in Gali No. 10 of Majlis Park. Eyewitnesses were quoted as saying it was parked there by a man wearing a white 'bush shirt' and black trousers. It had happened about an hour before midnight on the night of 30 August. The man who parked the car was tall, slim, and 'wheatish' in complexion.

It was first parked in a nearby lane, Gali No. 9, by the Government Girls Middle School.

Is this Gali No. 10? the tall and slim man, who emerged with a black bag in his hand, asked an eyewitness, Jeetender, a worker at Ayodhya Textile Mills.

No, this is No. 9, Jeetender replied. Why do you ask?

Because I have to see a person called Anwar.

I know where Gali No. 10 is but there's nobody called Anwar there, Jeetender replied. And he would know, he insisted, because he was from the neighbourhood—he lived in Gali No. 11 but slept outside the shop of his father in Gali No. 9.

'OK, I will find him myself,' said the man, and returned to the car.

He drove off to Gali No. 10, and parked the car.

Some in the locality spoke of a tall man with a black bag in his hand walking on to Gali No. 2—and away into the darkness.

■

This car quickly became the cynosure of all eyes, investigation—and news.

The police's forensics team literally had a field day with it. The car, which appeared to have been washed inside and out, was still a hive of tell-tale detail. They found bloodstains on the back seat, and a clump of hair. They lifted prints from the back seat and front seats. They found two sets of plates in the trunk of the car, one that read HRF 5411; the other set read DEA 1221. They were found tucked under the rubber mat.

Other evidence comprised a black bag which contained a check shirt.

More details boosted the car as a vehicle of circumstantial evidence. The left parking light was broken. So was the antenna for the radio. The left side had dents. The windows still had prints even though the car had been washed.

All this seemed to match eyewitness accounts of a mad rush by the abductors of the children—and the evident panic that had likely followed the crime.

The two door handles at the back were intact. (This would provide slim defence at court in a few months.)

Pieces of the jigsaw began to fit. This was the same car that was reported as stolen from Ashoka Hotel on 23 August—the date would subsequently be revised to 19 August. Cross-checking the information given by the owner, the police checked the reading—20,699—and deduced that the car had been driven for 300 kilometres or so since being stolen.

The police looked around for HRK 8390, the plates that Inderjeet Singh reported as seeing when he chased after the car with the two clearly distressed youngsters in the rear seat. Had these plates been jettisoned? Was there another possibility?

Who could tell?

There were more accusations thrown at the police for its sloth. Residents of Adarsh Nagar had reported the presence of the car to the police control room at 7 a.m. But a 'flying squad' arrived only at 9 a.m., giving plenty of time for onlookers and street urchins to imprint their own curiosity onto the car. The deputy commissioner of the police of the district, Rajinder Mohan, showed up at 11 a.m. Actual forensic work on the car began at 1:30 p.m.

Perhaps the folks from naval intelligence, who had joined the investigation on account of Captain Chopra being who he was and his former role in Bombay as a JAG officer, would have a story to tell. They were scanning all possibilities as partners with the police in this joint hunt for the killers of the children of one of their own.

■

But there were no leads there; the search was pro-forma, to hunt down possibilities with a view to close chapters. The captain, as had already been communicated to investigators and the media-world-at-large by his family and friends, did not work in any capacity in the navy that could breed such revengeful hostility towards his children.

'All this is selling, isn't it?' a friend of Captain Chopra sneered at media persons who showed up at the Chopra residence, looking for anything—clues, even a slim trail with the barest crumbs to follow—that could explain motive.

Invasive public interest, as ever, battled intensely private grieving.

Military courts don't work like civilian courts, this friend snapped at journalists. In any case, in his advisory capacity, the captain often offered advice to both the prosecution and the defence. Meanwhile, the friend continued his tirade, the media was distorting reality by publishing anything they could get in the name of news.

Such friends also stood firm as gatekeepers to Roma and Madan Chopra, shielding them from the media's untiring need to know personal things about the family, especially given the parents' reluctance to share such things.

Five days after their children went missing, two days since their corpses were discovered, and two days after their funeral, Roma and Madan Chopra had retreated into the only haven they knew—their apartment.

They would occasionally step outside, drawn by students who arrived to offer their messages of grief and solidarity—children like their own.

As Roma did, when she came outside just after the family friend shut out the media that day. It was to hear a group of college students offer their condolences. She acknowledged their message with folded hands, a wordless namaste, and returned inside.

That she even had the strength and grace for such gestures seemed to amaze visitors and onlookers.

AND THE WORLD TURNED...

There remained a world beyond Geeta and Sanjay, beyond the massive overhang of the death and a collective distress.

A boy had gone missing four days earlier.

Bludgeoned by the rush of news of Sanjay and Geeta, the police got to it a little late—and so did reporters of the crime beat who necessarily had a symbiotic relationship with the police. The father of the boy, Raju Thakur, had told the police that his son hadn't reached his school the previous Monday, 28 August.

Thirteen-year-old Raju had left his home in the middle- and lower-middle-class neighbourhood of Netaji Nagar, an area dense with housing for government employees, for the walk to his school in Safdarjung Enclave. Raju never arrived.

All the world now had of him was the description supplied by missing persons bulletins. Dark complexioned, wearing navy blue 'half pants' and a white shirt.

A girl had escaped her abductors that very day, the 31st, when news of young Raju arrived. Veena Yadav, a seventeen-year-old, had managed to jump out of the van in which her abductors were transporting her when it slowed at a major junction.

The drama had begun an evening earlier in the modest ground floor apartment of the family in Ashoka Road, another government residential hub. She had screamed in alarm as, while she bathed, there was an attempt to break the window to the bathroom. Hearing her cries, her father, a brigadier in the army, and two relatives rushed out. There was nobody. But the family filed a report with the nearest police station, in Tilak Marg.

After the family had retired, there was similar disturbance by her bedroom. Her alarm led to another unfruitful chase, and a second complaint to the police. The police advised them to wait for the morning. Nothing could be done before that.

In the morning, she took a bus to her 'polytechnic' in South Extension, a neighbourhood that had several of such career-oriented institutions primarily aimed at female students. As she walked to her polytechnic—Veena would later recount—someone grabbed her from behind and placed a cloth over her face, at which point she became unconscious. When she regained consciousness, she found herself in rear seat of a van. There were two drivers in the front seat.

Despite her grogginess, she managed to yank open the door and jump out of the van when it slowed to a crawl at a roundabout—it turned out to be on Raisina Road, a thoroughfare that ran northeast from a roundabout near the Parliament to the Janpath 'circle' not far from Geeta and Sanjay's intended destination, All India Radio.

Veena managed to walk home. The brigadier again filed a report with the police. The family let the media know about a curious thing. There was rumour at Veena's polytechnic that she was a friend of Geeta's. Had that buzz attracted such attention?

Veena wouldn't say much because she was in shock, and sedated.

Some in the police evidently shrugged it off, even suggesting that there could be more to a seemingly copycat abduction—an attention seeker. There weren't any visible injuries on her; and Veena had declined medical examination.

In greatly distressed Delhi, doubt carried the day over benefit of the doubt.

■

And the world turned.

Even as Delhi's citizenry remained dazed with the deaths of Geeta and Sanjay, there was business to conduct that only Delhi could do. Would India buy the Anglo French SEPECAT Jaguar? Was it as Raj Narain said—this Janata maverick whose stiletto was implacably pointed at his political colleague and foe, Prime Minister Desai? Narain, who insisted a 'caucus' and 'pressure group' had eased the way for the Jaguar, and that 'a commission had been distributed as a consideration' for the deal, wanted to know if the prime minister's son, Kanti, had piggybacked on an official visit of the prime minister to Great Britain to cut a deal on the side. Even the defence of the country appeared to have a dark side.

Desai, meawhile, had no time for such accusations, He was away playing statesman, trying to dial down the perennial tensions with Pakistan. It took the death of a statesman to get Desai to talk business with Pakistan's military dictator Zia-ul-Haq.

As we know, Kenya's president, Jomo Kenyatta, had passed on 22 August. After several days of lying in state, it was time for a grand funeral for that post-colonial icon. Desai and Zia joined that procession.

After the funeral on 31 August, when Delhi remained in uproar over the deaths of Geeta and Sanjay and parts of the city had begun to be inundated by epic floods, Desai invited Zia, Pakistan's chief martial law administrator and till a year earlier the country's army chief, to ride in his limousine to the Nairobi Hilton. There, the two went to Desai's suite and engaged in talks for a little less than an hour.

Desai invited the general to India. Zia accepted. There was talk of 'economic and technical cooperation' between the countries. It would help, went the foreign office opinion. The bilateral nadir of 1971 caused by the fracture of Pakistan after its genocidal machinations in East Pakistan, and the subsequent birth of Bangladesh, appeared to have emerged from the enveloping darkness with the signing of the peace agreement in Shimla in 1972 between Indira Gandhi and Zulfikar Ali Bhutto, a key person behind the policy of genocide in the eastern province. Now Indira was electorally deposed and Bhutto militarily so—he was in jail on a murder charge; not the charge of agreeing to a final solution in soon-to-be Bangladesh but, like Indira, a politician tripped up by hubris.

Now the public bonhomie between the usually cussed Desai and the canny Zia offered a window of opportunity to mend ties and try to move on. There was talk of an Indian delegation visiting Islamabad to resume talks on smoothening bilateral trade. Fight-fight, talk-talk.

Without missing a beat, upon his return to Delhi the following day, Desai visited the wounded Vajpayee in hospital, who by then had decided to postpone a two-day official visit as foreign minister to Nepal. Then, after a day of tending to affairs of state, Desai hosted an iftar party at his residence for 500 guests, prominent Muslim citizens of Delhi and politicians across party lines.

The prime minister and his cabinet colleagues would have a busy schedule. It had also rained incessantly in northern India, flooding Punjab and fifty districts of Uttar Pradesh; there were reports of floods and inundation from central and eastern India.

Delhi's weekend was one of intense wet. It had rained nearly all of 1 September, a Friday, in Delhi and thrown traffic out of gear. Saturday brought more rain, and strong gusts; the weather wouldn't let up till late into the evening. Like the day earlier, commuters would be stranded till midnight or more. School buses were running late, so schools were greatly disrupted. Short circuits led to several dozen electrical fires breaking out across Delhi, in particular central, northern, and eastern Delhi by the Yamuna, all massively waterlogged.

The Yamuna was in spate. The river was expected to soon breach the high-water mark recorded a couple of monsoons earlier. Within the week, helped by hard rain in the region north of Delhi, the Yamuna expected a 'flood wave', cautioned the Central Flood Forecasting Division. (It wasn't a giddy forecast as events would soon bear out; in any case, Delhi seemed to have enough on its plate without additional disruption of lives and livelihoods.)

Into this mayhem stepped the reclusive Jayaprakash Narayan, with an act of compassion. JP to familiars and commentators, the Opposition giant of the Emergency years and moral leader of the pushback against the Indira–Sanjay brand of absolutism—and now the ignored moral compass of the Janata government in a manner not unlike Mohandas Gandhi once Partition had been decided and acted upon—sent telegrams of support to both Vajpayee and Captain Chopra, who were with this act linked by a bridge of some irony.

Geeta and Sanjay were never far.

MEMORIES

A few days after the funeral of Geeta and Sanjay, the journalist Arati R. Jerath visited Madan and Roma Chopra at their residence in Dhaula Kuan, which had become a receptacle of grief and a simmering anger. The parents took Jerath to Geeta and Sanjay's room.

The captain looked around the room, full of photographs and the children's lives. Geeta's 'Love Is...' posters and Sanjay's pictures of planes. His books stacked on a desk. His bongo drums. Her guitar. Their clothes neatly stacked in the cupboards. Sanjay's school satchel, which his father gently picked up and cradled.

It proved too much for him.

'And see these bongo drums, these are Sanju's,' the captain gestured at them. 'He used to play the drums and his sister played the guitar. It was so beautiful.'

Roma Chopra cried softly, continuously.

The captain resumed his reminiscing. There was little else to do now.

'Geeta was such a playful child, fond of sports'—and of dancing and Western music. 'Sanju wanted to join the navy,' the captain recounted, but they had 'dreams of a good company job' for him, apex ambition for a young upwardly mobile professional-to-be.

His emotions now in check, the captain went back to the living room which had since the 26th overflowed with visitors; since the 29th the crowds had increased manifold. People whom they knew as family, those who had no idea of anything but the tragedy, government officials—politicians and bureaucrats—arrived to express their platitudes and some, it was plain to see, genuine sympathy.

'We are very grateful to all those who have shared our grief in this dark hour,' the captain told Jerath. 'People have been coming from all over Delhi, people whom we have never met. I have no complaints against anybody....'

He walked on towards the visitors and then suddenly turned to Jerath in anguish, an angry parental logic now bursting at the seams of his usual structured calm after the days of hellish tension and grief. 'We members of the defence forces give a lifetime to you people. In return we expect protection for our children. You expect us to do our duty but you have failed in yours.'

And Roma Chopra cried her river of tears.

WHERE IS BILLA?

Delhi Police had doubled down—and was seen to do so with regular briefings and assertions.

The police had 'definite clues' about the killers, the additional commissioner of police in charge of security, G. S. Mander, announced to the media on 1 September. Several people had been questioned after the discovery in Adarsh Nagar of the stolen and abandoned Fiat. He declined to confirm the number of people questioned but that didn't prevent the media, eager for every scrap of information from any available police contact, to offer word through that definitive yet anonymous and speculative phrase: 'It is learnt'.

It is learnt that three people were arrested and questioned. It is learnt that one of them is a woman. It is learnt that she was from Bombay but married to a person from Delhi. It is learnt that she is 'believed to have been close to Billa'.

Some assertions were layered with authority: 'It is reliably learnt....'

Additional Commissioner Mander threw in some standard phrases which added to the drama, like the murders having likely been committed by 'hardened criminals'. Then he added some mystery, by declining to detail the 'exact' number of such hardened criminals involved in the crime as it would 'hamper' investigations.

But he did say that fourteen crime branch officials were on the case, that the deputy commissioner of police was running the investigation, and that they were all waiting with bated breath for the result of forensic examinations of the abandoned Fiat.

Several 'police parties' had been despatched across the country, Mander said, but declined to share what these 'different parts' were.

He said many citizens had come forward to share information. 'Some of it was useful,' he divulged with seer-like mien, 'and some not.'

The frenzy for news and the frenzy for being seen to be serving up law and order had reduced such daily briefings to the banality of foreign office briefings, in which the talks of India's leaders with those of other countries, even the ones with which India had ongoing issues and bloodletting, was always described by deadpan diplomats as being 'cordial and fruitful' and based on 'shared histories and cultures' going back a hundred years, or several hundred years, or several thousand—sometimes dramatized as 'time immemorial'.

Mander and his colleagues were in a tricky place. The police were hard-pressed for answers and qualifiers in an environment where they had, for practical purposes, lost the trust of citizens. Every answer or non-answer was scrutinized; and the hyper-attention of the media, equally hard-pressed for fresh information, pushed some journalists into adopting a combination of information and conjecture for their daily interrogation of public servants in public interest.

Had the police pinned the blame too soon on Billa? Why had it taken two days for the criminals to dump the car when logic dictated that they would ditch the car at the first opportunity? Why had it taken the police six days to trace the car when they had information about the car's theft and subsequent reports? And why six days? The police actually had nine days—because the owner, Ashok Sharma, had reported it as being stolen from the street outside Ashoka Hotel as far back as 19 August.

If the Fiat had indeed been cleaned by the killers, then how had the police and its forensics team discovered hair and bloodstains in the car, on the seats?

If the car was abandoned at night, why had it taken the police until the morning to find it? Why would one of the suspected killers, tall and slim, strike up a conversation with someone from the neighbourhood? Did he want that person to take a good look at him?

Time lag, the possibility of sloppiness by the killers and the possibility of sophisticated forensics techniques had no place in such storytelling. The media, like the public it provided for, demanded absolutes.

Additional Commissioner Mander stuck to his guns. This was *the* car. The police had 'definite proof'.

That didn't seem to matter to many civic leaders, even legislators who were part of the government. MPs like Mrinal Gore of the Janata Party demanded a 'revamping' of the structure of Delhi Police. She spoke at a gathering organized by the Citizens for Democracy in the capital. She had eminent company—Khusro Faramurz Rustamji, a member of the National Police Commission and a highly respected police officer, women's-rights activist Premila Dandavate, and Supreme Court lawyer Gobinda Mukhoty—who offered a radical suggestion to revamp-or-disband.

There was another development.

Courtesy of Bombay Police, on 1 September several newspapers in Delhi splashed mugshots of Billa on the front page. It showed front and profile images of a stocky, square-jawed man with thick brows, a pencil moustache and thick hair brushed back with a lick of hair on his forehead, and a go-to-hell frown.

The man whom the police in much of India appeared to be looking for now had a price on his head for his arrest—5,000 rupees.

This was announced by the police commissioner of Bombay, the city which had taken on the search for Billa with an intensity driven by what seemed to be a matter of prestige—how could a thug from *our* city do what he did? Maharashtra's junior home minister, Bhai Vaidya, informally met reporters and shared his 'confidence' that Billa would soon be tracked down.

It turned out that Billa had managed to escape from police detention, or 'lock-up', in Bombay earlier that year on 1 May, when he was under the jurisdiction of detectives of the Criminal Investigation Department (CID).

In a domino effect, the city's taxi business had taken a hit; Billa was described as a person who preferred to steal cabs literally as vehicles for his crimes. Cinema halls reported lower business for the evening and night shows which typically ended close to midnight. Theatres reported lower attendance for evening shows.

■

A day later, it was drama as-was-now usual.

Vajpayee, still stunned from the attack at the Boat Club was moved from Willingdon Hospital to the All India Institute of Medical Sciences, which all of Delhi, and much of the country, knew both as an acronym and phonetically as AIIMS.

But his colleagues in government had moved on. They appeared to be more concerned about the growing tensions within the ragtag Janata Party, a gathering of widely divergent ideologies now that the primary goal of ridding Indira of her throne was achieved. The Janata Parliamentary Party had resolved to meet for a three-day session; 150 party MPs had demanded it. There were urgent matters raised by these MPs to discuss, stressed the party's general secretary Murli Manohar Joshi. The party's shattered image of unity and pre-poll propriety had to be 'refurbished'. Socio-economic plans for India had to be kickstarted. And there was the tricky matter of discussing the conduct of 'certain individuals' who behaved in a manner 'derogatory to the party interests'.

Party heavyweight Charan Singh, who resigned from the cabinet as home minister in July as had his hell-raising colleague, Raj Narain, from his position as minister of health and family welfare, had assured his colleagues he wouldn't seek to split the party. Everybody in the Janata Party knew that during the meeting the following day of the party's national executive, Prime Minister Desai, increasingly rocky in his position, would try to present a show of strength and unity with colleagues Chandra Shekhar and Defence Minister Jagjivan Ram—tainted by a sex scandal involving his son, Suresh, the same as Desai's son Kanti, besieged by accusations of impropriety by using his father's position to leverage several business deals, appeared to daily taint his father's office and credibility.

Kanti was 'misusing' his father's office, some commentators—both from the Opposition and the ruling dispensation—offered behind the anonymity of media 'sources'. The Press Trust of India, a co-operative news service that had learned to swim both with and against the tides of India's power dynamic, offered a flashback—remember when, in 1968, a time when Desai was finance minister of India, accusations of impropriety had been raised against Kanti's 'business dealings'? The quite fearless socialist and political activist Madhu Limaye had, at the time, suggested to Desai he send his son back home to Bombay. Asked of it now, Limaye, a general secretary of Janata Party and a person who wouldn't hesitate to range himself against powers-that-were, and, certainly, the prime minister, didn't deny it. Nothing personal against the prime minister, he clarified, it was all to do with his son.

On the following day, later there would be denial of this via the media quoting 'reliable sources' that Kanti Desai would not be moving back to Bombay, all of it was fabrication.

And so it went, dawn to dusk. Delhi in thrall to itself and India dragged along by Delhi—and, besides everything else that was going on—quite enraptured by the fascinating horror of two names which, even a week earlier, almost no one knew.

Geeta Chopra. Sanjay Chopra.

CONJECTURES

The prize for information that would lead to the arrest of the killers of Geeta and Sanjay was raised to 20,000 rupees—a reward jointly offered by the navy and Delhi Police. The chief of naval staff, Admiral Jal Cursetji, announced a reward of 10,000 rupees on behalf of the navy. The other half was offered by Police Commissioner J. N. Chaturvedi. It was altogether four times what Delhi Police had initially offered, but that promise of 5,000 rupees hadn't yielded results.

Additional Police Commissioner Mander, the face of the police for most public briefings, faced flak, including media queries for raising the amount—was it an admission of Delhi Police being clueless about the whereabouts of the suspects despite its claims of tracking down the car thought to have been used for the double murder?

He backpedalled in the face of media impatience. 'The establishment of the identity of the culprits did not necessarily mean it was easy to catch them.'

'They are hardened criminals,' he added, underscoring the police line since the discovery of the corpses on 29 August.

Be patient, Mander counselled. We haven't yet received results from the Central Forensic Science Laboratory of the evidence collected from the Fiat; it would take a while but we'll get there. The police also pulled back from their earlier certainty of suggesting Billa as more than a mere suspect. As if suddenly conscious of prejudicing a future case, they now held back on naming him the murderer. There just wasn't adequate evidence yet, not even substantive circumstantial strands that would hold up to legal scrutiny.

Many in the media, meanwhile, diligently strove for escape velocity from verification and circumspection. For answers, and to fix culpability, the press continued to fly kites—any rumour was worth a story, any gossip front page material. It wasn't a particularly proud moment for some of India's best-known newspapers and magazines, published from Delhi in both English and Hindi. Several of them went with dribbles of gossip merged with trickles of information and hyped up conjecture to sensational suggestion, and these would run the next day mostly without a by-line even for major stories. It was an outcome of competitive reporting when a 'beat' reporter felt obliged to feed a hungry newsroom and a hungrier editor; and all done without any thought that they might be providing fodder for a future legal defence team.

As we have seen, weekend editions of newspapers huffed that Billa's modus operandi was to steal taxis and then abduct couples from outside cinemas and theatres, basing their indignation on what Bombay Police had been claiming. Billa, this modus went, would then use some pretext to take on board an accomplice who would sit beside Billa in the front passenger seat. They would then take the couples to convenient places—'lonely places'—by frightening the couple at knifepoint. The male would then be dumped, and Billa and his accomplice would 'speed away to molest the woman'. To go by this telling, there was no economic motive, just a macabre, demonic lust for entertainment: 'If Billa had been involved in the Chopra children's murder—considering the car used for the crime was a stolen one'—as a major newspaper described it—'he would have believably forced Sanjay to get down from the car.'

The *Hindustan Times Weekly* of 3 September offered more analysis, such as it was. 'Even if one were to believe that Sanjay resisted that (as there are ample signs to show it) and that he had been killed in the process, what could have been the need to kill Geeta also? The post-mortem report had revealed that she had not been molested.'

The post-mortem report had also offered a caveat that the private parts were too decomposed to offer conclusive evidence of molestation, but the media generally erred on the side of conjecture, not caution.

'Normally there should not have been in any need to kill her too, unless there was a special motive behind that. What could this be?'

Normally.

There were plenty of 'motives' floated. One was: there were men behind the men, so to say, and these puppeteers were described as 'wayward sons of top notchers'. So, was the 'introduction' of Billa as a suspect, a case of a criminal 'in one hand' and a crime 'in the other' an attempt to make both fit?

Why would Billa, who primarily robbed and treated rape 'only as a secondary issue', kill the teenagers? Neither Geeta nor Sanjay had been robbed. And if it was indeed kidnapping, aren't such ventures typically bolstered by a little homework? Why bother picking up the children of a middle-class naval officer and, as a postscript, look for riches to squeeze?

Some in the media attributed such theorizing to 'private conjecture'. It appeared to be an all-source approach, so to say—including ideas typically thrown up during news meetings—to fill voluminous column-inches of newsprint and provide the gruesome mystery with any and all momentum.

Wouldn't a sophisticated, hardened killer like Billa work with some sophistication? Why hack at Sanjay as an attacker-killer clearly had, why not just an elegant slash-kill that was more 'sophisticated' and 'less obvious'?

And was Billa at all in Delhi on 29 August? Wasn't he reported as being seen in Bombay that day?

How could the police be convinced even before the vehicle was found that the car used for the murder—the lime-green Fiat, not mustard as was being reported—was the one stolen near Ashoka Hotel on 19 August? And why ditch it in a crowded 'low income' neighbourhood when losing it in the parking lot of a cinema or a shopping complex would be more innocuous, less prone to quick discovery in a city where both lime-green and mustard Fiats were in plenty?

False number plates were found in the car, as well as a 'tool of the crime'. If that seemed improbable, the police did say that hardened criminals too can commit errors. That was too much for at least one newspaper. It harrumphed, sarcastically chiding the 'sophisticated' and 'hardened' criminal: 'To this extent, Mr Billa?'

'Novices in the art,' dismissed another media conjecture, describing the slapdash manner of leaving large breadcrumbs across swathes of Delhi, and the abundantly manic violence the post-mortem examination of Sanjay and Geeta revealed. The killers took on more than they had bargained for. They panicked.

This was the circumstances-out-of-control school of thought.

And 'one group' of investigators, as the stories circled back a point of suspicion from the first day since the discovery of the bodies, reflected the teach-her-a-lesson school of thought.

Geeta had rebuffed some in her own 'circle'. Her abduction was payback. Her death was an over-reaction. Sanjay's death was collateral damage. Here this school merged with the circumstances-out-of-control school.

Sanjay was the circumstance out of control. At 5 feet 10 inches, in the boxing team of Modern School, fit, and ready to give the abductors hell.

At least that part seemed to fit with the post-mortem report.

DELHI DISQUIET

The search for Billa and Ranga went up another notch. No tip was unworthy of a follow-up.

On 2 September, Bombay Police tracked a tip that brought them to Bombay Central Station. The word was that Billa was planning to take the Pashchim Express to New Delhi.

Billa, whose photograph was now displayed at petrol stations across the city, wasn't on that train. It left for the capital, delayed by an end-to-end search.

Calcutta Police were keeping a watch on 'vice dens' and even 'posh hotels' for Billa. The police commissioner of Madras assured the public that Billa's photo and description had been supplied to police stations across the city—indeed, across all Tamil Nadu. The police in Gwalior in the northern tip of Madhya Pradesh remained on alert.

Some passengers were looted on the Sabarmati Express between Kanpur and Jhansi by an armed gang. One of them was arrested and queried as to whether he was Billa. He was not.

Would Billa make a run for Pakistan? So that he did not, the Border Security Force was alerted to keep watch from its posts along the long and open western border that ran along Rajasthan and Gujarat. Rajasthan Police claimed that it had ramped up vigilance in Jaipur and the towns closer to Delhi, Alwar, and Bharatpur; and along the state's borders with Haryana and Punjab. The railways and road link between Delhi and Jaipur was broken on account of flooding caused by the heavy rains, and even the route from Jaipur to Delhi via Bharatpur was cut off. Things were bad in vast parts of the state, but no matter, the police would do whatever it could to keep their eyes peeled for Billa.

With pressure building for results, the cynosure turned to other matters—with Delhi Police again at the receiving end of a sickened and, evidently, a sick society. Geeta's and Sanjay's murders remained unsolved along with a clutch of murders over the previous few years. These unlovely memories were now dragged through the muck of recrimination.

What of the murder of young Kiran, all of six, whose body was found on 23 August 1975—a blue riband year for unsolved murders in Delhi along with the crushing onset of the Emergency? The daughter of Mohan Singh, a butcher, was found on the day of Raksha Bandhan stuffed inside a cupboard at a higher secondary school for girls in West Patel Nagar. Kiran wasn't a student at the school, and the school had been closed that day.

Not long after, a fifty-year-old engineer in the Central Public Works Department was walking towards his home in R. K. Puram, the sprawling neighbourhood of government housing in South Delhi, between the inner and outer Ring Roads. R. Nagarajan was accompanied by his wife. Nagarajan was attacked by a couple of unidentified men. He died of stab wounds. No robbery. No evident motive.

What of the young no-name boy, about ten, who was found hanging from a tree near the railway tracks just to the east of Delhi Zoo? That was on 15 October 1975.

In the same month, there was the killing of a mother of three girls, pregnant with her fourth, Ajinder Kaur. The thirty-two-year-old was discovered bound, gagged, and burnt—and stabbed, as it turned out—in her home in Rohtak Road. Several motives from foeticide to general assault by her spouse, family, or neighbours were lit in investigative neon, but her murder remained unsolved.

Kailash, all of seven, was found dead with several stab wounds on 1 November 1975, in Bhuli Bhatiyari Sarai opposite Jhandewalan Extension, a few short kilometres north of where Geeta and Sanjay were found. Clues, and yet, clueless.

The litany of unsolved killings continued into 1977.

11 January. The double murder of the Mehra couple, G. S. Mehra and his wife, in plush Maharani Bagh in southeast Delhi. A locked entrance mystery.

9 June. Two young girls with stab wounds found dead in a ditch in Mehrauli, not far from the Qutab Minar.

2 September. A twenty-four-year-old housewife killed during the day in Green Park.

18 December. A triple murder. Mohini Sawhney in her bungalow in the exclusive enclave of Southend Road. Attacked by a pack of burglars, maintained the police. Her maid and a security guard were attacked too. All three died. Unsolved.

These unsolved murders reflected a cross-section of citizenry, from relatively high up the ladder of society to those brought low by circumstance. Largely forgotten, tucked away into the psychologically expedient compartments of file-and-forget, flashes of news that had outlived their cycle of curiosity and horror, they were now offered as proof of both police apathy and ineptitude. These deaths added weight to the unease and despair caused by the heartbreaking death of the siblings.

Geeta and Sanjay.

Unsolved.

Delhi's disquiet grew.

▪

Another day in Delhi, and disquiet had turned to danger—not from criminals but criminal neglect of the environment.

The capital, and the country, were in the throes of a climate-crisis as had not been seen in a generation.

Along with the sprawling, teeming neighbourhood of Jahangir Puri in northwest Delhi, within sight of Coronation Park, the site of the opulent Delhi Durbar of 1877, 1903, and 1911 for the British Indian empire to celebrate itself as a large part of its Indian empire starved or remained destitute, was going under water. So were twenty-five villages in Delhi—the city that continued to grow around the villages it couldn't entirely displace.

The army was tasked with evacuating 200,000 residents of the capital. The deluge that had in the past days destroyed more than 8,000 houses and swept away 1,500 and more people in West Bengal's

Midnapore district, in a horrific combination of rainfall and flash floods caused by release of water from barrages and large dams, had served as a rude wake-up call.

Haryana was already ravaged by the Yamuna. Residents of the cantonment town of Ambala were speaking of the rains and floods as being the worst 'in living memory'.

Now the floods had followed the fabled Grand Trunk Road down south to Delhi. Alipur Block, which lay about midway between the border with Haryana and Jahangir Puri, was already witnessing traffic disruption along the GT Road that passed through the area.

Meanwhile, the target of the ire of students at the Boat Club rally for Geeta and Sanjay, foreign minister Vajpayee, was better. The doctors at AIIMS had provided a health update. The foreign minister seemed to be as robust as a strain of E-coli bacteria was to several antibiotics—tetracycline, ampicillin, and chloramphenicol, 'in that order'—as a team of researchers at Lady Hardinge Medical College had just announced.

As ever, Delhi was full of tender mercies.

▪

And what of Geeta's and Sanjay's killers?

Nothing.

What of the clues, the forensic evidence?

Still nothing.

'We do not expect the police to snatch the wanted criminal out of the blue,' wrote Raj Gill in his well-read 'Delhi affairs' column in the *Hindustan Times*. 'We also cannot set time limits for the resolution of a criminal case howsoever important it may be. Because we cannot overlook the human and incidental factors that can as much hamper as help the police investigation.'

But we cannot, Gill wrote, overlook shoddy police work as exemplified by the case of the Chopra children. We cannot overlook the fact that when citizens come forward to offer help, they are instead dealt 'hours of interrogation and harassment' for the simple act of helping the victim of an accident, or for reporting a 'dead body'.

Maybe it was time for the top brass, who justifiably complain about much of the police force being diverted for 'VIP duty' and 'bandobast' for uncountable political rallies, processions, and protests, to get on the ground and actually see what's going on, the readiness, preparedness of the force to protect and serve the citizens of Delhi and New Delhi, the region of the national capital?

For the citizens, with the citizens—always. That was the ask. The police would need to deliver.

PRESSURE

By 4 September, there was still no firm word on the killers of Geeta and Sanjay. Billa continued to be painted as the prime suspect but in a way that again exposed a missed opportunity by the police—this time in Bombay.

Some Bombay Police officials—identified as 'highly reliable sources'—set about leaking to the media that it was '100 per cent sure about Billa's involvement'. They offered two reasons for this claim.

One was the fingerprints from the Fiat—interchangeably the Premier Padmini, but that wordy name had yet to catch on—their colleagues in Delhi had shared. These had been 'verified' in Bombay and they were now 'certain' about Billa's involvement. Following journalistic norms, the media added the prophylactic of 'alleged' as a prefix to Billa's involvement, but that didn't diminish the effect of the claim. Two personnel of Delhi Police who had been camping in Bombay left for the capital that day with their colleague's verification of the prints.

The second reason was the claim that Billa was in Bombay, and had been there since 29 August. Again, Bombay Police was 'certain' of it, had information of where he might be, but had tripped up with the arrest.

The story—the theory—went like this.

Billa had gone to the neighbourhood of Govandi in east Bombay to collect twelve hundred rupees he was owed from a person in a 'hut.' He took with him an associate, Luis. The police, who had prior information of this, caught Luis but Billa gave them the slip. A canny Billa had sent Luis on ahead.

All this was sourced to another associate of Billa, Jugal Kishore, who was interrogated in police custody. Jugal Kishore had cut and run from Billa when he learned of his true identity—and he had subsequently squealed to the police.

There was investigative trivia too. Falsifying car plates was a thriving business, as evidenced by the abductors of Geeta and Sanjay—more precisely, users of the car that was believed to be employed in the abduction.

As investigators in Delhi looked beneath the layers of the repeatedly painted-over plates they had found in the Fiat recovered in Majlis Park, four sets of plates provided eight sets of numbers: HRK 8930. DHA 3548. MMB 3538. DHI 281. DEA 828. DEA 1221. DHB 9337. RJA 7.

Delhi Police continued to chase every angle, from questioning real estate agents in Majlis Park and the greater Adarsh Nagar area to following up on the slimmest threads that involved the navy.

They interrogated a former lieutenant in the navy. He had been imprisoned in 1975 and sentenced to two years of hard labour on charges of espionage, passing official secrets to 'enemy agents'. Captain Chopra, as an officer in the Judge Advocate General's branch, had been present during the trial. Delhi Police wanted to be sure the cashiered and disgraced officer did not bear a grudge against the father of Geeta and Sanjay. Captain Chopra hadn't been part of either the prosecuting team or the judge's bench, but one had to be sure to strike a suspect off the list.

■

Meanwhile, a stunning eyewitness account of an ENT specialist had literally fallen into the lap of the police. Dr M. S. Nanda lived in Anand Niketan, not far from Dhaula Kuan, and, on the evening of 26 August, had been on the way to his private practice in Connaught Place. Like many in his neighbourhood, he found it convenient to hook a left onto Ring Road, curve west-northwest towards the Dhaula Kuan roundabout, and then take a right onto Sardar Patel Marg to reach the junction at Willingdon Crescent and follow that curve north and east, via Baba Kharak Singh Marg, past Gole Dak Khana, to Connaught Place.

That is how he had come by two teenagers, a girl and a boy, at the Dhaula Kuan 'circle'. According to his statement to the police, he had given the two a lift all the way to Gole Dak Khana. He then went on his way, naturally oblivious of the horror to follow, including the subsequent forced backtracking—according to eyewitness reports—of the siblings along much of the route they had taken while travelling up to central Delhi from Dhaula Kuan.

Supposition suggested that Geeta and Sanjay's rush to reach All India Radio by hitching another ride instead of walking the remainder of the relatively short distance of a few hundred metres to their destination, albeit in steamy, overcast weather, did them in.

Now Delhi Police appeared to be leaning hard on Dr Nanda to squeeze him for information, to clear him or to associate him in some way with the murders. It had got so bad that the doctor, according to some accounts, had complained to the prime minister.

That was bunkum, the doctor clarified on 4 September. The crime branch had indeed questioned him several times, and intensely, as was expected in the circumstances, but none of it amounted to harassment. And he certainly hadn't complained to the prime minister.

He went as far as to say that he had indeed given a ride to a young boy and a girl, but they seemed a lot younger to him.

It was a bit of a coincidence to have collected another set of teenagers, a boy and a girl, and given them a lift from where Geeta and Sanjay usually hitched rides to where they were looking to go—precisely to the point from which they appeared to be abducted. But the doctor stuck to his story. (His backpedalling in a time of great stress, police questioning, and public scrutiny would again add to complications for the prosecution later on, but that development was still months away.)

■

As ever, there were other horrors, small and big, that continued to mark Delhi even with the overarching attention generated by the deaths of Geeta and Sanjay and the hunt for Billa and an accomplice.

On 1 September, a schoolboy, Ravinder Singh, had gone missing.

The seventeen-year-old Sikh boy—his missing persons' report had him wearing a maroon patka, a white shirt and blue trousers—had as usual left for school from his home in Ramesh Nagar in West Delhi, not far from the Ridge. He had left school at 12.30 p.m., and never reached home.

In Kingsway Camp to the north, near the North Campus of Delhi University, two men had been shot dead inside a general store. The two were the driver of the store's owner and a friend. They had been drinking after hours. Two more men had arrived to join the first two. The shutters were lowered. Then at half past midnight on 3 September, the owner, who was outside with a helper, heard shots fired. When he went in, he saw his driver and his friend lying dead. The assailants threatened him and asked him to not go to the police, forced him to take off his shirt, found some other clothes, wrapped the corpses in them, and took off.

Usually, such news would make the inside pages of newspapers. In the days and weeks since a post-Geeta and -Sanjay world, every crime with a twist was front-page news.

DELUGE

It was as if the Yamuna was conforming to the dictates of two of her mythological relations, her mother Sanjana, the goddess of the clouds, and her twin, Yama, the god of death. Pushed by the ecological depredations of man, the Yamuna remained hellish. More than a hundred villages in Haryana's Karnal district, due north of Delhi, were flooded. The waters of the Yamuna and several offshoot canals and distributaries had now encircled Delhi. Najafgarh in the west of the capital was already under water. So was nearly the entire quadrant of the city's far northeast Delhi as seen from Alipur.

Residents of areas to the south of the city that lay close to the Yamuna, nouveau-upscale Maharani Bagh and New Friends Colony, besides Okhla and the area around Jamia Millia Islamia, were asked by the government to move out—where to, was left unsaid. Anywhere they could. The four bridges that stapled the west bank of the Yamuna to the east bank were to be closed.

Even though troubles appeared to be evenly distributed among Delhi's wealthy and not, all facing the Yamuna's wrath—Kalindi's wrath, to go by the evolving etymology of ancient India—Delhi's worse-off and the poor would, in a time-honoured tradition, bear the brunt of upheaval.

To bring some order to the chaos of post-Partition Delhi, the Delhi Development Act was passed in Parliament in 1957. That birthed the so-called Master Plan, envisaged by the central government. It was formally approved in 1962. The Master Plan called for a massive expansion of government-led and private housing, infrastructure, and facilities—from shopping centres, parks, and cultural hubs to several colleges and hospitals.

Delhi had duly mushroomed. From scant urban centres—Delhi was always an agglomeration of numerous villages both distant and cheek-by-jowl with modern housing—it now had 43,000 acres of urban space. By 1981, estimated the Delhi Development Authority, commonly known as DDA, urban space would explode two and half times to 1,10,000 acres. The ongoing land acquisition by the government was already staggering in volume, gorging on villages and commons alike.

But in the middle of all this relative order of a sort, lay inherent unease. Pushed by the designation as the British imperial capital of its Indian empire, and then the flow of the Partition, urban Delhi, according to an estimate by the Town and Country Planning Organisation, had gone from a population of a little over 200,000 at the turn of the century to around 5 million. Now discussions were ongoing to sort out as many as 500 residential hubs, 'colonies' in peculiar Delhi-speak, that were unauthorized. These covered 7,500 acres, DDA estimated, some packed with as many as a thousand people to an acre. That brought a proposed solution via another Delhi-speak verb, 'to regularize', which would then, theoretically, bring such neighbourhoods orderly municipal facilities of sanitation, water, and electricity. DDA marked nearly the entire and vast 'trans-Yamuna' area, on the east bank of the Yamuna, for 'regularization' of such neighbourhoods and for development. Some areas in the west bank too came within that purview, as did parts of north and west Delhi.

But the weather, and the Yamuna, wouldn't wait. Those in this 'irregular', teeming, heaving Delhi were the most vulnerable to disasters, most prone to displacement piled on despair.

But even as the Yamuna wreaked havoc on Delhi, she would be responsible for a major twist in a grisly tale. Her wrath would contribute to delivering up the suspected killers of Geeta and Sanjay.

'CONFIRMED'

The chaos of information and the anticipation of denouement began to peak around 6 September. The police across jurisdictions appeared to go head-to-head in a feeding frenzy of leads and conclusions.

Billa now had an accomplice, Delhi Police formally announced at a crowded press briefing. His name was Ranga. There was an alias, his real name: Kuljit Singh. Billa and he were involved in the abduction and killing of Geeta and Sanjay.

'Confirmed.'

It was a 'theory' but it was 'confirmed'.

They had pieced that together from various angles of investigation, Delhi Police claimed. The analysis of the fingerprints lifted from the Fiat in Adarsh Nagar had also arrived from the Central Forensic Science Laboratory in Hyderabad.

Forensics had come a long way since William Herschel, a British-colonial civil servant in Bengal's Hooghly district, in the mid-nineteenth century realized the uniqueness of fingerprints and developed the early techniques of fingerprint-based identification. It took until the 1890s for the colonial police in Bengal to greenlight fingerprinting for anthropometric databases—for identification related to record-keeping and, eventually, crime. Forensics gradually grew to include handwriting, footprint, and ballistics analysis, along with other disciplines, with Calcutta establishing India's first post-colonial forensic science laboratory in 1952. The Hyderabad establishment, India's first national forensic laboratory, came about in 1967, managed by the Intelligence Bureau. It had since been co-opted into a national police research bureau along with the lab in Calcutta. Even so, by the time the fingerprints on the Fiat came to the attention of the lab in Hyderbad, it was still a modest operation, housed in a poky rented building on Chirag Ali Lane in the Abids neighbourhood of the city.

Rajinder Mohan, head of Delhi Police's crime branch said that the forensics laboratory had confirmed that the blood in the car matched the blood groups of Geeta and Sanjay.

Besides, the police had other 'scientific evidence' too that tied together the 'theory' that Billa and Ranga had a hand in the crime.

Billa, one knew of from the descriptions and theories shared by police forces of Delhi and Bombay and both transmitted and transmuted by the media. And there was word that the help of Interpol had been sought as a pre-emptive measure in case Billa made a run for Pakistan, or to Nepal using the vast open border with India. This Billa is a chameleon, he is quick—the police underscored at every opportunity. He is also multilingual, packing fluency in Hindi, Punjabi, and Marathi.

So who was this Ranga?

Mohan wouldn't say any more in the interest of ongoing investigations, but in the meantime, the inspector general of police of Punjab, D. S. Dhanewalia, had told media in Chandigarh that Ranga had been arrested in Ludhiana.

That was news to police in Delhi, but they seemed to have other ideas in Ludhiana, a hub of woollen knitwear exports, primarily to the Soviet Union. They had Ranga, that city's police insisted. Indeed, they had arrested him on 5 September and on 6 September, a judicial magistrate had given Ranga over to police custody for a couple of days in order for this Ranga to be taken to Delhi. He would thereafter be brought before a magistrate in the capital and the judicial transfer process would take its course.

This Ranga had been arrested, Ludhiana police said, on the basis of a letter found on him—another version had this Ranga being arrested on account of a supposition that he looked like Ranga. Anyhow, this letter had been written by a jailed convict in Delhi; he urged Ranga to return to Delhi as he would soon be out. Besides, this Ranga had admitted to being in Delhi on 26 August, the day of the double murders of Geeta and Sanjay. He claimed he had even acted in the movie, *Ranga Khush*—a 'Bollywood' thriller released in 1975 about a runaway, rapacious bandit called Ranga that would in 1978 accrue a dubious cult rub-off.

Dhanewalia, the inspector general in Punjab, also mentioned that Ranga had denied he had anything to do with Billa.

And he mentioned that the real name of 'Ranga' was Pawan Kumar.

Chaos reigned....

■

...As did knee-jerk action.

With each telling, Billa and Ranga appeared to assume the mantle of criminal superstars of mythical proportion.

Apparently, they were everywhere.

On the night of 29 August, the date on which the bodies of Geeta and Sanjay were discovered, two men had made off with a truck full of furniture intended for the town of Mirzapur in eastern Uttar Pradesh. The truck was parked near Old Delhi Station. Two scruffy men approached the truck's handyman—'cleaner' in the trade's terminology—hit him on the head with a blunt object and drove off with their loot. The truck was found three days later in Delhi's eastern suburb of Shahdara, across the Yamuna.

The cleaner, Sukhdev Singh, identified Billa as one of his attackers when crime branch detectives showed him photos of Billa and Ranga. Sukhdev Singh's word was later dismissed as 'naïve', as, unable to clearly describe his attacker he was perhaps eager to be associated with the biggest ongoing manhunt in India, with the faces of the two key suspects who were by now household news.

Meanwhile, Punjab Police's Ranga—the Ludhiana Ranga—was dismissed by Delhi Police. At a press conference Delhi's additional commissioner of police, G. S. Mander, disabused his colleagues' notion by saying he was 'not the Ranga' the capital's police were looking for. After scrutinizing the description sent on by their colleagues in Punjab, they figured the Ludhiana 'Ranga' was 6 inches or so shorter than their 6-foot-plus suspect.

Commissioner Mander also dismissed a 'Billa' arrested by the police in the western Indian city of Baroda as the 'wrong' man.

In any case, he said, teams of detectives had fanned out to various locations in an effort to trap Billa and Ranga. Several people had offered information about the two, but he couldn't, naturally, share such details as that 'might hamper the arrest'.

While the murmurs of police incompetence kept growing, there was also now talk of administrative incompetence—a fallout spurred by the Yamuna's unleashed force.

Even though the Yamuna floodwaters had begun to recede, large areas of northwest Delhi were still reeling from the deluge. Boats were the only recourse to distribute relief materials in Adarsh Nagar. As recently as 5 September, officials of the central ministries of railways and power and irrigation, and the Delhi administration had met to consider an extreme measure—blowing up the old railway bridge on the Yamuna as a tactic to lessen the chances of it being a barrier to the enormous water flow; or there could be the risk of the bridge diverting floodwaters to the bunds lining the eastern bank of the Yamuna, breaching these bunds, and flooding vast areas of eastern Delhi and about 600,000 inhabitants.

The swollen Yamuna had taken its curse downriver: Mathura was inundated, Agra was on alert—as were keepers of the Taj Mahal which lay by the river that was usually a slow-moving ribbon of sludge in the dry winters and scorching summers. And now the Ganga had joined in the overflow; the battle to save Varanasi and Allahabad was on.

In the middle of this climate crisis, the horrified fascination that fuelled media-driven public engagement with Geeta and Sanjay, and which had now been ghoulishly transferred to their suspected killers, would need to wait just another day for a boost. Yamuna-in-rage would have a part to play in it.

And when that day arrived, it defined bizarre.

WEATHER REPORT

In the cosmic scale of crime, it could be said that the weather did in Billa and his accomplice.

All through the beginning of September, floodwaters continued to ravage or threaten the region of the national capital, particularly the north and east.

By 5 September, the Delhi 'A' frequency of All India Radio broadcast intermittently as floodwaters inundated transmitters in Nangloi in northwest Delhi. The station Delhi 'B', and the popular Vividh Bharati programme and Yuv Vani—for which Geeta had gone to record a programme of Western music on the day she was killed—went off the air. Along Mall Road near the university, transmitters that beamed the programmes were waterlogged. Eighty per cent of the residents of the north-western neighbourhood of Jahangir Puri had been evacuated, and close to half the population of Model Town, not far from the university, was also awash.

Kingsway Camp, the avenue and transit facility made for the Delhi Durbar of 1911, and the vast area that hosted tame Indian maharajas and rajas and nawabs, and, later, its unpretentious and more urgent use as a transit camp for several hundred thousand refugees of Partition, was at risk. By evening the Inter State Bus Terminus at Kashmere Gate, a destination known mostly as ISBT, was flooded, its services at a standstill. It appeared as if nothing would stop the Yamuna, the level of which by that day was recorded rising at 10 centimetres every hour as it cleaved through the capital, the rate just shy of 8 feet a day.

Bridges across the Yamuna were packed with a continuous stream of people who were escaping the areas of Delhi referred to as Trans-Yamuna; some Anglophile students at Delhi University referred to such areas as 'Trans-Yam', the same as the stationery hub of Kamal

Nagar near the university was 'K-Nags', Defence Colony morphed seamlessly to 'Def Col' or, more universally, as 'Defence', while South Extension was a relatively tame 'South Ex'. All government-run schools in Delhi were to be shut for the next four days, after which the status would be reviewed. There were reports from some residential areas of the relatively well-off offering passers-by—albeit passers-by on rafts and boats—one hundred rupees for each stranded child they helped to bring down from rooftops.

For a while, floods played havoc with inequity. There was ghoulish activity in places. Delhi Police put out a warning against flood-voyeurism: they would detain those who came near flooded areas 'merely to watch or for fun's sake'.

Things had got so bad that in some parts of Delhi even the dead and the grieving would have to wait. One of Delhi's biggest cremation grounds at Nigambodh Ghat, by the Yamuna, was closed. It looked to be at least a week before there would be any chance of it reopening.

The crisis had escalated so exponentially that Prime Minister Desai took to an Indian Air Force plane for an 'aerial survey' of the capital and its surroundings. Sections of the medieval-yet-modern Grand Trunk heading northwest were identifiable only by the landmark neat row of trees on either side. The stadium in Model Town looked like a swimming pool. As he flew towards the southern periphery bordering the industrial towns of Faridabad and Ballabhgarh in neighbouring Haryana, it was as if east-central Delhi was a vast lake, strewn with building islands, and bridges linking waterways.

The next twenty-four hours would decide the fate of much of Delhi.

And the devastation spread east, along the Ganga and its riverine web of tributaries and distributaries—big sister and numerous cousins to the Yamuna. Allahabad and Varanasi were placed on alert. The army was alerted to be on a disaster-management standby along the Ganga's course through Bihar. (And news continued to arrive from West Bengal and Orissa, from Gujarat and Maharashtra, of major flooding and disruption. A million were affected in Bengal, and daily, dozens died. Nearly all major rivers in the other states were in spate, and flowing above what in the business of hydrography and flood control was called the 'danger mark'.)

The rains and the deluge travelled south along the Yamuna, to Mathura and then to Agra.

What the rains and flooding also did was massively disrupt road and railway networks across northern and central India. Roads and tracks were submerged in floodwaters. Several bridges were damaged or simply washed away. The Railway Board announced to the media that the railway bridge between Ghaziabad and Sahibabad to Delhi's east, across the border in Uttar Pradesh, had been washed away—the generally tame Hindon River was in uproar. An epic-minded correspondent with the *Indian Express* was on one of the last trains to leave Ghaziabad for Delhi. 'It reminds one of the Biblical times when the world was submerged under a sheet of water as God expressed his displeasure with mankind,' he wrote in apocalyptic distress. 'Coming by train from Ghaziabad to Delhi, the floods are evident in all their fury. Where, less than three days back, there had been green, smiling fields, now there is only a vast sheet of water on both sides of the railway track, the fields and villages have been submerged under the muddy Jamuna water which every minute covers one more foot of land.' What little land remained was packed with displaced residents—human and cattle.

Traffic on this immensely busy artery that straddled the railway routes between eastern India and Delhi—and beyond to points on the great northern plains like Ambala, Chandigarh, Amritsar, and Jammu, and the charming stations of Pathankot and Kalka in the Himalayan foothills—was being routed via Tundla south to Agra and then back up north to Delhi. Besides, the two railway bridges over the Yamuna in Delhi had been closed to traffic from the afternoon of 5 September. For the foreseeable future there was no way out for east-to-west trains but this detour.

By 8 September, only two east-to-west trains were running on this depleted route—this detour—the Amritsar-Howrah Mail and the Kalka Mail between Howrah and Kalka. Word came that even this detour might need to be closed because a railway bridge between Tundla and Agra was threatened by floodwaters. But that slim lifeline remained open for the moment.

And that led to the Kalka Mail, on its run from Howrah to Delhi, to take this detour on the evening of 8 September.

■

In this universe of uncertainty, there appeared to be one certainty. The Chopra family's river of tears flowed relentlessly. Lament had become an understatement.

On 8 September, the same day as the Kalka Mail continued its delayed, detoured, and tortuous run towards Agra and Delhi—and a rendezvous that appeared to define fate and certainly defied logic—Saraswati, grandmother to Geeta and Sanjay and mother to Captain Chopra, passed on in Chandigarh. Her husband, Shanti Sarup, said his wife had died of heartbreak. She couldn't bear what had happened to her beloved grandchildren.

Grandmother Saraswati's passing was the fourth death in the family in forty days.

First came the death of her daughter. The funerary duties had fallen to Captain Chopra.

The captain had only just completed the kriya, the thirteen-day cycle of funerary rites for his sister when, bare days later, he lost both his children.

And here he was for the funeral of his mother, a day after completing the kriya for his children.

THE TRAIN

Janardhanan Nair, a soldier with the 6th Regiment of the Corp of Engineers of the Indian Army, was on the Kalka Mail, in a coach reserved for army personnel. He had boarded the train in Allahabad along with his boss, Naik B. Gandhi—the rank an equivalent of corporal—and other colleagues. The coach carried soldiers from other regiments too, heading home or to their units in the near-constant movement that is life in the armed forces. Nair and his colleagues were headed to their new deployment in Rajasthan.

The slowed Kalka Mail had slowed some more after being diverted from its usual route at Tundla Junction. By the time it passed the Yamuna Bridge Station in the suburbs of Agra to cross a dangerously swollen Yamuna over to its western bank and the teeming main city, it was around 11.30 at night on 8 September.

The mood wasn't light. The train was seven hours behind schedule, and the uncertainty of the weather and floods made the prospect of reaching any destination a gamble. As it neared the bridge, the Kalka Mail slowed to a crawl; floodwaters had risen dangerously close to the tracks.

Nair, from balmy coastal Calicut in faraway Kerala, and his colleague Muthupandian, from the bustling inland temple town of Madurai several hundred kilometres further to the southeast, could hardly believe what happened next.

A man jumped onto the steps to the door of the coach, and finding it locked, clambered through the adjacent open window.

The soldiers instantly went on alert. Thinking he was a robber they pulled the man inside.

'After beating him a little we made him sit down,' Nair would recall.

Incredibly, another man, taller than the first, followed through the window. He too was dragged in by the soldiers.

Then, to coax confessions from them the soldiers beat their two prisoners with belts and batons. The two appeared stunned and cowed since the time of their helter-skelter entry through the windows into a coach full of soldiers—clearly an oversight caused by their desperation, and the dark. The two claimed to be army personnel as soon as they realized they were in a coach reserved for the armed forces. As unlikely as that story was, given their manner of entering the coach, they were asked to produce military identification. The questioning began when they were unable to produce any.

After an hour or so of being jostled, beaten, and questioned, the two owned up to robbing eight hundred rupees from a person. A white Rexine bag the shorter of the two had brought with him lay by their side.

The soldiers then upped their investigative quotient. They had bought newspapers before boarding the train at Allahabad. Newspapers across much of the country had for some days carried photos and descriptions of Billa and Ranga as released by police. Now the soldiers again looked at their newspapers and wondered if their cowed yet stubborn prisoners weren't the two accused of killing Geeta and Sanjay.

One of them noticed a scar on the forehead of one of the prisoners—they had read news of a person answering to Billa's description as being injured in a scuffle with the Chopra children inside the Fiat. Eyewitness accounts at Willingdon Hospital had reported two people, one with an injury on his forehead, showing up on the night of 26 August to be treated; the one with the injury had received stitches. They later disappeared after giving a false address and false assurances about returning the following morning for a police enquiry.

In their fightback the children appeared to have left a damning mark as emphatic as a pointed finger.

The man the soldiers took to be Billa denied he was Billa. He was beaten some more.

The man then admitted to being the face in the papers but in a roundabout way: if his captors thought he was Billa then how could he deny it? But he denied having had anything to do with killing the children.

The taller of the two, whom the soldiers now took to be Ranga, remained mute. He suffered the occasional beating.

The soldiers then opened the Rexine bag. In it, Nair and Muthipandian discovered a toy pistol, a live .32 cartridge, what turned out to be a master key designed for Fiats, a set of small tools for cars, couple of railway tickets. One was issued on 30 August for a journey from Bombay Central station to Delhi, and another was issued on 8 September for a journey from Etawah to Agra. Two wristwatches were also found in the bag.

A search of the small bag held by the taller captive yielded a driving licence for a Kuljit Singh—Ranga's given name as shared with the media—and a kirpan with bloodstains. The police would add to it (to supplement what media persons who tracked down the soldiers in Delhi narrated to their readers) a dagger with a 13-inch blade, a 'gupti', a white shirt, and a pair of black trousers.

Despite the protestations of their captives, the soldiers were now increasingly convinced they had Billa and Ranga in their hands. The kirpan and the driving license in 'Ranga's' birthname were giveaways in addition to 'Billa's' scar. They were both secured with ropes taken from the bedrolls of the soldiers—that and aluminium trunks painted black being standard equipment for travelling soldiers.

The soldiers stopped at the next station to alert railways staff and insisted they would hand over the captives only to army personnel. Then they went back to beating and interrogating the two men for the four hours it took for the Kalka Mail to reach Delhi. By then it was 3.30 a.m. on 9 September.

'BILLA AUR RANGA'

The soldiers couldn't find anyone from the army at the station, no military police to take charge of the captives whom, they were by now convinced, had to be Billa and Ranga. The army contingent took the captives to the room at Delhi station which functioned as a police post. Through all the questioning, beatings and exposure of their belongings, their captives had strenuously denied they were Billa and Ranga. Perhaps the police would be able to make more sense of things.

Head Constable Sri Chand was the duty officer, seated on a chair, relaxed, not an unusual posture for those working the graveyard shift at the station.

His eyes nearly bugged out of their sockets when he saw the two captives brought into the room. The head constable's unit had been warned about the two key suspects behind the killings of Geeta and Sanjay. A colleague of Nair and Muthupandian, A. V. Shetty, a sepoy with the 6th Engineers like them, recalled the constable leaping to his feet and exclaiming: 'Yeh toh Billa aur Ranga hai!'

This is Billa and Ranga.

Shetty, his boss Gandhi, a gunner from a mountain brigade, Gokul Singh, and a retired lance-naik, a rank junior to naik, helped Sri Chand and his police colleagues secure Billa and Ranga inside the small police post. They waited for Delhi Police's crime branch personnel to arrive—Sri Chand had meanwhile alerted his SHO, station house officer, who in turn had alerted the crime branch.

The soldiers would soon be named for sharing an enhanced reward of 50,000 rupees for the capture of Billa and Ranga announced by Delhi's police commissioner, J. N. Chaturvedi; and they would also be asked to remain in Delhi for some days to aid the investigation. The other army men, mostly serving soldiers and some retirees among them, had remained behind to guard the group's luggage. In any case they had to remain together as they were all heading to Rajasthan on the same travel warrant. But there was a certain thrill in being instrumental in the capture of a pair of headline criminals, for more than a week India's most wanted.

Billa and Ranga.

And, soon, to be joined in hyphenation. Billa-Ranga.

The two finally broke upon the police checking their personal effects and offered yet another story which, along with playing misunderstood victims, would soon become their hallmark. They boarded the Kalka Mail in desperation—so they claimed—with the intention of robbing passengers and, with their loot, heading south to Madras.

The crafty, shifty, desperate, and yet awkward twosome's journey into India's lexicon of loathsomeness as the very definition of evil had truly begun.

THERE YOU HAVE IT

Word of the arrest of Billa and Ranga went viral courtesy of the police, media, and word-of-mouth.

Before crowds could gather in large numbers at the railway station, the crime branch of Delhi Police transferred the two to its offices in Dev Nagar, in the Karol Bagh area of west-central Delhi. But several hundred people converged there, raising slogans to lynch the suspected killers.

They were then taken away to an undisclosed location by the police, who had a tough time wading through crowds baying for the blood of the killers. As packs of journalists frenetically chased the story, top officials of Delhi Police went to the ground. They avoided the media for a while to strategize about how to deal with their star captives.

Meanwhile, word arrived from Bombay that Billa's fiancée, a twenty-one-year-old Gujarati girl he had met in the city's Sion area, was in the Arthur Road jail, in custody on the charge of possessing stolen property. That crime under Section 411 of the Indian Penal Code paled before the juicier crime-beat gossip that Billa had actually married the girl, Sushila, at the shrine of a Muslim saint in suburban Kalyan.

And that paled before the news of the interrogation of Billa and Ranga by the police. Public briefings by the police and tactical leaks within scant hours of their arrest ensured this interrogation made it to the front pages of nearly every major and minor newspaper the following day. It was as if, after nearly two weeks of cumulative ineptitude and cluelessness, blow-by-blow accounts of the investigation were as exculpatory for the police as they were necessary to assuage the anger and frayed nerves of the citizenry.

Just hours after Billa's and Ranga's arrest Police Commissioner Chaturvedi and his senior colleagues provided a brief version of events, attributing these to the interrogation pitched to the public as a confession.

He said Billa and Ranga offered a ride to Geeta and Sanjay near the Convent of Jesus and Mary, a school not far from the circular structure of the post office—also the roundabout linking five major and minor roads; a major link, Ashoka Road, goes past the Gurdwara Bangla Sahib on to the roundabout at Patel Chowk, where a turn to the right would bring them to All India Radio. Perhaps the children were running late, and even if it didn't look like it would rain that evening, they wanted to hitch a ride that would have saved several minutes of walking. That tied in with the initial statement of Dr Nanda, the physician who had given the children a lift from Dhaula Kuna to Gole Dak Khana.

The car brought them to Patel Chowk but instead of continuing right at the roundabout, Billa drove the car back the way they had come and carried on towards Kali Bari and Shankar Road—which crosses the Ridge to connect to Rajinder Nagar.

Geeta and Sanjay, already protesting, began their fightback—'struggle', as the police commissioner put it—at this time. Geeta slashed at Billa with a kirpan. According to crime branch detectives, Geeta was in turn stabbed several times—half a dozen was the number conveyed—and for a time the fight went out of her.

Sanjay kept fighting back until the Fiat reached Upper Ridge Road.

The commissioner said Billa and Ranga had confessed to murdering Geeta and Sanjay.

Afterwards, they went to a petrol station to wash down the car to remove bloodstains, and travelled to Moti Nagar to hole up for a while. There they changed the registration plates, and then drove to Ram Manohar Lohia Hospital to get Billa's cut seen to. After receiving the stitches and misleading hospital staff about the cause of the injury, they slipped away to their hideaway room in Gali No. 3 in Majlis Park, in northwest Delhi.

Billa left for Bombay on 27 August, the day after the children were killed—the commissioner said.

Billa then hung around in Bombay, stole a car from the parking area near the Taj Mahal Hotel and the Gateway of India in South Bombay, and, spooked by word that the police there were looking for him, made his way back to Delhi. He then headed to Agra, where, Commissioner Chaturvedi continued, he had the stitches to his forehead removed at the clinic of a doctor with a private practice. Ranga meanwhile stayed back in Delhi, in the Majlis Park hideout—the Fiat would be found there two days after the bodies of the children were discovered. He joined Billa for the Agra segment of their murderous escapade.

Commissioner Chaturvedi then threw in a couple of more twists. The Rexine bag found in Billa's possession, he said, had Arabic letters that spelled the name of Mohammad Abdul Ghani of Barkas Pan Shop. It strengthened the suspicion that Billa was behind the murder in Bombay of two Arabs.

He followed up this suggestion with one that few in the crowded media briefing would buy. Delhi Police's sources had let them know that Billa and Ranga were holed up in Agra—and they would likely come to Delhi 'today'.

The commissioner then announced that Billa and Ranga would be produced before a magistrate sometime that afternoon.

With that, the commissioner wrapped up his there-you-have-it briefing.

Only, it was far from there-you-have-it beyond the arrests, a clearly hurried interrogation and presentation for public benefit and edification of the police. The key dates were still vague. These would begin to be pieced together after more questioning, and corroborated to establish a case for the prosecution. For now, there remained several gaps in the whodunit.

Indeed, even the whydunit. The motive for Billa and Ranga killing Geeta and Sanjay, let alone giving the siblings a lift, was still a point of speculation.

VOYEURSHIP

In the absence of information, media and crime voyeurs alike fanned out to the two courts where in their opinion Billa and Ranga would most likely be arraigned before being taken into judicial custody: at the Tiz Hazari courts complex near ISBT in north Delhi, or the courts at Patiala House by India Gate in the heart of the city.

By two in the afternoon, the crowds numbered in the thousands at Tis Hazari, which people tagged as the most likely destination. At 5 p.m., when there appeared to be no sign of the crowds dispersing, the police and local administration implemented Plan B. They took Billa and Ranga to the New Police Kotwali in Daryaganj, in the old city, not far from where they came into the hands of the police at Delhi Junction—Old Delhi Station. The chief metropolitan magistrate, P. K. Jain, lived less than 2 kilometres away, and could conveniently visit the kotwali to take a call on the next steps for the suspected killers.

Word spread fast.

Within minutes of their arrival at New Police Kotwali crowds began to gather. In half an hour, conservative estimates placed onlookers at 400 hundred in and around the small station in the cramped neighbourhood. Crowds supercharged daily with front-page news of the newest and, for two weeks, the biggest drama in town, rushed the police station. Several screamed for Billa and Ranga to be hanged in public.

After the magistrate arrived at 5.30 p.m., Billa and Ranga were taken, handcuffed and in chains, to the room where the temporary court would be held. It took fifteen minutes for the magistrate to decide to hand them over to police custody. Formal charges and a trial were several weeks away.

After their turn in front of the magistrate, Billa and Ranga were asked to participate in an identification parade. Both declined. It was in any case pointless. Their photos had been splashed across newspapers for several days—Billa's more than Ranga's. Identification was a done deal in this trial by media. Formal culpability for the crime would find its own judicial course.

At around five minutes to six, the two emerged into the narrow corridors along with their police escort.

Billa and Ranga made a curious pair. They skulked along, manacled, in their distinct mini-universes with their police escorts. The suspected killers looked tired. Billa, referred to as 'chhota', the small one, was in a green shirt and wore dark trousers. He looked tense. So did Ranga, at six-foot-one-inch much the taller of the two. He wore a white kurta-pyjama.

The photographers went into a frenzy.

That revealed a set of character traits—at least in public. Neither Billa nor Ranga attempted to lower their faces or raise their manacled hands to shield the faces. They faced the little forest of photographers up front and personal. They were brazen in this amped up, dubious limelight. It was their moment.

But where Billa hovered between expressionless and occasionally scowling, Ranga smiled for the photographers.

That's what the world saw of them the next day in the papers. A deadpan Billa, almost shrunken in the crowd. And a tall, nervously—as one account described it, 'wolfishly'—smiling Ranga, framed by a group of policemen and investigators as they crowded around one of their star captives.

Ranga was the showboater, belying his nervousness with smiles for photographers and even the crowds baying for their blood. This twitchiness, this tendency to show off, would become a Ranga hallmark, part bravado and, perhaps, part wonder at being this famous in infamy, before he would quieten as execution approached, and pass this showboating, this nervous bravado, to his colleague as if it were a psychological last will and testament.

Captain Chopra heard the news of the arrest of Billa and Ranga on the evening of 9 September at the home of his parents in Chandigarh. He sat expressionlessly in the living room not far from the body of his mother, his eyes swollen with a lifetime of tears and grief as a newscaster announced the arrests on All India Radio, in Punjabi.

He gestured vaguely in the direction of the radio. He had heard enough. An attendant switched off the radio.

It was now time for the captain to see to his mother. But even here he would be publicly reminded of his children in the most achingly inadvertent way. A correspondent for the *Indian Express* recorded that moment:

> Capt. Chopra comes out of house to help his mother's body into the funeral van. And just as the members of the family pay their last respects to the departed woman, a relative, addressing his son says, 'Sanjay, tum bhi pair choo lo (Sanjay, you also touch her feet).' Captain Chopra looks up, turns towards the man, stares awhile and returns to the entrance....

WE KNEW IT!

Information, much of it speculative or shared and sometimes leaked by the police after their hyper-interrogation of Billa and Ranga, came in a torrent.

They had always intended to return to Delhi—we knew of it; we were tracking them. They had made a down payment of 150 rupees for a small flat in Anand Parbat, for occupation from 9 September. Their arrival was just a matter of time.

'Under constant watch' was the phrase often used by investigating officers in their interaction with the media. Two hundred plainclothes police had been keeping a watch on all trains originating from both Old Delhi and New Delhi stations, and they tracked every train that passed through.

Where regular beat police couldn't make up the numbers, Delhi Armed Police personnel were drafted into the watch for Billa and Ranga. As unlikely as it might seem for them to use planes to get about, crime branch personnel were on watch at Palam Airport.

They were crafty, you never knew what they might do. See how Billa showed some smarts at the hospital when he went to have his slashed forehead attended. Procedure for suspicious cases called for thumbprints. But in a sleight of hand Billa managed to effect a partial thumbprint of his right thumb—the convention for women—instead of marking his left thumb for the print.

Even so, and with all the conjecture, that was an odd but useful clue. As the net of investigation spread, they had begun to tally the clues, and matched that partial print to a thumbprint from the getaway Fiat. Indeed, entire palm prints. Billa's prints matched with those. A palm print belonged to Geeta; they had matched it with prints taken from her house. Disparate bits of the crime were all beginning to come together as composite evidence, the police insisted.

■

Speculation was mixed with whatever arrived as fact to the media—the main channel to carry news from the justice system to the public. In the initial days of the spotlight on the suspected killers, several major media houses offered disbelief as analysis.

Meanwhile, the police went with ransom as the main motive.

'However,' questioned an article in *India Today*, underscoring an existing media theory, 'it seems incredible that two highly experienced, hardened criminals would kidnap two teenagers without any prior information as to their background, their families and their financial standing. Further, it is obvious that if the Chopra children belonged to a wealthy family, they would hardly be thumbing a lift, especially with two suspicious-looking men, at that time of the evening.'

'The most likely theory,' continued the article with a giddy breathlessness uncharacteristic of the magazine that had set a benchmark for sharp reportage just three years into its existence, 'is that the Chopra children were forcibly abducted with the intention of sexually molesting the attractive, seventeen-year-old Geeta Chopra. There was no question of premeditated murder, and they were stabbed because of the unexpected resistance they put up.'

And once the stabbing proved to be fatal, Billa and Ranga panicked, dumped the bodies, and took off. They then went to Willingdon Hospital to get Billa's wound treated—the one inflicted on his scalp by a defiant Geeta as they, with her younger brother besides her, careened along in the Fiat to their collective doom.

CONSPIRACIES

Absurdity increased as the media and police, in their hesitation to consider it for the crime it was, and hesitation to consider Billa and Ranga as the blunt and bungling instruments they appeared to be, began investigations to pin several unexplained incidents on the two—some from several years earlier.

On 24 September, news arrived of a 'party of crime investigators' who would soon arrive in Delhi from Madras in an attempt to close a loop: 'The Madras city police has yet to solve the mystery surrounding the wife of a company executive last year and the disappearance of a 14-year-old girl in 1974.' The reason, as a report by United News of India explained, was that 'Billa had taken up his residence at Anna Nagar, a locality in the city, for some time when he was wanted by the Bombay police last year.'

At a stretch, Billa could be questioned about the death of a lady in Madras in 1977, a year he was there, but the disappearance of a girl in 1974? It was accepted as being logical in the general villainy of things.

Three days later, on 27 September, a loop unrelated to the Chopra children was actually closed by a frantic Delhi Police still red-faced over the murder of the siblings, when they quickly arrested the alleged killers of a company executive, Shana Ramchand. This did not arrive without a public relations blip and vocabulary issues when it came to describing female innerwear.

On the evening of the 25th, a Monday, the day the lady's murder had been detected, police had initially released her name as Shana Ramachandran, a Tamil twist to a Sindhi name. Ramchand had been a secretary with Union Carbide, and lived in a quiet part of South Extension Part II—the neighbourhood along the southern arc of the city's transport girdle, the Ring Road, and sandwiched between the vast complex of AIIMS to its west and a housing complex for mid-level bureaucrats to the east.

The prime suspect, Ram Singh, from a village near Almora in the hills of Himachal Pradesh, had worked part-time at Ramchand's apartment in a building she shared with other ladies who were paying guests. Ram was twenty-two, like his accomplice, Hari Singh, and both were evidently in need of money.

To hear Delhi South District police chief Dr K. K. Paul tell it, on that Monday the two, on the pretext of delivering bread, had let themselves into the ground floor garage Ramchand used as her living room. They then locked the room from the inside before beginning a search for things to steal. Ramchand had by then returned from work and was presumably in her bath, because subsequent interrogation of the two revealed that, upon hearing noise in that room, she emerged from the bath in a 'bikini'.

A scuffle ensued and Ramchand was stabbed. There was a deep wound to her neck and bruises upon her body, signs of the lady resisting.

Her two attackers—killers—escaped, in their panic leaving behind their slippers. Other residents at the paying-guest residency investigated and discovered the body, including a lady who told police Ramchand had mentioned that she would shower before dinner—it had been so humid that evening.

Police went to the room Ram and Hari Singh shared not far from Ramchand. The two weren't there but a letter was discovered with an address in the west Delhi locality of Tilak Nagar. That is where they were discovered within hours, on the morning of the 26th.

Crime solved. Ergo: Delhi's police were alert and on the job.

▪

That bit of news done and dusted, a hungry media looked for any and everything to keep this story of the year—Geeta and Sanjay and the now hyphenated Billa-Ranga—on the boil.

Towards the end of September, *India Today*, which had up until then offered several stellar, detailed accounts of the investigation, uncharacteristically jumped in by providing a platform to speculation. It muddied the already murky waters around the investigation.

The speculation involved the publisher and editor of an obscure weekly, *Tuesday Post*. Avinash Dubey, the publisher, and Surinder Vats, the editor, claimed that the investigation into the killing of Geeta and Sanjay was little more than a cover-up by every level of government from the police upward. They actually said this towards the end of September at Tis Hazari Court, in the Kashmiri Gate area of North Delhi, where they sought anticipatory bail—in anticipation of being arrested by Delhi Police.

They claimed that Billa and Ranga were hired for a small sum by the real triggers of the killings, the son of a cabinet minister in the central government and the son of a senior army officer. The minister's son had been in love with Geeta, and was livid at being repeatedly spurned by her. The army brat actually lived in the same apartment building as the Chopras. He too faced rejection. Geeta had slapped him several days before she and her brother were abducted and killed.

Dubey and Vats claimed in their conversation with *India Today* that all this information came to them by way of a detective agency they hired in Bombay in early September for a fee of 500 rupees a month. Pandit Detective Agency delivered this dirt by virtue of 'certain documents' it had obtained.

They have more evidence, the two journalists claimed. They had a pair of bloodstained trousers that belonged to the army officer's son—gory, sure-fire proof of his culpability. They claimed to possess an interview with Billa taped several days before his arrest. In it, they claimed Billa detailed the plotting of the elaborate crime, and also claimed that Delhi Police were framing him for the murders.

The journalists went a step further and claimed—via Billa, their Deep Throat, as it were—that the dozen soldiers credited with apprehending Billa and Ranga were in on the cover-up. Billa had told them, so Dubey and Vats claimed, that the soldiers had actually brought Billa and Ranga all the way from Bombay.

To cut to the chase—the minister whose son was a rejected

suitor found out about the investigation. He offered to buy out the evidence for 200,000 rupees. The journalists declined. The crime branch immediately stepped in—the allusion was that the minister set the wolves on the hapless journalists. They raided the premises of *Tuesday Post* on 3, 19, and 22 September. They would tell all, they claimed, in the weekly's issue of 3 October—if they, naturally, managed to remain out of jail.

It was altogether bizarre, with loopholes and degrees of improbability to tire a Sherlock. A tiny fee to an agency in Bombay that managed to crack wide open one of the biggest puzzles in India. The astounding claim of a suitor-neighbour of Geeta who remained out of reach at a time the Chopras were trying to move heaven and earth, so to say, for justice. The claim of the bloodied trousers of one of the key conspirators and assailants. The claim of the taped interview with Billa. There was also Billa's alleged claim to Dubey and Vats of being escorted by the soldiers west from Bombay by train, when that train, the Kalka Mail, actually originated in quite the opposite direction—east—in Howrah, the main station that serves Calcutta, and the soldiers who captured Billa and Ranga boarded the train in Allahabad.

There was no promised article in *Tuesday Post*. The two claimants faded. But it was hardly the end of bizarre stories or the tragicomedy of errors the entire sordid episode had quickly come to be.

By the end of September every aspect, supersized or minute, was under scrutiny. And the envelope was extended by the contradictory confessions provided by Billa and Ranga, in turn sieved to the media by the police through announcements and leaks.

A great part of the confusion was sown by Billa and Ranga who, to add to their obvious albeit nervous glee at being in the spotlight, seemed to possess enough smarts and cunning to provide conflicting versions of their crime—whether to implicate each other in a case of dishonour among criminals or to deliberately cause chaos, or both, wasn't clear.

Was Geeta sexually assaulted? The media didn't shy away from using the word 'rape'. The post-mortem report diminished that possibility and the police's announcements negated the possibility. Yet Ranga claimed to the police—and in turn the police claimed to the world at large—Billa had raped Geeta in the Fiat.

Were these really the 'callous, clever and hardened criminals' the police had showcased in the immediate aftermath of the discovery of Geeta's and Sanjay's mutilated corpses on the Ridge and right up until their incredible arrest. Or were they just hopped-up desperadoes who, on a whim, took on much more than they could handle, made a hash of things and—spectacularly, ludicrously—ended their run by jumping into a coach full of alert soldiers?

They behaved like start-up criminals, not individuals or a team that would be welcomed at the high table of criminal masterminds—as the police had projected them, partly to cover up their inability to track down the killers and partly to downplay snafus. Their very bungling behaviour enabled the police to move from clue to clue that Billa and Ranga left less like breadcrumbs and more like entire loaves of bread; even though the police themselves often behaved as if they were clueless.

Indeed, police eagerness led immediately to another complication. Even though ace lawyer Ram Jethmalani was being spoken of as being imminently engaged as counsel for the prosecution, he and the entire prosecution would encounter the defence's counter of prejudice. There was the massive splash of the photos of Billa and Ranga being released to the media, and the two being projected as killers without conclusive evidence let alone advancement and conclusion of the trial. With that ready bias, any identification parade or process would be meaningless in the eyes of the law. Some commentators used 'pre-conditioned' to describe the case against the two.

The construction of that case was expected to begin sometime in November.

RANGA'S CONFESSION

Who were they, these suddenly infamous folk, now hyphenated? What led up to the murders? Why did they do what they did—abducting two teenagers, killing them? Who, precisely, did what? How much was Billa, how much Ranga?

Much of the answers, obfuscations, and deflection lay in the confessions of Billa and Ranga—deflections to artfully project the other as primary planner and executioner. Their lives were finally laid as bare as each would permit, each would paint.

Ranga's confession to a magistrate ran to thirty pages—compacted into typewritten sheets from the eighty-three pages of notes recorded by the magistrate. It could, as noted later by judges, be broadly grouped into five areas:

Ranga's antecedents, and this included his association with Billa which began in Bombay. Their crimes in Bombay. Their activities in Delhi before kidnapping Geeta and Sanjay. The 'kidnapping, rape and murder of Sanjay and Geeta'. And what they were up to in Agra before their surreal arrest.

Ranga's career graph ran from being a runaway from his home in Panipat, due north of Delhi in Haryana, to a truck driver's apprentice, to a driver, to a driver of taxis in Bombay. Along the way, he came by a dealer in contraband alcohol, Raj Kumar. Ranga did the odd job for Raj Kumar and, he claimed, was soon given the charge of managing the operation. Then came an introduction to a man called Sham Singh; he urged Ranga to begin his own line of business in contraband alcohol.

Sham Singh introduced him to Billa—rather, an alias of his, 'Bengali'—who, he was told, owned a taxi. Ranga mentioned he had no idea that Bengali carried a reputation, at least a recognized name, in that city's seething underworld.

One day in early August 1978, the month that would quickly begin their countdown to doom, Bengali took him for a spin around noon. Ranga drove. They travelled to the northern suburb of Juhu in his taxi. There Bengali changed the number plates of the taxi. Ranga, seemingly naïve, was curious as to the reason. He was told that was a preferred modus operandi when planning a crime; the prep helped to dilute or escape any subsequent suspicion. They drove around till 2.30 p.m. Then they stopped in front of an 'English' school.

Their mark was a schoolboy. Bengali got down from the taxi and asked Ranga to return after a while. When Ranga returned, Bengali 'lifted' a boy and deposited him in the taxi. Ranga was asked to drive off—Bengali insisted that they go to Virar Lake. There, he replaced the previous number plate. At that time Bengali told Ranga they would demand a ransom of 300,000 rupees from the boy's father.

They went on to Ghatkopar in eastern Bombay. Ranga said that is when Bengali handed over the custody of the child to him, and tasked Ranga with the child's custody; he was to be kept at Ranga's place. Bengali left after ensuring the boy was asleep. He also told Ranga that the boy would be killed if the child's father didn't cough up the ransom. By Ranga's telling, the amount of ransom had been scaled down. It was now 50,000-rupees-or-else, a sixth of the declaration made only hours earlier.

Here Ranga projected himself as an angel of sorts.

When there was no word of any ransom-related communication for two days, Ranga assumed the boy would likely be killed. The getaway taxi now became the taxi of deliverance—he drove the boy home, deposited him there, and sped away.

The following day the mastermind, Bengali, learnt of it, and was livid. He roundly abused Ranga. Sham Singh, the go-between, was also told of it. He too berated Ranga.

Ranga and Sham Singh began to drink.

During their inebriated conversation Sham Singh repeatedly asked Ranga his reasons for having 'disobeyed' Bengali.

And during this exchange Bengali was revealed to Ranga as

Billa—a dangerous man. Sham Singh too was revealed to him as one half of a dangerous team—'Two Arabs' had 'recently' been murdered by Billa and him. Ranga was counselled to not bring up that matter with Billa.

Even with his panicky—or peaceable—act, evidently Ranga was co-opted into the Billa-Ranga team; inadvertently, according to Ranga. He stayed over at Billa's for a night because he was afraid the boy might guide the police to his place. He then made a faux pas. Ranga mentioned that he had seen an imported tape recorder at Billa's and asked its provenance. Smuggled goods, he was told. Ranga went motormouth at this point and retorted that it had belonged to the Arabs 'whom Billa and Sham Singh had killed'—Sham Singh had said so. This set Billa on edge.

The following morning an anxious Billa, with Ranga in tow, rushed to Sham Singh's house. The purpose was to ensure Singh stopped being indiscreet with their inside story, as it were. Upon reaching, they discovered an absent Singh; his wife said the police had arrested him the night before.

This spooked Billa. His concern was twofold—Sham Singh could confess to the murder of the Arabs and also spill the beans about the kidnapping of the boy. Ranga too was spooked.

From then on for about a fortnight it was a blur of activity—a mix of run-hide-run, bluster, threats, a series of capers. And then, finally, the killing of the Chopra children.

It began, Ranga said, with them making a quick run to Billa's place to collect whatever was of value. This they kept in the taxi. Ranga's place was out of bounds too; the overhang of the kidnapping was still fresh, and with Sham Singh in custody they couldn't take chances.

They went instead to a restaurant, Tasna, and attempted to keep their goods with an acquaintance of Ranga's, Jugal—he too had an alias: Bhedoo. As Jugal wanted no part of what had gone down, the two went to Ghatkopar and found a room to store their things. They spent that night in the taxi.

The following morning, they again met Jugal, with a request to find them a room.

Billa was introduced to Jugal as Anwar. Jugal suggested that they leave town and head to Delhi to escape the heat that had begun to stalk them. A visit to the room where they had stashed their things convinced them of the need to quickly leave Bombay: the area was crawling with police. They managed to retrieve their belongings and drove off to Surat. After a drive shy of 300 kilometres, they reached Surat on 15 August.

There Ranga, Billa, and Jugal—now a trio that would last for a few more days—ditched the taxi near a cinema and, after, they took a bus to Ahmedabad, about 260 kilometres to the north.

They then switched to a train to Delhi and reached the capital a day later, on 16 August. They checked in to Room No. 5 at Gautam Lodge in Fatehpuri—an old Delhi neighbourhood between the teeming areas of Sadar Bazar and Chandni Chowk. They used assumed names.

Their first order of business on 17 August was to purchase two sets of number plates from Karol Bagh, a residential neighbourhood to the west of the business and shopping hub of Connaught Place. They had fake registration numbers painted on the plates. Now they needed a car.

They went on a trawl and found one in Moti Nagar, a few short kilometres further to the west, where Jugal had a place. Billa and Jugal broke into the car. They drove it around for 3 to 4 kilometres and, in the process discovering the car was not in good shape, ditched it after retaining their stock of number plates. (Here Ranga mentioned a brief interlude of a day, when he visited his home in Panipat to have his sister tie a rakhi on him; he returned to Delhi the same day after this episode of family bonding.)

Ranga resumed the trawling for suitable cars and marks with his colleagues on 19 August. They began roaming Connaught Place. Around noon they perked up when they noticed a Fiat car park and its driver emerge and walk off. The car's plates read DHE 828. As soon as the coast was clear Billa and Jugal broke into the car. Ranga said he was then asked to bring along the bag containing spanners and meet Billa and Jugal at the shop in Karol Bagh from which they had purchased the number plates. It took Ranga an hour and a half to retrieve the bag and rejoin his partners.

Now DHE 828 was replaced with plates that read DEA 3548. They took the car for an extended spin to properly check it out. It turned out that the pickup wasn't up to their mark—a healthy initial speed was as crucial as anything for a getaway vehicle.

In it, they went to Ashoka Hotel in the hope of stealing a 'really good' car—a good possibility in the vicinity of the sprawling luxury hotel at the northern edge of Delhi's diplomatic enclave. Ranga recalled that Billa stopped near another Fiat. This wore the number 'DEA 1221 or 2112'. Billa carjacked it.

He drove it behind the car stolen earlier—now being driven by Ranga, accompanied by Jugal. Jugal led them to his place in Moti Nagar. There, number plates were again swapped. DEA 3548 was transferred to the car newly stolen from Ashoka Hotel. The car stolen previously, the one which lacked good pickup, had its original plates put back. As a further precaution the grills of the two cars were exchanged. Then the first car was dumped near a large open drain that skirted Moti Nagar. The Fiat wearing DEA 3548 now became the car of choice, and the criminal crew drove it back to their den.

They roamed about for the next three days, Ranga recounted. On 22 August, an impatient Billa asked Jugal to zero in on a mark with money. Jugal suggested they rob his uncle. Perhaps not, Billa replied, because they would need to kill the uncle and everyone else at home.

He didn't care for his uncle, Jugal retorted; he had no problem with his uncle and his uncle's family being killed. He even provided a sketch of his uncle's house. With instructions to keep a lookout, Billa and Ranga left Jugal in the car and went to the uncle's house. Billa carried a sword.

The foray didn't yield much, Ranga said. There wasn't anyone at the place, and after searching everywhere they found a hundred rupees, maybe a hundred-and-fifty, from the pocket of a shirt. They took that, and a few shirts—'two-three'.

This meagre haul wasn't the only surprise. Upon their return to the street Billa and Ranga discovered Jugal had disappeared with the car. Jugal surfaced the following morning, with the car and a companion, Kewal, in tow. Jugal explained to a furious Billa that he had to leave quickly because a chowkidar had shown up. There was more, Jugal said: He would now have to leave for Bombay because his nephew there had died.

Let's all go to Bombay, Billa suggested; Delhi wasn't turning out to be useful. Nothing was working out. They would all catch a flight, Billa said, there was always Indian Airlines.

But Billa got into a murderous mood on the way to the airport. He set about removing the handles of the doors. He then had Jugal stop the car. He told Ranga that Jugal and Kewal would now need to be killed. Billa took out a knife. By now Jugal and Kewal had begun to cry, fearing for their lives.

Why kill them? Ranga asked. Because they might get us both into trouble, Billa replied.

Spare them, Ranga pleaded in his self-confessed angelic mode.

Fine, Billa finally agreed. But Jugal and Kewal would each need to kill someone. Those murders would trap them criminally and act as insurance for Billa and Ranga.

It was evening by the time they reached Buddha Jayanti Park to search for suitable victims. They spotted a couple. Billa gave instructions for them to first be looted and then for Jugal and Kewal to kill them. The crew surrounded the couple. Billa grabbed the man; that set the woman to weeping. (Billa would in some days mention the incident in his confession, adding a dash of bravado along with his habitual flash of a knife: 'It was not difficult for me to kill that person had I desired so, but I did not do that.' Among several other aspects, this would ultimately doom him—but more on this a little later.)

This was evidently too much for Ranga and Kewal. They made an excuse to slip away from the scene and made towards the exit of the park. It was also too much for Jugal: he made a run for it. Billa showed up shortly after and told Ranga and Kewal that Jugal had disappeared. With Billa's plans gone awry, the targeted couple received a new lease on life.

Billa, Ranga and Kewal then drove off to Paharganj and took a room at Mini Guest House.

That night, Kewal made a run for it. He told Billa and Ranga that he needed to buy paan and while they were all out, he managed to slip away.

That rattled Ranga and Billa. They quickly returned to the hotel and checked out of their room. They again changed the car plates: the new plates read HRK 8930. That night they stayed put in the car. The following morning, 24 August, they managed to hire a room in Majlis Park for 160 rupees a month. They paid two months' rent in advance.

They continued to roam about Connaught Place on the 25th. It was Janmashtami, Ranga said, a holiday. They were on the lookout for a couple to offer a lift to, with the intention of overpowering them, and forcing them to take Billa and Ranga to their home. Billa and Ranga would then rob the place. There wasn't any talk about what would subsequently happen to the couple.

They were unable to find any marks.

That brought them to 26 August, the day things would change forever for them and two teenagers and everyone in their orbit—shake an entire city, a country.

Billa and Ranga began their search in the morning, Ranga said. (Billa would say of that day they mostly spent trawling Connaught Place in search of victims: 'I had a talk with Ranga and asked him that we will start committing robberies in the houses here as well as in the manner in which it was done at Bombay. I told him that we will now provide a lift to someone in our car and then we would commit robbery.')

The entire day went in scouting about for just such an opportunity. Nothing.

At 6.20 in the evening, when they reached Gole Dak Khana, 'a boy and a girl'—'the deceased', the appeals court judge would later add to the description—asked for a lift.

It was perfect. The handles of the car had already been loosened in anticipation. The boy and girl looked well-off—surely they were from a prosperous family.

Billa and Ranga went along the roundabout that encircled the five-road hub in the middle of which sat the circular post office. Billa stopped the car near the boy and girl. Where did they want to go? he asked them. They spoke in English. Exchange over, the boy and the girl sat at the back—the girl sat behind Billa who was in the driver's seat. The boy sat behind Ranga. As the left rear door shut, the loosened window and door handles came off. Billa quickly took these and kept them with him.

He drove off on one of the roads that spoked out towards Patel Chowk, another circle hub. Billa went around it, and turned back the way they came, towards Gole Dak Khana. At that time Billa reached back and pulled out the handles from the rear right door. Now the boy and the girl began to question Billa in English, asking him where he was taking them.

'Billa started abusing them and asking them to shut up,' the magistrate recorded Ranga as saying.

The boy and girl began to fight back. The girl caught hold of Billa's hair. The boy began to repeatedly kick Ranga.

The only way out was for Ranga to frighten the boy. He took out a kirpan. The boy attempted to snatch away the kirpan and that fetched the boy some cuts—'three-four'.

Meanwhile Billa continued to circle Gole Dak Khana. The boy and the girl were shouting at this time but they couldn't be heard because the windows were all up and the handles at the back were removed. In the melee the girl and the boy managed to shift the gear into neutral. The car stopped for a minute, perhaps two. Billa managed to get the car moving again, and began to snake his way towards Buddha Jayanti Park.

At one stage, Ranga said, the car was followed by a Sikh man on a scooter. This worried Ranga. He told Billa that the 'Sardar' might be determined to follow them. Ranga suggested that the best way out might be for them to simply let the children out of the car and then make their escape. Billa flatly refused.

They finally managed to get on the road that led to Buddha Jayanti Park—'Buddha Garden', the appeals court judge would note. The road was empty. The 'Sardar' had evidently given up the chase.

Ranga again asked Billa to let the children go. Billa refused, again. They reached the parking lot of Buddha Jayanti Park. Here Ranga paid 'eight annas'—fifty paise—as parking charges to the attendant of the park.

By now the children were exhausted. The boy asked for water. No water, Ranga replied, only Campa Cola. He got out of the car and brought back three bottles of the cola purchased from a nearby vendor. The boy refused the cola. He likes ice cream, the girl pleaded, could he be given an ice cream? Ranga bought an ice cream—he didn't clarify what kind—and then a second, for the boy.

Billa now asked Ranga to change the number plates of the car. Why not let the children off and then drive away before changing the plates, Ranga suggested, or the children might note the changed number?

They were live snakes, Billa said. With a gesture he indicated to Ranga that they had to be killed. Ranga remained in the car while Billa changed the number plates. These now read DHI 280.

Billa then began to question the boy and girl, and asked what their father did. He was a captain in the navy, they replied. That prompted Ranga to say there was no point in trying to rob the captain's home as there was a risk the officer might shoot them. And, in any case, he said, there couldn't be much to rob in a naval captain's house.

The girl asked Billa why they were being held. Billa spun a tale that included a role for the girl. They were waiting for a jeweller to arrive from Bombay. This jeweller would leave Palam airport and reach their vicinity around 8.30 p.m. The plan was for the girl to intercept the car by asking for a lift, at which point the car they were all in would be used to block the jeweller's car. The jeweller would then be robbed and, that deed done, there would no longer be any need for the girl and boy to be detained. They would be freed.

This assurance quietened them.

As they waited, a security guard came by and asked them to leave. Billa gave him some baksheesh and sent him away.

Now Ranga again suggested the children be freed, but Billa refused.

Somebody else—Ranga wasn't clear as to who—came by after a while and asked them to leave.

Billa drove off towards the airport. At Dhaula Kuan junction, the children again asked to be let off. Ranga interceded too, but Billa again declined. He turned back towards the park, and stopped at a place to buy more ice cream. Thereafter, they parked the car on a 'kacha' road.

Billa continued with his ruse of the girl being used to entrap the jeweller—while she requested that car for a lift, the boy would remain out of sight.

Now Billa and Ranga got down. Ranga was asked by Billa to take out the bigger of the kirpans, about 3 feet long, from the trunk and deposit it a little further away in the bushes, and return to the car. Like the smaller kirpan, that kirpan too had been purchased at Chandni Chowk and been sharpened at Nai Sarak, not too far away.

Ranga again asked that the children be freed. Billa refused. He asked Ranga to comply with whatever he was asked to do.

▪

Now we read Ranga's words as conveyed by the magistrate who recorded his confessional statement in September 1978:

> *I returned after placing the kirpan at a distance of 100 yards from the vehicle. When I returned, Billa asked me to make the boy sit at a distance. When I was taking the boy with me, Billa followed us. The boy was made to sit on the place where the kirpan was lying. Billa asked him to lie down.*
>
> *The boy replied that he was comfortable and that there was no such need. He was sitting with a piece of cloth keeping on the injury on his chest, which I had given to him. Billa asked me as to where that (the sword) was. I replied that it was in the bush*

on the front. I ... brought the sword. Billa asked me that he may be done away with. I lifted the sword and aimed to hit. The boy was shivering and ... the sword-blow hit ... the left arm. The boy started raising an alarm ... 'Mat Maro, Mat Maro, Kyon Martey Ho?' (...Do not kill, Do not kill ... and ... why do you kill me.) Billa snatched away the sword from my hand and addressing me as 'Behande Khasman' stated that neither I knew anything to do nor I was capable of doing anything. Saying this he started killing the boy. He went on striking wherever he could. He made the boy bleeding profusely. For 10 minutes Billa continued to kill the boy. I kept aloof thinking that he may not give a blow to me as well. In haste I left my Chappals over there. After throwing away the sword over there Billa went away.

Billa questioned me as to what I was seeing and directed me to drag him away at some distance. I caught hold of the arms of the boy and placed him amongst the bushes. That was a lower-level place. I broke some branches (of the bushes) and placed the same over him. Thereafter I wore my chappals and cleaned the kirpan with the help of grass and approached the car and kept the sword standing against the rear bumper of the car.

By now Billa, according to Ranga, had turned his attention to Geeta. The magistrate's bureaucratic flourish removed none of the chilling revelations in Ranga's confession:

(At this stage the accused laughs and states) *The girl was naked in the car and was raising a hue and cry but some of her voice was being heard outside. I approached the road and stood over there in order to see as to whether the voice was being heard over there or not. Billa was engaged in sexual intercourse with the girl on the back seat in the car itself. Billa was naked. All his clothes were lying in the dickey outside the car whereas the clothes of the girl were lying on the ... dash board inside the car. After 10/15 minutes I returned whereupon Billa came out. Billa told me that I should also do the same (sexual intercourse). I told him that she will give a kick and consequently I shall be flat. Billa again persisted that I should do. I told him that as I was tall, it was not possible to perform it inside. I suggested to him that in case the seat was taken outside, I would do it. The seat was taken out and was placed by the dickey. The girl was perspiring profusely when she was taken out. The girl slipped from the seat as the seat was having slope. 4/5 times she was made to lie on the seat. A lot of dust had fallen on her. I kept back. Billa questioned me as to whether I had done my job. I replied him in the affirmative. Billa asked me to let him do the sexual intercourse again. Billa again went for sexual intercourse. At that time I was putting on my clothes.*

Geeta then fought back—Ranga's confession stated:

> *The girl lifted the sword and struck it against Billa. Billa happened to place his hand on the sword, as a result thereof the sword struck slightly and he was saved. The sword had struck Billa on his forehead. The girl in its naked position ran towards the road. I ran and caught hold of her while she was naked. Billa aimed to kill her in her naked position itself. I suggested to him to let her wear the clothes. I told the girl that we had made her brother sit with the [guard] ... and that half an hour time had been given. I questioned the girl saying that in case he sees her naked, what he will say? She wore the Jhagula (coat) and I helped her in wearing the pants. I suggested to her that I should take her to her brother and that she should go away from there. I was taking her to that side towards which her brother was lying dead. I was on the right-hand side of the girl. Billa gave a signal to me and I got a little ahead.*
>
> *Billa struck the sword with full force against her neck and as a result thereof she was no more alive.*

That blow might have been the fatal one, but Geeta still had life—and spirit—left:

She took a turn and fell down. Billa gave 5/7 more blows to her. She was raising alarm to the effect 'Hai, Hai'. I caught hold of her by one side and Billa caught hold of her by the other side and threw her away amongst the bushes. On return we started the car. Billa tied down a handkerchief on the portion where he was given a blow. There is a pump near the circle towards Karol Bagh. We made provision of water for the car and threw away 2/3 boxes of water on the back seat where there were slight stains of blood.

■

Now Ranga drove the Fiat after this cursory carwash. It was imperative they visit a hospital to get Billa's bleeding head seen to. A backstory was needed—and agreed upon—if they were questioned about the cause of the injury, Billa would say that he came by it while walking near Bangla Sahib Gurdwara. Thugs had attacked him, beaten him up, and robbed his watch.

Ranga asked passers-by about medical facilities and hospitals nearby while sticking to the story. One of them suggested a government dispensary in Moti Bagh, quite far from where they were. Another suggested they visit the government-run Willingdon Hospital as the attack made it a 'police case'. And so, nearby Willingdon Hospital it was. They drove there.

Billa and Ranga decided to hide in plain sight. They parked the car and went into the outpatient department of the hospital. Here Billa identified himself as Vinod Kumar. Ranga too used an alias—Harbhajan Singh. After Billa's injury was stitched up and bandaged, the doctor on duty suggested he get himself admitted. It was crowded and a separate bed wasn't available; Billa would have to share a bed with another patient. Billa demurred and said he would rather go home, and promised to return to have the stitches removed.

He then had a short conversation with Sub-inspector Ram Chander of Delhi Police—his injury was a case for the police. Billa stuck to the story and added a layer by providing a fictitious address—

as did Ranga when the sub-inspector queried him. Ranga too added a layer to his lie as he explained the reason for his accompanying 'Vinod'. He was the chauffeur of a big seth, he said, and he came by the injured 'Vinod' on the road. 'Harbhajan's' businessman-boss, whom he described as owning (the very real) Century Rayon Mills, had instructed him to bring the injured 'Vinod' to the hospital.

The plates of this car of deliverance read DHI 280.

The sub-inspector didn't probe the story but accompanied both of them, in that car, to the scene of the concocted crime. They then took the policeman to his police station and promised to show up the following morning at ten for the sub-inspector to pursue more questions.

Billa and Ranga then headed home to Majlis Park. Geeta's undergarments were still in the car. These Billa got rid of. One piece was thrown onto a passing vehicle—so claimed Ranga, although it seemed like bizarre behaviour piled upon bizarre behaviour. The other undergarment was dumped into an open sewer.

On 27 August, they went to Kingsway Camp in North Delhi, not far from Delhi University, to have the DHI 280 number plates repainted to HRF 5411. That night they drove to a petrol pump to fill the tank, and managed to leave without paying the bill. Billa had by then adopted a disguise—he put on a turban so he could pass off as Sikh.

Billa took a train to Bombay from New Delhi station the following afternoon, 28 August, around four. It was an attempt to deflect any heat from the police.

Ranga hung about in Delhi for two more days. During that time, he bumped into an acquaintance, Bhanwra. The underworld network had heard of a Bombay Police officer, Manak Shah, having come into town along with several colleagues—so Bhanwra told him. Ranga's immediate instinct was to again change the plates to insure against Bhanwra snitching. The plates now read UHD 8034.

Later that night—the 30th—he drove the car to Gali No. 9 of Majlis Park and, as a device to reduce any suspicion, asked a couple of locals the way to Gali No. 10, where he had to meet a person called 'Anwar'. He parked the car in Gali No. 10 and headed to the room Billa and he had rented, in Gali No. 3.

When he went to check on the car on the morning of 31 August, Ranga saw the area crawling with police. Numerous onlookers had gathered.

Ranga took off for the railway station to meet Billa who was expected back from Bombay. That rendezvous didn't work out, but he found Billa waiting for him upon his return to their den in Majlis Park. He filled Billa in on what had transpired during Billa's short absence from Delhi.

They also bumped into their landlord—who told them that police had 'traced the car in which the children had been killed'.

The net was closing. Billa and Ranga stayed over that night but left as soon as they could the next morning, and checked into a guest house using false names. They left for Agra by bus soon after. It was 1 September. They carried with them the instruments of death: the smaller kirpan in an attaché case—'attaichi' in North Indian parlance; the larger kirpan rolled inside a mat.

Agra was a blur: a rush from a small hotel to a small rental. Meanwhile, they procured a 'country' pistol—plentiful in northern India's improvised cottage industry of weapons. They would travel with this weapon—a plan proposed by Billa—to Madras and rob Billa's former employer.

Then came the train ride that would be their undoing. As we know, they hopped onto a train near Yamuna Bridge. The coach they attempted to enter was packed with military personnel. Billa was the first to enter. Ranga said the sight of soldiers prompted him to jump off the footboard of the crawling train, and quickly conceal the pistol under a stone before entering the coach.

Both were queried about their identities and their purpose. It led to an altercation ending with both Billa and Ranga being tied up by the soldiers. Upon their arrival at Delhi Railway Station, they were handed over to the police.

Geeta and Sanjay Chopra, the siblings whose story became the story of Delhi, and of India, in 1978.

Kidnapped teenagers untraced

Hindustan Times Correspondent

NEW DELHI, Aug. 28—Police tonight were looking for a 17-year-old girl Geeta Chopra, and her 15-yearold brother, Sanjay Chopra, who were allegedly kidnapped on Saturday evening while on their way to All India Radio.

The two had left their Dhaula Kuan Service Officers Enclave house for the Radio Station to record a programme there. But they never reached AIR and have been missing since.

Police Commissioner J. N. Chaturvedi today announced an award of Rs 2,000 for giving information being helpful in finding the two teenagers.

The police suspect that a yellow or light orange-coloured Fiat car was used to kidnap the two. Some passersby are said to have seen the car near the Gole Dakhana and Willingdon Hospital. They heard someone crying for help.

A police party went to Panipat following a report that the kidnap car had been found abandoned there.

The Delhi police denied that the car used in the Dhaula Kuan abduction had been traced.

Geeta Chopra

Sanjay Chopra

A *Hindustan Times* report from 29 August 1978 on the missing Chopra siblings. The report ran on p. 3.

CRIME CIRCULAR
WANTED ACCUSED
DETECTION OF CRIME BRANCH C.I.D., BOMB.
LOOK OUT FOR ESCAPED PRISONER

Jasbir Singh (alias Billa)

Kuljeet Singh (alias Ranga)

All India Radio, where Geeta was headed to record the show 'In the Groove'. Sanjay accompanied her.

©Amrin Naaz

The Ridge, where the bodies of Geeta and Sanjay were found.

A building belonging to Sikhs burning in Daryaganj during the anti-Sikh riots of 1984.

BILLA'S CONFESSION

Billa's confession, recorded in early October of 1978, was nearly as detailed as that of Ranga.

He broadly corroborated the statement of Ranga about their activities in Delhi. He differed slightly on several details, and also mentioned an unsuccessful bid to rob cash from a dairy—it was passed up as too many people were present. According to him, they also ditched a plan to rob a jeweller, Mehra & Sons, after reconnoitring the vicinity and deciding that 'this job' was 'not...worth doing'.

Investigators noted—as judges would later—that Billa also broadly corroborated the aspects of kidnapping Geeta and Sanjay, and the injuries inflicted upon Sanjay by a kirpan-wielding Ranga, their arrival at Buddha Jayanti Park, querying them about their father, and the elaborate ruse and deflection involving a fictitious jeweller, the purchasing and feeding of ice cream and Campa Cola, of Sanjay accepting the ice cream, the drive towards Palam before returning to the vicinity of Buddha Jayanti Park and parking on a 'kacha' road.

But just as Ranga painted Billa as being the key actor in the molestation of Geeta and the killing of the siblings, Billa flipped the major role in the entire sordid affair onto Ranga.

According to Billa, Ranga did it all, even speaking of creating a ruse to take Sanjay away to kill him by pretending to take him away for handing over to the 'Gorkha'—a Nepali security guard at Buddha Jayanti Park.

For instance, in Billa's telling Ranga suggested that Geeta should be raped. Billa sought to dissuade him, even reprimand him, because their primary motive was to secure funds. But Ranga insisted, Billa said. So, giving in to that urge, he urged Ranga to ensure Sanjay was taken away from the spot so that, to quote a judge's future interpretation of the confession, 'she should not be raped in the presence of her brother'.

Billa said that he had given Sanjay several Mandrax tablets to dull the pain from his cuts—a detail Ranga had omitted—and it explained Sanjay's relatively somnolent state after initially resisting their kidnapping so strenuously that Ranga cut him for it.

Billa also painted Geeta with an unsalutary, demeaning brush.

In Billa's own words—as recorded by the magistrate who took his confessional statement in September 1978:

> *Ranga suggested that we should move from there at the earliest but I was waiting for Sanjay to sleep first. Ranga told me that he would take Sanjay (away) on the pretext of [taking him to] the Gorkha. Ranga first opened the dickey of the car, and brought out something which I could not see on account of darkness. After [one or one and a half] minutes, Ranga came back and after opening the door (of the car) told Sanjay to come and he (Ranga) will leave him (Sanjay) with Gorkha. Ranga took him away. Geeta and myself were left in the car. Geeta enquired of me as to why Sanjay had been sent away. I told Geeta not to be so innocent. I further told her that she was doubtful about us at the time when the tablets were given that the same were intoxicant. It will be useless to waste time in such discussions, and that why nothing was done with you in the presence of Sanjay.*
>
> *Geeta told that it was not a good idea. She neither expressed her willingness nor her unwillingness. The clothes were removed and I did my work (committed the rape on her) inside the car. I put on my clothes, and then Ranga came over there. Ranga told that he would also follow suit, the actual words being 'Woh Bhi Aisey Kare Ga'. I told him that he himself should talk to her. Ranga first did the job (committed the rape on her) inside the car, and then took out the seat of the car outside and again did the job (committed the rape on her). After the work was done ... I enquired from Ranga the whereabouts of Sanjay. He told me that I should ask this question later on.*

Billa said that stirred Geeta into action:

> *Geeta got suspicious. Thereafter, the girl picked up the sword which was lying by the side and attacked me with the same which hit on the left side of my forehead. I then felt all dark for about 2 seconds. When I was able to see, I noticed that the sword was in the hand of Ranga, and the girl was lying down (on the ground). I saw Ranga giving sword blows. After the above occurrence, I enquired from Ranga as to what he had done. He replied that he would tell the same later on. I told him that I wanted to know immediately. Thereupon Ranga informed me that when he had taken Sanjay away the latter picked up a quarrel, and he (Ranga) had killed Sanjay. He further told me that if I happened to be there in his place, I would also have done the same. The girl was picked up and thrown inside the bush.*

The confession returned to broad corroboration with Ranga's statement when Billa's story arc mentioned their visit to Willingdon Hospital and the interview with the sub-inspector of police. The corroboration extended to the episode about filling petrol and then slipping away from the fuel station without paying for it; and his subsequent departure for Bombay by train.

Billa maintained that he reached Bombay on the evening of 29 August. Soon after his arrival he stole a taxi with the plates MRK 7118. He called upon an acquaintance, Luis, to reconnoitre the area around his house. While he was waiting for Billa to arrive, the police took Luis in.

Billa saw him being apprehended and took off. He abandoned the taxi, hopped on a train to Delhi—bribing some policemen before he did so. Then his meeting with Ranga upon arrival, the realization that Delhi Police were after them, their desperate flight to Agra, the days at a lodge there, the purchasing of a pistol and, with a mind to reach Madras, the bizarre entry into a coach reserved for the military, their apprehending by the soldiers and subsequent handing over to the police in Delhi.

In all of this, Billa was merely an accessory, he maintained. The key instigator, the main culprit, was Ranga all the way.

Within a couple of months both Ranga and Billa would retract their confessions—first Ranga, then Billa. The legal battle for their lives would be added to the frenzied information being circulated in the public domain.

COMPETITIVE NARCISSISTS

As preparations for their trial continued, and as the trial commenced, Billa and Ranga settled into a life of mutual animus in Tihar Jail—the largest jail in the capital. From all accounts, they couldn't stand each other and ran the other down at every opportunity—perpetuating their blame-the-other stand from the confessions. Even the eventual retraction of their legal confessions within days of each other, a clear prompt from their state-mandated legal defence teams, did not reduce this hostility; they would carry it to the end of their days.

Billa remained reticent and withdrawn, with minimal interactions with others, reflecting the sullenness in the much-circulated police mugshot and the now-famous newspaper photos of his arrest in Delhi and visit to Tis Hazari. Ranga, given to occasional exultations of 'Ranga khush' as if he had adopted the title of the Bollywood movie—Ranga is happy—as his mantra, was the determinedly, even somewhat manically upbeat of the two, engaging in the routine jail-day activities in Tihar.

In their world that was now all about spikes in public attention, and their speedy permanence in India's cornucopia of notoriety, Billa and Ranga shared the space with another star villain, Charles Sobhraj. The son of a French-Vietnamese mother and a Sindhi father, Sobhraj had cut quite a figure as a confidence-trickster, robber, and murderer in an arc from Greece to Hong Kong, and several countries in between. Arrested in Delhi in 1977, he was one of Tihar's ace residents when the killers of Sanjay and Geeta were transported there, strutting about as if he owned the place, with special concessions, such as the facility to cook his own food, and a retinue of inmates at his beck and call.

To Billa's and Ranga's instant legend of a few weeks' vintage,

Sobhraj's infamy was a legend cooked over a slow fire for several years, the stew increasingly thicker and murkier. There were accounts of his first brush with the law in India way back in 1971, when he had tried to pull a fast one at the Ashoka Hotel in Chanakyapuri, using a dancer as a dupe by offering her a lavish contract at his non-existent chain of hotels, and eventually using her as a prop to rob a jeweller at the hotel of a million and a half rupees worth of diamonds and other precious gems.

Comedies of error were quickly centre-stage. He was arrested in Bombay. After being taken to Delhi, Sobhraj, who fortuitously had an attack of appendicitis, was transported to Willingdon Hospital—(where, years later, Billa would have his head wound treated). Here, Sobhraj was handcuffed to a hospital bed. Two policemen watched over him. He escaped after slipping off the handcuffs. It remained unclear as to how, let alone how he had escaped from the policemen. He made his way to Delhi Junction—Old Delhi station, where Billa and Ranga would in some years arrive as arrested suspects—in striped hospital pyjamas. That's how the two duped policemen, who were sent there as the manhunt spread, discovered Sobhraj. He was at the ticket counter.

He was promptly arrested. This was followed, surprisingly, by his release on bail. Unsurprisingly, Sobhraj skipped bail and disappeared.

A trail led to Pakistan and more killings. By 1975, after a murderous run in Kathmandu, he had collected Marie Leclerc, his Canadian girlfriend and a key accomplice by this time, and an Indian sidekick, Vijay Chaudhary. The trio duped, drugged—Mandrax being the soporific of choice—and robbed their way through a string of tourists, hippies included, back in India. A run in Thailand followed this run in India.

The Serpent, as a moniker now described him, returned to India sometime in 1977—to Delhi.

Stories would emerge from Barbara Smith, a twenty-two-year-old Sobhraj lure turned approver. They took to drugging and robbing tourists in Ranjit Hotel near Ajmeri Gate, and such. Then Sobhraj miscalculated: overkill, as it were.

Travelling back from Agra with twenty-two tourists, he joined them for dinner at Vikram Hotel, across from Moolchand Hospital in the Lajpat Nagar locality. He offered them soporifics pretending these were antidotes to spicy food and iffy water. The party duly swallowed the pills in their concern to avoid the dreaded Delhi Belly, and promptly fell about insensate.

The dosage was too much. Sobhraj was the only one up and about. Hotel staff cornered him and handed him over to the police. He was taken to Tihar Jail after his conviction in August 1977 by a judge of a lower court in Delhi for 'having attempted to administer intoxicating drugs to members of a French tourist party'.

▪

The Serpent was quite the diva. His hissy fits had even travelled up to the Supreme Court of India—as would mercy petitions by Billa and Ranga that, as we shall read about shortly, triggered intense debate and even threatened a crisis between the judiciary and the executive. It was as if Sobhraj was a warm-up exercise in Tihar's string of marquee convicts. And, as with Billa and Ranga, nearly every legal pitch of Sobhraj attracted India's judicial crème de la crème.

Indeed, on 7 April 1978, less than five months before Geeta and Sanjay were killed, three judges of the Supreme Court, Justices V. R. Krishna Iyer, D. A. Desai, and O. Chinnappa Reddy, delivered a judgement in a case brought by Sobhraj against the superintendent of the Central Jail in Tihar. The lawyers for and against were also legal luminaries—even if some occasionally lived in disturbing shadows. N. M. Ghatate, known for his association with several key politicians, and S. V. Deshpande, stood for the petitioner Sobhraj. Additional Solicitor General of India Soli J. Sorabjee and Girish Chandra argued for the respondent—the superintendent of Tihar Jail.

In triggering this legal circus which played to fascinated galleries, Sobhraj sought less secure wards, better facilities and better company, and invoked Articles 14, 19, and 21 of India's Constitution—which variously dealt with equality before the law, freedom of speech and expression, and protection of life and personal liberty.

As if aware of their audience and the media attention Sobhraj with his chutzpah inevitably brought to nearly everything he did, the judges took seven pages to deliver their judgement. After five pages of meandering that seemed to be aimed at sending up Sobhraj with their collective dignity and sense of humour intact, they reserved scathing sarcasm for the last two pages.

> Charles Sobhraj...goes on hunger strikes but medical men take care of him. Ward 1, where he is lodged, gives him the facilities of wards 13 and 14 where he wants to be moved. He has record of one escape and one attempt at suicide and Interpol reports of many crimes abroad. There are several cases pending in India against him.... Now he seeks the other extreme of coddling as if a jail were a country club or good hotel. Give me finer foreigners as companions, he demands. Don't keep convict cooks and warders as jail mates in my cell, he rails. Remove me from a high security ward like Ward I to a more relaxed ward like Ward 14 or 13, he solicits. These delicate and genteel requests from a prisoner with his record and potential were turned down by the Superintendent....

'The court must not rush in where the jailor fears to tread,' the justices maintained in purple flourish, clearly enjoying their moment dealing with their self-important star criminal.

'Petition dismissed.'

■

It had proved difficult to keep Sobhraj out of the news through the year, even as Billa and Ranga were regularly headlined as ace villains—perhaps precisely because they were headlined as ace villains. It was as if the competitively narcissistic Serpent, whose modus operandi seemed to range from amateurish stumbles to smooth operator, yearned for the spotlight.

In September 1978, even as Billa and Ranga were headline news, Sobhraj got word to the media that he had landed a juicy deal from a publisher overseas for his autobiography. That piqued interest and earned Sobhraj media space.

Even so, and despite his antics and demands for five-star treatment, Sobhraj would just have to contend with being just another star convict in a jail of star convicts and star undertrial prisoners—even those beyond his self-declared social pale as Billa and Ranga.

In any case, it appeared that Sobhraj, Billa, and Ranga were eminently suited to life in Tihar, a horror by several accounts. There would soon be a flap in the capital because of a few convict whistleblowers. One, in jail for robbing a bank van, got the word out of torture of another prisoner by a jail warden; it involved using chili powder on a baton and inserting it into his anus. Rakesh Kaushik, a convict serving life for the murder of a doctor's wife managed to smuggle out an account of the hellish life in Tihar. Mandrax tablets were openly sold and jailers took a skim—the same as they did off the prisoners' welfare canteen—and made money by even selling ice slabs to prisoners during Delhi's scorching summers.

Word of it all reached the Supreme Court via media and a writ petition, and triggered an order to clean up Delhi's jails—India's jails.

In 1979, a reporter from *Indian Express* spent four days in Tihar posing as a petty criminal. This corroborative experience would later be encapsulated in *India Today*: 'His eyewitness reports on life inside portrayed a living hell: a decrepit, dangerous underworld of lethal weapons, violence, homosexual assault, drug addiction and blatant connivance of jail officials who seemed to thrive on all crime.' The business of 'selling favours' seemed to be booming, managed by a tag team of convicts and warders. '... (F)rom hashish to homosexual sex with juvenile delinquents,' the magazine article noted, 'the ruling network also extorted whatever money undertrial prisoners (who constitute the bulk of the prison population) brought in.'

Naturally, there were reprisals for whistleblowers. Word arrived to the media that while Kaushik wasn't attacked directly, an associate of his, Srinivas Sharma, was. Inmates led the attack. Their leaders led them. Along with 'Sobhraj, it was said,' added the article in *India Today*, quoting a fact-finding enquiry on Tihar by an advocate appointed by the Supreme Court—'"ruthlessly mauled Sharma and broke his nose" and had it not been for the warder "Sharma's neck would have been slit" as the assailants were armed with knives.'

As ever, Delhi remained surreal. A palette within a palette. Planet within a planet.

JUDGEMENT DAY

In some ways, the day began with a sense of foreboding. By most accounts Prime Minister Desai's days were numbered. It was a matter of mere months, if not weeks, before the infighting and jostling within the heaving Janata conglomerate triggered his exit. There was no shortage of candidates for the spoils of power. A name doing the rounds for India's next premier was that of another dogged, truculent aspirant, Charan Singh.

But such tectonic shifts were insignificant in everyday, everyperson Delhi. Here, 7 April 1979 began with a sense of anticipation. For ordinary citizens the capital's sun revolved around the Tis Hazari Courts, a hulking, utilitarian, box-like four-storey building not far from the transportation and wholesale markets of Kashmiri Gate, a history-infused neighbourhood that also housed the Nicholson Cemetery—the address of many who died during the so-called Sepoy Mutiny of 1857. Tis Hazari too had its slice of history, the name stretching back to a time in the late eighteenth century, so claim some accounts, to a band of 30,000 Sikh troops who camped there for several months as they held sway over the crumbling Mughal empire of Shah Alam II.

The complex, already creaky just twenty years into its existence, contained endless dusty and dank corridors and a warren of offices and several hundred courtrooms that adjudicated on both civil and criminal cases, matters of life and death—even divorces—and certified births and deaths and marriages and divorces with rubber-stamp regularity. Cramped lawyers' offices and sheds packed with those soliciting consultations and typewriting services peppered the front and the sides of the court complex. Entering it was akin to entering a holy town and being mobbed by touts and facilitators who offered divine blessings at a price; as the principal lower court for Delhi, Tis Hazari's mien wasn't dissimilar.

Additional district and sessions judge, M. K. Chawla held court in one of Tis Hazari's larger rooms on the first floor, but that was a figure of speech. The judge's raised perch was the only uncluttered part of the courtroom, which was lined with overloaded cabinets and shelves lining the room. Premium space there belonged to the prosecution and defence—and the defendants. What little space remained was jammed with the media and the public.

Onlookers packed the corridors, and lines snaked down to the ground floor. Several hundred people lined the roof. Watchers crowded every window. Leading to the very real danger of injury, several dozen piled onto the roof of the portico—the prime viewing area. It had been that way since Billa and Ranga entered the court premises at mid-morning to hear their sentences.

It would be that way until Billa and Ranga exited a couple of hours later, fresh from their sentencing—to be hanged till death for the murder of Geeta and Sanjay on 26 August the previous year.

As soon as a sombre Judge Chawla passed the sentence to an uncharacteristically subdued Billa and Ranga, a relay of shouts—'phansi ho gayi'—worked its way through the corridors outside the courtroom and, it appeared, to every corner of Tis Hazari and spilled onto the crowds gathered outside.

They've got death.

They were whisked away through teeming crowds onto police buses and then to the death row of Tihar Jail.

In a country where justice sometimes took a lifetime to be delivered or denied, it took less than eight months since the murder of Geeta and Sanjay for their killers to be brought to book.

FACTS OF THE CASE

Billa's and Ranga's defence team immediately appealed the sentence at Delhi High Court, extending the life of this cause célèbre.

But as far as that court was concerned, the evidence had stacked up against Billa and Ranga for various timelines over August and early September of 1978.

In their order on 16 November 1979 in the case of appeal listed as *State vs Jasbir Singh @Billa and Kuljeet Singh @Ranga* Delhi High Court Justices V. Misra and F. Gill listed twenty-eight of such 'facts' that 'stand proved' against the 'appellants'—Billa and Ranga.

These, delivered as a recap by the judges, were derived from a mix of witness testimonies, evidence, signed confessions of the convicts who seemed to be canny or clumsy (driven it appeared by the exigencies of their defence), and post-mortem reports. These altogether served to summarize the chain of events to a country still wounded by the memory.

This is how the granular evidence, both circumstantial and not, looked to Justices Misra and Gill.

Billa and Ranga exited Bombay when they realized that the city's police had way too much interest in them. This impelled them to travel to Delhi—where they arrived on 16 August. Upon arrival, they went about their business using assumed names and providing false addresses. Besides, Billa had a 'habit' of stealing cars. That expertise came in handy as proved by the ease with which Billa and Ranga obtained several number plates with fictitious registration numbers.

Their threatening intent—and murderous intent, as it turned out—became clearer when they purchased two kirpans and had them sharpened.

The judges rolled out the sequence of events and evidence:

Ashok Sharma (listed as Public Witness No. 40) lost his Fiat car with registration of DEA 1221 on 19 August from the premises of Ashoka Hotel. The 'appellants'—Billa and Ranga—hired a room at House No. B-314 in Gali No. 3 at Majlis Park from its owner Sohan Lal (Public Witness No. 31) on 24 August; and pre-paid rent for two months.

'At about 6.15 p.m. on 26 August Sanjay and Geeta left their house at Dhaula Kuan for going to the All India Radio and thumbed a lift up to Gole Dak Khana.' And, on the same day, between '6.30 and 6.40 p.m. Sanjay and Geeta were kidnapped by the appellants in the stolen car' which at the time displayed the registration number, HRK 8930. Thereafter, 'Sanjay and Geeta were seen struggling with the appellants in the car and shouting for help.'

Sanjay received a 'bleeding injury' on his shoulder in the car. At about 6.45 p.m., Billa and Ranga, with the kidnapped children in the car, were seen travelling towards Shankar Road.

Around 7.30 p.m., 'Ranga bought three Campa Colas and two ice creams after parking the car in the car parking area of Buddha Jayanti Park, Upper Ridge Road.' Subsequently, 'at about 9.30 p.m.' Sanjay and Geeta were killed in the jungle of Upper Ridge Road at a place 'between Buddha Jayanti Park and Shankar Road Upper Ridge Road roundabout.'

Later that night, around 10.15 p.m. Billa, 'who had no head injury at the time of kidnapping the children,' arrived at Willingdon Hospital sporting a head injury; at the time Billa and Ranga drove a car with plates that read DHI 280. The two provided false names and addresses and 'falsely stated' that the injury was caused by robbers.

After Billa's wound was stitched up and dressed, they left the hospital an hour or so later—with Billa 'going against medical advice'. And, as it happened, after duping Sub-Inspector Ram Chander; they told him of a 'non-existing place of robbery' and promised to report to him the following morning.

On the morning of 27 August their landlord in Majlis Park, Sohan Lal, questioned Billa about the head injury. He was told that Billa got the wound when he tangled with the small fan tacked to the inside of the car. Three days later, on the night of 30 August, Ranga was seen parking a car which displayed the registration, DHD 7034 in a lane—Gali No. 10—a little away from their rental flat. The next morning police seized that car. Billa and Ranga had meanwhile, and quite 'suddenly', left their flat for which they had paid rent in advance for two months.

They then went to Agra and 'lived at different places under assumed names'.

Ranga was later found to be in possession of a kirpan (listed as Exhibit P21), while Billa had a 'sword' (listed as Exhibit P22) recovered from his possession. The injuries on Sanjay's body were caused by sharp-edged weapons and, 'according to medical opinion' the 'Exhibits P21 and P22' could have made them. Geeta's injuries were attributed to the possibility of 'Exhibit P22' causing them.

The viscera of Sanjay contained 'milk products' which tied in with the suggestion that he had eaten ice cream 'shortly before his death'.

Geeta's innerwear was missing from her body.

And, while Billa and Ranga 'do not tell us what they did with Sanjay and Geeta'—each blaming the other—all of 'their explanations have been found false'.

In conjunction with these twenty-eight points was an array of claims, advanced by Billa and Ranga's defence teams, that were judged again as either false at worst or untenable at best.

Both Billa and Ranga, the record showed, had confessed to their crimes in the presence of a magistrate who had showed them due process.

■

Justices Misra and Gill then systematically went about disproving nearly all aspects of the appeal, beginning with the argument offered by the defence counsel that Billa and Ranga's confessions were coerced and, consequently, untrue and inadmissible as evidence of guilt in the trial.

Both Billa and Ranga had confessed their crimes to P. K. Dham, the metropolitan magistrate. No matter that the confessions were subsequently retracted during the trial as being 'neither voluntary nor true', or that 'each appellant has made an exculpatory statement as regards the actual murder and blamed the other for the same'.

The sequence of events was clear to the judges. The two were arrested on 9 September, and produced before the chief metropolitan magistrate ten days later, on the 19th. At that time the investigating officer made an application to the chief magistrate that Ranga wished to make a voluntary statement, and that it be duly recorded under the relevant Code of Criminal Procedure—Section 164, which accords authority to various levels of magistrates to record statements and confessions. The chief magistrate accordingly directed Dham to hear the confession.

Dham made it abundantly clear, as part of due process, that Ranga was not legally bound to confess, and that his confession could be used as evidence to implicate him—even bring the death sentence. Ranga insisted. Indeed, the judges observed, to ensure he had time to consider his decision Ranga was sent to judicial custody for two more days 'to think over the matter'.

On 21 September, at 10 a.m., Ranga appeared before Dham. He was clear he wanted to make a statement. His handcuffs were removed. Jail guards were asked to leave the room. Curtains in the courtroom were drawn. Dham took care to ensure no policeman was 'in sight or within hearing'. He permitted only a reader and stenographer to remain. The doors were bolted on the inside. At this time Dham again reminded Ranga that he was under no compulsion to confess, and it could trigger a chain of events that could lead to death penalty.

But Ranga 'insisted' on a confession. He was then given another hour to think things through—and, as he did so, was seated on a chair near the magistrate's dais. After this hour was up, he was again asked by Dham. Ranga again agreed—it was agreement, not acquiescence. So, at 11.45 a.m., Dham proceeded to ask him the 'usual questions', and recorded Ranga's confessional statement.

All along, Misra and Gill observed, Ranga assured the metropolitan magistrate that 'nobody had put pressure on him to make a statement nor anyone had assured or promised him that on his making a statement he may be forgiven or made an approver or his sentence reduced'. Equally, Ranga was clear that neither the police or jail staff had threatened him to make the statement.

It wasn't possible to record the entire statement on that day, so at 4.20 in the afternoon Dham stopped the process, certified the unfinished statement, and sent Ranga back to judicial custody with instructions that he be produced in court the following day.

The recording of the confession resumed on 22 September—with Ranga again cautioned by Dham as to the implications of his confessional statement. The entire statement was recorded by Dham in his own hand and the 'necessary memorandum/certificate was duly given by the Magistrate'.

Ranga retracted his statement two months later, on 20 November.

■

Meanwhile, Billa's confessional journey took a slightly different chronological arc.

His status changed from being in the custody of the police to the custody of the courts several times between the day of his arrest on 9 September and 17 October. He went from the custody of Delhi Police to the court, after which the chief metropolitan magistrate handed him over to Bombay Police for their ongoing investigations, but with instructions to bring Billa back to Delhi on 16 October. That done, he was back in judicial custody.

On 17 October, Billa applied to the chief magistrate requesting his statement to be recorded. As he had with Ranga, the chief magistrate directed Billa to Magistrate Dham. On the 19th, Billa was brought before Dham. As with Ranga, Dham agreed to the request that Billa be unfettered—he saw to it when Billa was brought before him at 12.45 p.m.

Dham ensured similar privacy and security for Billa as he had for Ranga just weeks earlier. As with Ranga, Billa was cautioned several times about the possibility of his confession leading to his implication, and a death sentence. As with Ranga, Dham gave Billa a little time to think over matters. At 2.15 p.m., Dham again asked of his intention. 'Billa said he wished to make a statement and it was made clear to him, that he was not bound to make a statement; had not been threatened, pressurized [sic], persuaded or duped to make a statement; and that he was making a voluntary statement.'

That went on till 4.15 p.m., and resumed the following day at 10.40 a.m. with all precautions and protocols followed as before, including giving Billa an extra hour to think things through, consider his decision to continue—or not. The recording of the statement continued until 3.05 p.m.

On 27 November, a week after Ranga retracted his confession, Billa retracted his.

■

A reason for the retractions, Ranga and Billa's defence counsel argued—and here Justices Misra and Gill paraphrased—was that the appellants 'had been given beating (sic) every day by police while in police custody and they had been threatened and tutored to make the statements.'

The defence team had brought on assistant superintendent at Central Jail, Tihar, Bachan Singh (listed as Defence Witness No. 3) and had him testify that Billa and Ranga were kept in solitary and watched over by a special security detail. That detail was used to argue that there were therefore, opportunities for beatings and coercion away from any witness, and it is 'thus argued that the confessions were not voluntary'.

Here, the judges flatly dismissed the accusation and quoted precedent in a case at the Supreme Court to maintain that keeping someone in solitary does not necessarily affect a confession made by that person. 'There is not an iota of evidence on record to show that the appellants had been given beatings by the police or anyone else.' In any case, they maintained that Magistrate Dham had given both Ranga and Billa ample opportunity—several opportunities—to consider their decision to offer confessional statements.

Here the judges decided to rub it in a bit. When the two were produced before the trial court the previous year on 25 October 1978, and then again on 6, 10, and 15 November 1978, there was no mention of solitary confinement and beatings in jail. It took until their court appearance on 20 November for Ranga to 'move' an application retracting his confession. Billa applied, as we have read, to have his confession retracted a week later, on 27 November.

Ranga's application hadn't mentioned anything about the police 'beating him'.

Billa's application retracting his confession had a long-winded explanation that would remain a part of his legal defence till the very end of his life.

The judges noted the content of that application. Billa was on the run from Bombay and had taken shelter in Delhi. Ranga and he considered committing robberies but were unsuccessful; and then decided to rob some goldsmiths. Before they could, they read in the papers that they were being accused of Geeta's and Sanjay's murders. That spooked them, especially the part about a reward, so they took off for Agra. After the arrest Billa decided to make a statement 'the police would desire'—as the High Court judges noted. 'Therefore, he made the statement confessing the guilt'.

But at no point did Billa, like Ranga, accuse the police of hitting—'beating'—him, even as they both retracted their confessions. 'Evidently,' ruled Misra and Gill, 'the allegations of police beating etc., are an after thought [sic].'

They were certainly kept in separate cells, and in fetters. While keeping them in fetters appears extreme, jailers had resorted to it—and the jailer Bachan Singh admitted to doing as much—because, as improbable it might seem, Billa had tried to make a break for it by attempting to cut through the fetters as well as the iron grating of his cell. He had gone on a hunger strike after that failed attempt.

He had once escaped from custody in Bombay, the judges noted. Who could take a chance that he might do so again, even if he was kept in solitary in one of India's best guarded jails? But even such relatively harsh measures—the 'necessity' of such measures—could not be taken as 'amounting to any coercion or threat affecting the voluntary nature of the confessions made by the appellants'.

The judges also dismissed as insubstantial the claim of the defence that Magistrate Dham, even though he had briefed Ranga and Billa with 'detailed warnings', had neglected to mention that they would not be handed back to the custody of the police—as opposed to the custody of the court—if they did not make a statement. The suggestion was that both Billa and Ranga might have felt threatened by the possibility of being handed back to the police, so they decided to make their statements.

The judges conceded that Dham would have been better off actually informing Billa and Ranga of this detail, that they would remain in judicial custody for the time, but that this didn't have a bearing on their statements because it was abundantly clear to both that they were in the custody of the court under direct orders of Dham and the chief magistrate who had directed Billa and Ranga to Dham's care.

DEFENCE / OFFENCE

Billa's and Ranga's defence fought every inch of the way with every twist and nuance at their disposal.

Justices Misra and Gill pushed back.

They used a series of precedents to hold the convicts to their own account; and which was then buttressed by what judges held was irrefutable, independent evidence.

Ranga's and Billa's withdrawn confessions had to be seen in this light, they maintained: 'A person accused of an offence must in terms admit [to] the commission of the offence before a statement can be termed a confession. Any statement which is wholly exculpatory or only admits a fact which is incriminating would not amount to confession. A confession properly recorded by a Magistrate and duly proved carries great weight and may be used against the maker. However, where a confession is retracted it needs corroboration.'

There was plenty of it, the judges held and offered more precedence (*Nand Kumar and others v. State of Rajasthan*, among others). Courts generally considered it 'unsafe' to convict an accused person on the basis of his retracted confession, noted the judges, except where 'the truth of such confession is established by corroboration in material particular independent evidence'. Each case needs to be decided on its 'own facts and circumstances'.

And when the prosecution presents 'reliable evidence' which is 'independent of the confession' and which is also not 'tainted evidence' as that of an accomplice or a co-accused, and this establishes the truth of 'certain parts' even in the retracted confession—these 'integrally connected' parts, as the judges put it—it needs to be seriously considered. Indeed, a 'prudent judge of facts would think it reasonable to believe, in view of the established truth of these parts, that what the accused has stated in the confession as regards his own participation in the crime is also true, that is sufficient corroboration'.

'More than this is not needed, less than this is ordinarily insufficient.'

In the case of Billa and Ranga, the corroborative evidence was deemed as being more than enough. To buttress their judgement, they quoted another precedent from Rajasthan (*Shankaria v. State of Rajasthan*):

> The court laid down that when in a capital case the prosecution demands a conviction of the accused primarily on the basis of his confession recorded under S. 164, of the Code of Criminal Procedure, the Court must apply a double test:
>
> (1) Whether the confession was perfectly voluntary?
> (2) If so, whether it is true and trustworthy?
>
> It is only after the first test is satisfied that the question of applying the second test arises. While ruling that for judging the reliability of such a confession there is no rigid canon of universal application, it was observed: "Even so, one broad method which may be useful in most cases for evaluating a confession may be indicated. The Court should carefully examine the confession and compare it with the rest of the evidence in the light of the surrounding circumstances and probabilities of the case. If on such examination and comparison, the confession appears to be a probable catalogue of events and naturally fits in with the rest of the evidence and the surrounding circumstances, it may be taken to have satisfied the second test.

There was nothing to mitigate the circumstances, maintained Justices Misra and Gill, as they went about systematically dismissing several points raised by the defence.

Even if one took into account that Billa and Ranga had volunteered their confessions, were there any inculpatory aspects—which imputed guilt—among all the aspects the defence maintained were exculpatory, which diminished or dismissed guilt?

The defence held that, as Sanjay had 'shown' his 'bleeding injury' to Inderjeet Singh, the doughty Sikh on the scooter who later deposed as a public witness, then it follows that others must have seen it too. But nobody else had come forward to support this contention—which proves this aspect of the confession was 'false'—in other words, coerced.

'We do not find any force' in this contention, the judges observed. Just because no other person had seen the 'bleeding injury' of Sanjay, and that too in a moving car, it doesn't follow that Inderjeet Singh's statement wasn't credible. 'Indeed, we have already discussed the evidence of Inderjeet Singh and found it absolutely reliable.'

The police had concocted the story of Billa and Ranga buying ice cream, the defence maintained, after the post-mortem examination detected milk products in Sanjay's viscera.

Untenable, the judges ruled. The medical report was prepared on 22 September but was collected by the investigating officer only on 6 October. Ranga had made his confessional statement on 21 and 22 September.

'In other words, Ranga had made his confessional statement about purchasing ice cream for Sanjay from a vendor at Buddha Jayanti Garden even before the report of the viscera was prepared.' That's enough ground to reject the contention of the defence, said the judges, there's no doubt whatsoever that 'Ranga was making a true statement.'

The incident of Geeta being raped is false, the defence maintained. There is no evidence that Geeta put up any 'struggle or protest' and the police surgeon who performed the autopsy, Bharat Singh, is unsure if it ever took place. Indeed, the post-mortem report mentioned swelling of the genitalia, no evidence of injury to the vaginal wall, the hymen 'admitted tips of two fingers'—not unusual—there was no discharge, no injury to the perineum: all the aspects one looked for and recorded in instances of forced sexual intercourse or 'violent sexual act'. Besides, the body was in a state of decomposition so no definite opinion was possible.

On the contrary, the judges noted, this very fact of decomposition cannot rule out the possibility of sexual intercourse even though in his cross-examination Dr Singh had stated that Geeta was 'not used' to sexual intercourse. 'We cannot lose sight of the fact that, in the circumstances discussed above, Geeta was not in a position to offer any resistance to the appellants,' the judges maintained. 'According to Billa he had committed sexual intercourse while she was on the rear seat of the car. The rear seat of the car was taken out to enable Ranga to have the sexual intercourse. Therefore, there was no question of the back of Geeta receiving any marks.'

Besides, there was the 'glaring' circumstantial evidence of her innerwear missing: 'Geeta's dead body did not have these undergarments.' The judges pointed to Ranga's retracted statement about Billa noticing Geeta's undergarments lying in the back of the car, and how one was thrown onto a moving truck and the other into a drain.

Moreover, it was only after the confessions in which both Ranga and Billa mentioned rape did the police again ask Dr Singh for his opinion on the possibility of rape. The request by the police on 13 October 1978 and Dr Singh's response were both admitted in court as exhibits. The surgeon stuck to his original conclusion of his inability to state definitely on account of the advanced state of decomposition of the body.

'It is not possible,' Dr Singh replied to the police, 'to give (a) definite opinion whether sexual act was committed on the deceased or not.'

The fact that the police had followed the correct protocol after both Billa and Ranga mentioned rape was enough 'in these circumstances', noted the judges, for them to find the confessions about rape 'are true'.

The defence team also walked back Ranga's confessional statement about slashing at Sanjay in the moving car and injuring him. It simply did not happen, the defence maintained.

The judges dismissed the claim; there were twenty-one injuries, small and big, on Sanjay, as recorded in the autopsy. It was possible that five of the injuries, the pathologist maintained, had been made by the dagger and the remainder by the sword. (The judges clarified their definition of 'kirpan' and 'sword': 'We have seen the sword Exhibit P 22. It is a long kirpan but for the purpose of distinguishing it from kirpan Exhibit P 21 we are calling it a sword. The difference between a sword and a kirpan is that whereas a sword is straight, kirpan is bent at the end of its blade. This sword is more than two feet long, rather heavy and has a big handle.')

Of the injuries made by the dagger, those recorded as injuries 3, 6, 7, 8, and 18, numbers 7 and 8 were on the left lower side of the chest—the side visible to the rear left window of the car and therefore were likely the injuries that Inderjeet Singh saw as he followed the Fiat with the abducted, protesting and resisting teenagers in it.

And what of the remarkable act of parking the car in a parking lot of the park with every chance of an alarm being raised, the defence held? The imputation was: who would be so stupid as to do something like that? And so, the confession to this effect was 'false'.

Not necessarily, the judges ruled. People can behave unpredictably when at risk: 'Persons are known to lose their capacity to reason and think clearly'; they can act 'impulsively'; the role of the strong and the 'weakling' may be swapped. The judges didn't mention the aspect that Sanjay and Geeta could have been drugged—Billa had confessed to giving Sanjay tablets of Mandrax to calm him—but, even so, played up the aspect of two teens utterly shocked and bewildered.

'We cannot lose sight of the fact that the victims were teenagers leading a sheltered life. They were anxious to reach the All India Radio in time to take part in a programme. They had innocently thumbed a lift least knowing that it was to be their last journey. When the gravity of the situation dawned on them, they put up a struggle. They also shouted for help but in vain. On the other hand, Sanjay received injuries from a knife during the struggle. Having failed to free themselves from the clutches of their kidnappers and having realized that though many persons had seen them struggling none had rescued them, they must have resigned themselves to their fate. In these circumstances their only chance seemed to be to carry out the commands of the kidnappers and hope for the best relying on their promises. They would not have dared to risk their lives after having had the experience of the knife being used by one of the kidnappers.'

Besides, the 'desperadoes', as the judges colourfully described Ranga and Billa, ran little risk of discovery parking at a place where at that time of the evening there wasn't any other vehicle. Few visited the park so late. Moreover, who could overlook the fact that the two had actually managed to execute their 'nefarious' plan to kidnap the teenagers. And, moreover, Billa had on his 'own showing', and doing so by making a statement under Section 313 of the Criminal Procedure Code, had owned up to his facility for car theft during his time in Bombay, and was even prone to flashing a knife when 'thwarted in his designs'—'a dare devil ready with his knife' is how the judges somewhat dramatically underscored their description.

Crisis made people behave strangely, the judges reiterated.

'If one cannot predict the course of conduct of a victim whose life is suddenly imperilled, one cannot also assume that an offender would play safe and not risk going to a deserted parking place.'

Besides, Justices Misra and Gill observed again, Ranga himself had pointed to the very specific detail of the presence of the park attendant and the ice cream vendor at Buddha Jayanti Park. And Sanjay's viscera contained traces of a milk product, signifying he hadn't 'sufficient time to digest it'.

In their eyes, it all added up.

And, in any case, Billa and Ranga had sufficient time to consider their confessions while in judicial custody, and in court, and the nature of the confessions was entirely 'voluntary'.

Besides, what of the strange behaviour of Ranga as recorded by the magistrate who oversaw his confession—the judges reminded the court. When his confession was being recorded on 21 September 1978, Ranga had actually begun to laugh as he recalled the events of 26 August. 'The Magistrate has noted this fact at that stage of the statement itself. Ranga again started laughing after having described the ghastly killing of Sanjay and throwing his body in the bushes, and before narrating that he found the girl naked on the rear seat of car with naked Billa committing rape and the girl shouting.'

This, the judges held, only showed Ranga's 'depraved character' as he, 'evidently', took 'sadistic pleasure' while recounting the events. This manic behaviour also demonstrated to the judges that Ranga's statement 'has a ring of truth'.

The cries of helplessness by Sanjay 'asking for mercy', the description of rape by both Ranga and Billa—irrespective of who was painted as the key aggressor—descriptions of Geeta, even in her traumatized and disrobed state, to attempt an escape, the description of the ultimately 'ineffective' use of the sword by Geeta, all leave 'no doubt in our minds that this is true'.

Evidence and circumstantial evidence all tallied with confessions about Ranga and Billa's movements in Delhi, their 'apprehension' by military personnel, their underworld life in Bombay, and their run from Bombay to Delhi by way of Surat and Ahmedabad. These were all corroborated by their own statements, the judges maintained, and, therefore, entirely believable. Ranga had also mentioned Billa's murdering two Arabs and the episode of kidnapping the boy from school. In that regard, an inspector of Bombay Police—as Public Witness 101—had confirmed in court that Billa was indeed wanted for the murder of two Arabs. During his cross-examination, the inspector had stated that Bombay Police had a detailed description of Billa as a 'wanted person' for that crime, and that Bombay Police were on the 'look out' for both Billa and Ranga and had actually showed up in Delhi in their pursuit of the 'appellants'.

The cut on Billa's forehead, the visit to Willingdon Hospital by Billa and Ranga, and their giving false names, 'befooling' police officers, were all corroborated by their confessions and examination of witnesses all point to the 'appellants being the murderers'. And all this is evident irrespective of Section 30 of the Evidence Act, said the judges, which allows for a 'confession made by an accused' to be used 'against him as well as his co-accused'—and this is so 'even if the confession has been retracted later on'. Retracted confessions attract scrutiny of every fact and circumstance of a case, the circumstances of the confession, and the stage at which it was retracted. 'But once the court is satisfied that a retracted confession was in fact made voluntarily and was trustworthy, it can always be used not only against its maker but also against a co-accused.'

In any case, the confessions of Billa and Ranga truly differed only with who did all the priming for the rape, killings—and actually went through with the killings.

Ranga said it was Billa. It was Ranga, said Billa.

Either way both were complicit. And they did so with the intention, 'apparently' to 'destroy the evidence about [the] appellants' identity'. The confessions leave 'no doubt', said the judges, that 'each one was playing a part in finishing the victims'.

It all added up in the court's view even though, they said, they were 'conscious' that it was a case of circumstantial evidence. And, they said in their oblique manner, the chain of evidence had to be solid enough and 'so complete' that it should not 'leave any reasonable ground for a conclusion consistent with the innocence of the accused'.

Every chain in the link had to be established; and the chain itself 'must rule out a reasonable likelihood of the innocence of the accused'.

The judges cut to the chase. Ranga and Billa were seen with Geeta and Sanjay in the Fiat at Gole Dak Khana at about 6.40 p.m. and later on Shankar Road. They were also seen with Geeta and Sanjay at Buddha Jayanti Park around 7.30 p.m. The children died around 9.30 p.m. Billa and Ranga then both showed up at Willingdon Hospital around 10.15 p.m. Taken with their false explanations, including the debunked claim of Billa made later that he was in Bombay between 26 August and 31 August, the circumstantial evidence leaves 'no room for doubt that the appellants are the murderers'.

When it came to the pronouncement of upholding the death sentence given to Billa and Ranga, the judges scaled up the judgement to an existential level:

> It is submitted that sentence of death is cruel, barbaric, harsh and unjust, and the society has no right to take away the life

> of a human being. It is also submitted that since the sentence should be reformative and not punitive or retributive, sentence of death should not be awarded. In any case, it is contended, recent trends in judicial pronouncements and phonology show that death penalty being on its way out, it should not be awarded to the appellants....
>
> It is beyond the pale of controversy that judges in India are not the representatives of the people. It is the duty of a judge to administer the law as it is and not as he wishes it to be. It is rightly said that if a judge does not approve the law as it is, he owes it to his conscience to give up his job and seek livelihood in other walks of life. It may be that the death sentence is on its way out, but it has not yet been shown the door. It is very much alive and has not yet been killed.

Here, Justices Misra and Gill became quite lurid, punning on the matter of death and marrying it with commonplace and extreme public reaction for things visibly less murderous if not less painful, than capital punishment.

'Suffice it to say, that one should take a balanced view of things and should not show such undue concern for a murderer as if the whole law should be geared to his safety while forgetting what he has done,' they held. 'It is amusing to note that those very persons who wish the provisions of the Indian Penal Code providing for sentence of death to be a dead letter of law, are themselves the greatest protagonists of having persons found guilty of economic crimes hung by the nearest lamp-post.'

So, the point was not so much about a light sentence or a harsh sentence—as both pointed to a failure of justice. The point was about an adequate sentence. The answer may vary from judge to judge, as is natural. No two cases are alike, as is also natural. There cannot be a template response. As held by the Supreme Court and a tweak in the code of criminal procedure since 1974, 'special reasons are now required for awarding sentence of death'.

The justices here excerpted a precedence—the observations of a judge of the Supreme Court, V. R. Krishna Iyer, who had discussed capital punishment in a case pertaining to Andhra Pradesh.

Justice Iyer had spoken of the 'positive indicators against death sentence under India Law' of the day. Mitigating factors to not award a death penalty could be several: 'Where the murderer is too young or too old, the clemency of penal justice helps him.' Or in instances in which the 'offender suffers from socio-economic, psychic or penal compulsions' that may not be mitigating factors in law but can benefit from 'judicial commutation'—basically, it's up to the judge and his 360-degree view of the matter.

There could be other exceptions for the court to be 'compassionate'—all up to the judge—like a death sentence that has 'hung over the head of the culprit' for an 'excruciatingly' long period. Or, if others involved in the crime and 'similarly situated' have 'received the benefit of life imprisonment'. Or, if an accused was instigated to commit the crime and without premeditation.

Or—and here the judicial reach appeared to be somewhat tone deaf about gender stereotyping—where 'a just cause or real suspicion of wifely infidelity pushed the criminal into the crime'.

Justice Iyer along with his colleagues had observed in another case at the Supreme Court, that it became 'necessary to have a second look at the life versus death question, not for summarizing hitherto decided cases and distilling the common factors but for applying the Constitution to cut the Gordian knot.'

But if the crime was 'horrendous' the victim was 'hapless' and 'helpless' and there was the question of weapons and the 'manner of their use', and so on in a list of horror of horrors, this must 'steel the heart of the law for a sterner sentence'.

Basically, a judge had to balance the 'personality of the offender with the circumstances, the situations and the reactions and choose the appropriate sentence to be imposed'.

Justices Misra and Gill then embarked on the judicial equivalent of stream of consciousness.

Any 'special reason' to impose the death penalty, they said, extends beyond the crime to the criminal. 'The crime may be shocking and yet the criminal may not deserve death penalty. The crime may be less shocking than other murders and yet the callous criminal, e.g. a lethal economic offender, may be jeopardizing societal existence by his act of murder.' Similarly, the death penalty could accrue for a hardened murderer or 'dacoit' who 'relishes killing and raping and murdering to such an extent that he is beyond rehabilitation within a reasonable period according to current psychotherapy or curative techniques....'

Courts cannot be tasked to 'evolve' aspects of the death penalty using 'enlightened flexibility and social sensibility'.

Or, to make law by 'cross-fertilization from sociology, history, cultural anthropology and current national perils and developmental goals and, above all, constitutional currents'. It's up to Parliament to frame such laws that are 'consistent with the needs of the Society'.

Parliament designs, and the judiciary implements. 'It is for the court to administer the law as it stands.'

■

The judges didn't let their philosophical exposition mask their anger at Delhi Police—a memory of snafus and crossed wires over the investigation that for many citizens had faded. They severely censured the bumbling about and bungling that created a chain of inaction before the police post-mortem and after the discovery of the bodies of Geeta and Sanjay—also an act to which they made no contribution—went into hyperdrive in the search for the killers.

The judges would cuttingly term this frenetic activity as 'unusual efficiency'. After all, they would compliment the police in part, it was a blind murder to begin with, but the mystery was quickly unravelled and evidence collected to establish Billa and Ranga as the abductors and murderers of Geeta and Sanjay.

'Before parting with this case, we are constrained to observe that the lives of the two children could have been saved if the police had acted promptly,' Justices Misra and Gill scathingly observed, albeit in 20/20 hindsight. 'Non-cooperation by the public is a standing grievance of the police and public apathy is its routine excuse.'

In this case, there wasn't a 'dearth' of 'public-spirited person[s]' as demonstrated by Kula Nand, a chowkidar at Buddha Jayanti Park, who briefly queried Billa and Ranga, and Bhagwan Dass, who tried to help the children at Gole Dak Khana, and Inderjeet Singh, the junior engineer, who gave chase on his scooter.

Bhagwan Dass, for instance, did what a good citizen would do: he immediately informed the police control room. 'Evidently no importance was given to this information,' the judges reminded the world. The control room eventually passed on the information to the police station at Mandir Marg as a routine occurrence and 'washed its hands off'.

The police had vans—the flying squad—fitted with wireless which remained, or were supposed to remain, in constant touch with the central control room. These 'prowl cars' were designed to go into action within minutes of a crime being reported—and training had been given to do exactly that. Yet the flying squad remained grounded.

The control room received the message at 6.44 p.m. Mandir Marg police station deputed a police officer to investigate the matter at 7.05 p.m. for investigation. 'Surely the police did not expect the offenders to stay put in their car at Gole Dak Khana and wait for the police.'

Ergo, where was the 'flying squad?' There wasn't even a general alarm.

Inderjeet Singh didn't give up, the judges would note, even if his act of good citizenship was transformed into folly by a police officer at Rajinder Nagar police station. After he lost sight of the car, Inderjeet Singh went to the police station and filed a report. This report was recorded at 6.45 p.m.

The police at that station literally remained unmoved as the crime had not been committed 'in their jurisdiction'. It was an 'everyday excuse of the police for its non-action,' the judges would fume. Duty officers at Rajinder Nagar police station would inform the control room at 7.40 p.m., after nearly an hour.

To make things worse, the control room sat on both bits of information instead of tallying the two bits of information, correlating them and 'organizing a hunt near about Shankar Road'.

Had it been done, it could have led to a routine check of Upper Ridge Road, and that nearby place of quiet and hideaways, Buddha Jayanti Park 'and the car in question'.

'We can only trust and hope that the police of Delhi will take the public reports seriously and act promptly if they want the public to co-operate,' Justices Misra and Gill would caution. 'The public is likely to refuse co-operation till the apathy of the police lasts.'

■

After this outburst and a few more pages of talking precedents, the judges orbited back to Billa and Ranga.

They were young, the judges conceded. In his statement, Billa gave his age as twenty-two years. So did Ranga—although the trial noted that he 'appeared' to be twenty-four. In any case, young but seasoned in crime, as the courts have repeatedly noted. 'Nor was this crime committed in a fit of rage because of some altercation.'

They were also calculating in their choice of weapons, the judges said, masking their intent of using the camouflage of religion: '...it may be noticed that both the appellants claim to be Sikhs and thus entitled to keep a kirpan.'

Then they had the kirpans sharpened, elevating it from religious purpose to criminal intent. As a backup they had purchased hockey sticks—innocuous and could be kept without 'transgressing any law and effective in case of need'.

There was no hesitation for the judges to come to a conclusion:

> We are satisfied that the appellants are desperadoes who have no compunction in killing.
>
> They hit upon a most diabolical plan of cold-blooded, ruthless, cruel murders of two young innocent teenagers. Sanjay was hacked to death by both of them as is apparent from the post-mortem examination. He had as many as twenty-one injuries over various parts of the body, the injuries being the result of the use of the two kirpans carried by the appellants. Immediately after killing Sanjay. the appellants had

> no compunction in raping Sanjay's helpless sister by stripping her naked.
>
> After satisfying their beastly lust, they killed her and threw her body in the bushes. Evidently the appellants had a fiendish sadistic pleasure in committing the crime.

And so, they had arrived at a point where a 'conclusion is irresistible' that, with the 'elimination of the appellants' society would be infinitely 'better off' and safer. Indeed, they held, to award 'any other sentence except death sentence' would result in 'complete failure of justice'.

'We are in complete agreement with the special reasons given by the trial judge for awarding the death sentence,' ruled Justices Misra and Gill. 'The result is that all the appeals are hereby dismissed, and the appellants' convictions and sentences awarded to them are upheld.'

Billa and Ranga would be executed.

'Confirmed.'

ICARUS

Between transitions of the case that involved two of India's most notorious criminals, another transition of dark history had taken place. At one time the shift appeared to be inevitable, even preordained in the dynastic order of things: a meteorite-princeling who would be emperor.

But Sanjay Gandhi was dead. Just like that.

■

As it happened, Indira wasn't done with India—or India wasn't done with her—as the elections of January 1980 showed. After the spectacular implosion of the Janata Party, Sanjay had returned to the top of the food chain along with his mother; and he wanted to show he was boss.

He stormed to power in the same elections his mother used to storm back to power, politically decimating those who had evicted them from Delhi's seductive throne room just three years earlier.

Indira was again prime minister. Sanjay was now an MP from Amethi—finally elected to an office instead of genealogically claiming one. He, like his mother, was a winner in a chaotic politics that had since 1975 seamlessly adopted propaganda, misinformation, and disinformation as information technology of the day. It appeared that in just five years, India had been hooked to a habit of dictatorship it would wilfully shoot into its veins as if withdrawal—too much democracy—made it insecure.

As Billa and Ranga continued their repeated appeals to the courts to annul their execution to a life term in prison, a culture of sycophancy renewed itself at Sanjay's court. And, as with so many attitudes in politics, it seemed that this time around sycophancy had truly come to roost in post-Independence India. Sanjay was back as the unquestioned heir apparent to India-is-Indira-Indira-is-India—as the Congressman from Assam and president of the party during the Emergency years, Dev Kant Baruah, once spoke of his benefactor.

Such sycophancy would be topped by a president of India, Zail Singh, when he became Indira's chosen candidate for that post in 1982. 'If Indiraji had told me to take a jhadu and sweep the floor I would have done that too,' the soon-to-be head of state would say in gratitude. It would seem like blinding irony scant months later as many credited Singh with contributing to the chaos that had unleashed a political demon that would, in short order, peak in the desecration of the Golden Temple complex, the consequent assassination of a prime minister, and the structured witch-hunting of an entire people and the killing of many—staggering, seismic developments that would haunt India for several decades.

But enough of foreshadowing. Here was Sanjay, holding court—morning darshan, as it was called—with Congress stalwarts queueing to fawn over their once and future prince; future emperor. In April and May of 1980, the scorching sun competed with the son and lost: more than 15,000 politicians were pushing and shoving to fill a little over 2,000 seats in nine state legislatures headed to general elections that May and a large fraction were making a beeline for Sanjay's stamp of approval. The state assemblies had all been dissolved by presidential order earlier in February, within weeks of the Congress's landslide victory in New Delhi—in India.

The president of India was the executor of the government's will. And Sanjay was lord of the Congress's fate. Some said he was the true force behind his mother's return to power and premiership.

'You must understand,' explained Jagdish Tytler, a Sanjay confidante—there were ruder descriptions for those in that coterie—'that Sanjay Gandhi has a place in history.'

There were other acolytes who were synonymous with the excesses and exigencies of the Emergency and had stormed back with Sanjay as if they were storming heaven. Kamal Nath. Ramchandra Rath. Ghulam Nabi Azad.

Sanjay was being spoken of as the next president of the Congress. Rath spoke of Sanjay in the same breath as Nehru and the legendary Subhas Chandra Bose; both had been elected Congress president when they were young men.

Some openly spoke of him as an inheritor—a future prime minister. Indira, tough as nails, spoke impeccable French. Sanjay, her political hammer, spoke impeccable intimidation. Who could stop a man at a re-energized thirty-three but himself?

'It is only his mother's patronage,' griped Tarakeshwari Sinha, a leader in the Opposition.

Delhi—indeed, all India—appeared to be in thrall to a game of truth or dare.

■

And then Sanjay died, less than half a year after reclaiming the spotlight, just weeks after he was anointed secretary general of the Congress, the almost-crowned king of a brand of total politics—no give, all get—that would leave an indelible mark well into the new millennium.

Sanjay loved flying, an abiding passion of some years for which he would ascribe a 'terrific feeling'.

In particular, he loved to fly a brand-new two-seater S-2A Pitts biplane, painted red. It was stubby, sturdy, light and with a 200-horsepower engine with enough zing to make it an aerobatic favourite in America and the world over.

It wasn't his plane. It was parked at the Delhi Flying Club and it belonged to an entity owned by the Apeejay Group, which ran a tea, hospitality, and real estate business from Calcutta. But it was effectively Sanjay's plane. He flew it as he wished. He was obsessed with it, this new love which was just days old in receiving an airworthiness certificate.

On 22 June 1980, a Sunday, he had taken up his wife Maneka in it for a spin; and, also Rajinder Kumar Dhawan, Indira's personal aide and gatekeeper. Dhawan would later recall feeling 'dead scared' with the experience. Indira's resident yogi, Dhirendra Brahmachari, whom the snarky among gossipy Delhi had labelled a Rasputin whose presence in some ways symbolized a fallen city, had actually declined an offer of a flight with Sanjay when the two met at Safdarjang Airport—the capital's main airport until 1962, when commercial traffic began to relocate to Palam. The yogi had been on his way back from Kashmir in a private aircraft and Sanjay was priming the Pitts for a flight.

'I was a little apprehensive,' the jet-set yogi would later recall. 'I told him I would come only if he would avoid his kalabazi. I had heard about the acrobatics he had started doing recently.'

It was as if Sanjay mirrored his style of driving—fast, taking sharp turns, pushing the limits more if there were other occupants in the car; he seemed to enjoy rattling occupants. He flew as he drove—a speed nut, stunt nut, discomfiture nut. Switching off the engine at 4,000 feet. Diving. Flying to skimming distance of the ground. Sanjay literally threw caution to the wind.

Early on Monday, 23 June, he drove from the prime minister's residence—his mother's residence—on Safdarjang Road in a light green Matador van. He was dressed in his usual white kurta-pyjama and leather Kolhapuri slippers. He flew in this ensemble too. His elder brother, Rajiv, a pilot with Indian Airlines, had warned him against flying in slippers, besides other sage piloting advice. Instructors at the Delhi Flying Club cautioned him against recklessness too—but, were 'often too embarrassed to point out the hazards,' as Sethi, the chronicler of that peerless interview with Sanjay, would find.

But Sanjay did what he wished. He took off with a co-pilot, Captain Subhas Saxena, at 7.58 a.m.

Eyewitnesses later recounted the Pitts doing loops over the Ashoka Hotel, a few hundred metres to the northwest of Safdarjang Airport. At 8.10 a.m., minutes into the flight, the Pitts crashed in an area about 450 metres from his official residence at 12, Willingdon Crescent—the house to which Indira and her family had shifted after losing the elections in 1979.

A cook at a neighbour's bungalow, 15 Willingdon Crescent, spoke of the buzzing of the Pitts suddenly cutting out 'like a scooter grinding to a halt', and saw the plane lurch and then nosedive into a clump of trees by a big storm drain.

Indira arrived soon after, accompanied by Dhawan, her ever-present aide. Her car was parked a little way away along a dirt track near the site of the crash. She instinctively began to run. Mother Indira.

Then, instinctively, she slowed to a brisk walk. Prime Minister Indira.

Then she knelt to the body of her son which had by then been laid out on a stretcher. She saw Sanjay's battered face and broke down uncontrollably. Mother Indira.

An American stunt pilot would say of this low-level flying daredevilry even with Sanjay's proficiency in flying which more than one pilot vouched for. 'Flying hours mean nothing. Just because you have driven 500,000 miles in a car doesn't mean you can qualify to race in the Indy 500.'

But Sanjay had won back India for his mother. And for himself. He could be anything; India's Icarus, even.

It took eight doctors four hours to put Sanjay's and Captain Saxena's bodies back together before they were taken to their homes.

In the next days, Indira wore outsized black sunglasses, even larger than the ones she wore to attend India's first nuclear test in Pokhran, in the deserts of Rajasthan, in 1974. Except for another wrenching moment of public grief at her younger son's funeral, accompanied by Sanjay's widow Maneka and Rajiv's wife Sonia, she remained impassive through the thirty hours from Sanjay's death to his funeral. There was still a country to run.

But she grieved. 'Prime Minister Gandhi, who had ridden in an open jeep the length of the cortege, appeared composed,' Stuart Auerbach of *Washington Post* wrote in his despatch from a Delhi abuzz with conspiracy theories about the crash, including sabotaging of key controls. 'But friends said her eyes behind the dark glasses she has worn since her son's death were red and swollen from crying.'

Meanwhile, a great mess waited for its reckoning in Punjab. It came from the creation of a Frankenstein's monster in the charismatic Jarnail Singh Bhindranwale as a hard line, extremist pivot transparently engineered by 'New Delhi' to diminish the influential Akali Dal. The fallout would ultimately claim Indira's life—and, again, claim the soul of Delhi and the soul of all India.

Darkness after darkness.

MERCY PETITIONS

And the darkness after that. A serial darkness that threatened the neighbourhood—even Afghanistan, through which arrived so many invaders eyeing Hindustan's riches and Delhi's centrality in commanding the subcontinent's access.

Sanjay Gandhi's Icarus year saw the Soviet Union's invasion of Afghanistan from the previous year already mired into a bloody commitment. It had commentators, several of them American, gleefully—and ironically—declare it the Soviets' Vietnam. (Such commentary was prescient. That campaign bled the Soviets as it bled Afghans, and created an America-sponsored jihad that contributed to ridding Afghanistan of the Soviets, but it would lead to the onset of the Taliban and, subsequently, the staggering attack of 9/11 that changed America as it changed the world.)

At home, the year that Sanjay died also saw the rebirth of the dissolved Bharatiya Jana Sangh in a new avatar: the Bharatiya Janata Party. In a short nine years, it would lead India's social engineering through muscular politics and consequent rioting. Not long after, the party and the majoritarian ecosystem greatly benefited from the demolition of the Babri Masjid to stamp its identity politics on the nation.

While that particular trail of darkness would take some years to become evident to the country at large, there was a horror right at hand: 'Bhagalpur'. That one word summed up the horror of horrors highlighted by the watchful in the media. Over two years in 1979 and 1980, the police of this town by the Ganga in Bihar had poured acid into the eyes of thirty-one undertrial prisoners and convicts, proving yet again that the law of the land was often lawless. Bihar wasn't Delhi, but Delhi wouldn't flinch either. It was inured to atrocity exhibitions with its voyeuristic, insatiable fix of shock and awe.

Through these seismic or significant journeys, Billa and Ranga's on-again, off-again executions had become a sort of panem et circenses routine that played out as much in the highest courts of the land as it did in the public imagination.

Ranga's final petition for clemency—on which also rode Billa's fate—was dismissed by the Supreme Court, on 20 January 1982. Chief Justice Y. V. Chandrachud, Justice Chinappa Reddy, the judges who had reconfirmed the initial judgement of death on both Billa and Ranga back in 1979, passed the 620-word order along with Justice Ananda Prakash Sen. (Justice Sen would add a significant footnote to the annals of Supreme Court pomp: when he retired in 1988, he was lauded as the first Indian judge of the Supreme Court to decline a farewell function.)

Ranga's legal team had brought a petition against what was listed as *Lt. Governor of Delhi & Ors.*—'Ors.' signifying various agencies of the government of India. Rajendra Kumar Garg, V. J. Francis, Sunil Kumar Jain, and D. K. Garg stood for Ranga. (Billa was represented by the lawyers R. K. Jain and P. K. Jain.)

The attorney general of India, L. N. Sinha, K. Parasaran, India's solicitor general, and Milon K. Banerji, the additional solicitor general, stood against the convicts. The presence of all that firepower was in the end just pro-forma, a legal necessity—but the Supreme Court's shifting positions on the death penalty had for several months created quite the storm, and the government clearly did not wish to take any chances.

And Ranga—and, by extension, Billa—had been in the thick of it.

Indeed, their repeated moves for clemency had caused a series of flip-flops at India's highest court. It even created the environment for a constitutional crisis and drew the president of India into its vortex.

■

It had begun the previous year in April.

On 21 April 1981, while delivering their judgment on Ranga's original mercy petition, Justices Chandrachud, Sen, and Baharul Islam had passed the final step in due process on to executive authority, expecting that the president 'will dispose' of the mercy petition stated to have been filed by Ranga, 'as expeditiously' as the president 'finds his convenience'. The petition had been filed by Ranga's lead lawyer, Rajendra Garg, a passionate opponent of capital punishment.

Clemency was denied by President Neelam Sanjiva Reddy. He had been appointed president in 1977, a year before the killing of Geeta and Sanjay, and was fully aware of public anguish and outrage at the time.

A day before Billa and Ranga were to be hanged on 8 November 1981, Garg petitioned the Supreme Court questioning the president's power of pardon. He wished for an examination by the Supreme Court to gauge its worth: was such presidential pardon arrived at arbitrarily or was it justiciable—legally permissible to be debated and decided in a court of law instead of being held as absolute. 'Justiciable' of course being quite a distance from 'justifiable'—which is more in the domain of public opinion, or even, opinion driven by public discourse.

Justices Chandrachud, Sen, and Baharul Islam constituted a bench that admitted Garg's petition.

Just that act had triggered a reaction among the public which appeared to simply wish for Billa and Ranga to be hanged and be done with it. But the bench held firm.

'Since the question raised by Shri Garg is of far-reaching importance,' the judges observed, 'it is necessary that the question must be examined with care.'

'Many senior advocates privately held then that they felt the Supreme Court was going too far,' the journalist Chaitanya Kalbag wrote pithily of the conundrum. The court could have, they argued, 'told Garg that his question was interesting, but not worthy of being taken up in this particular case.'

The judges stayed the execution of Ranga and Billa. A furore ensued.

As Kalbag, an astute legal and constitutional observer, surmised in a series of perceptive articles, the repeated petitions raised points that queried the very foundation of the executive, legislative, and judicial powertrains. Was the president's mercy power justiciable or absolute? What of the executive's power? Could the executive's powers be disputed? And should the president, 'even though he is under advice of the Council of Ministers...give what is known as a "speaking order"—that is, a reasoned order listing arguments in favour of a particular decision.'

As an important subtext, the judicial fracas also set up a confrontation of sorts between the president's largely ceremonial authority and the pulls and pressures imposed by the government. This was most transparently displayed in the president having to, after a procedure of review, having to finally give in to the executive's wishes—by constitutional imperative—as with legislation proposed by the majority party or coalition in Parliament.

The implication: was the Supreme Court's decision to stay the execution actually calling to attention a flawed system which would prove that India's president was hamstrung and unable to make independent opinions that would stick; and the Supreme Court would need to intervene, impartially, to decide matters of clemency, for instance.

The next hearing of the mercy petition was scheduled for January 1982.

▪

From all available indications, public outrage meanwhile appeared to carry the day on 20 January, judgement day.

'Or perhaps the Supreme Court felt that examining the President's pardon powers implied a head-on collision with the Executive,' wrote Kalbag, 'at a time when relations between the Government and the judiciary are stretched to snapping point.'

The Supreme Court bench flipped their earlier order that stayed the execution '...a neat U-turn,' Kalbag wrote colourfully, scathingly.

Ranga would hang. In tandem, so would Billa.

The judges were—finally—emphatic:

> In fact, we do not see what useful purpose will be achieved by the petitioner by ensuring the imposition of any severe, judicially-evolved constraints on the wholesome power of the President to use it as the justice of a case may require. After all, the power conferred by Article 72 [of the Constitution] can be used only for the purpose of reducing the sentence, not for enhancing it. We need not, however, go into that question elaborately because in so far as this case is concerned, we are quite clear that not even the most liberal use of his mercy jurisdiction could have persuaded the President to interfere with the sentence of death imposed upon the petitioner, in view particularly of the considerations mentioned by us in our judgment in *Kuljeet Singh @ Ranga v. Union of India & Anr.*

The judges capped their order by quoting from previous judgments seeking clemency for Ranga—and excoriated both Ranga and Billa:

> We may recall what we said in that judgment that 'the death of the Chopra children was caused by the petitioner and his companion Billa after a savage planning which bears a professional stamp', that the 'survival of an orderly society demands the extinction of the life of persons like Ranga and Billa who are a menace to social order and security', and that 'they are professional murderers and deserve no sympathy even in terms of the evolving standards of decency of a mature society'.

There remained the final sentence:

> The petition is accordingly dismissed.

■

His cause, and case, were lost, but Rajendra Garg, Ranga's lawyer, would hold out for the last word in a conversation with Kalbag right after the order that would effectively shut every window for clemency.

'If one reads the orders of the Chief Justice of November 7 and January 20,' Garg told Kalbag, 'one cannot miss the complete collapse of the constitutional conscience of the highest court.'

In his battle against the death sentence, the eloquent Garg went as far as to compare the day's judicial absolutes as being similar to colonial imperatives. In these modern times, he held, the state had always to take the high road even if some citizens took the lowest of the low. Even with an unrepentant client against whom both evidence and public opinion were stacked to the rafters, Garg had hoped to show, wrote Kalbag, that executive clemency is 'no longer a Crown prerogative, but a constitutional power coupled with a duty.'

'When a man is hanged by the brute power of the State,' Garg lamented, 'something human dies within the heart of every man in that nation.'

But there was some moral recompense after all. A judicial review of the entire process might have had the opposite effect, reduced the room for case-by-case clemency.

'Thank God,' a top Supreme Court lawyer would tell Kalbag with some relief, 'the court has made it clear that it would not like to put the power of pardon within the limits of a rigorous judicial discipline by laying down rigid standards for its exercise.'

The judicial—indeed, judicious—retreat also walked back a possible confrontation between the office of a president appointed by the Janata government and the Congress-controlled legislature and executive at a time of political fragility.

RIGHT TO INFORMATION

Prabha Dutt, chief reporter with the *Hindustan Times*, had pushed hard for interviews with death row Billa and Ranga using every legal device at hand, and taken the Government of India to court in November 1981 in a move that became a cause célèbre for the media. Especially, as we have read, since the president of India turned down a plea of clemency by Billa and Ranga and refused to commute their death sentence to imprisonment for life.

It all crystallized to a journalist's right to information, and a journalist's role as amicus civi, as it were, a 'friend of society', in this case, to inform the public about a condemned person's last words to the world at large.

Dutt filed for a writ of mandamus 'or any other appropriate writ' seeking the Supreme Court to direct the respondents, in particular the Delhi administration and the superintendent of Tihar, to allow her to interview Billa and Ranga—requests the authorities had turned down. Dutt invoked Article 32 of the Constitution, which permits citizens to approach the Supreme Court to redress a situation if they felt justice had been denied them.

Dutt was now joined by colleagues representing the *Times of India*—this was her close friend, Rai—*India Today* magazine and the wire services Press Trust of India and United News of India. These organizations had also presented petitions similar to Dutt's. Prakash Patra, at the time a young crime reporter with *National Herald*, had meanwhile submitted a slew of petitions, to both the home secretaries of India and Delhi, the lieutenant governor of Delhi, and Delhi's director general of prisons. Patra wished for an interview and to also be present at the hangings. Patra spoke to me of this experience.

'Young man,' the horrified home secretary of India called Patra over to ask him, 'why do you want to watch such a morbid process?'

Journalistic necessity, Patra replied.

He was denied access to witness the hangings.

■

India's chief justice, Y. V. Chandrachud, sat in judgement of the petition, along with justices A. P. Sen and Baharul Islam, on 7 November.

The constitutional right to freedom of speech and expression as provided in a clause of Article 19 of the Constitution, which includes media freedom, is not an 'absolute right,' the justices maintained. Indeed, the Constitution doesn't provide for the 'Press' to have 'unrestricted access to means of information'. The press also needs to curb its invasive nature. The court went further: 'The Press is entitled to exercise by publishing a matter which does not invade the rights of other citizens and which does not violate the sovereignty and integrity of India, the security of the state, public order, decency and morality.' There is also no obligation accorded to the press by the Criminal Procedure Code, the court said.

They, so said the judges, didn't possess information—'data'—to be able to say that Billa and Ranga are 'ready and willing' to be interviewed. Equally, they had 'no data either that they are not willing to be interviewed' which would have made this entire petition moot. 'We are proceeding on the basis,' declared the court, 'that the prisoners are willing to be interviewed.'

After somewhat long-winded qualifications, typical of judgements as they can be used as precedent, the justices gave Dutt, the mover of the main writ petition, and her colleagues a way in. 'The right claimed by the petitioner in the present case, a newspaper reporter, to interview two convicts under sentence of death is not a right to express any particular view, or opinion but the right to means of information through the medium of an interview with them,' they held. 'No such right can be claimed by the Press unless the person sought to be interviewed is willing to be interviewed.'

And they could be interviewed under a provision—Rule 549 (4)—of the Jail Manual too, as it provided that a prisoner sentenced to death 'shall be allowed interviews and other communications with relatives, friends and legal advisers'. Media, though not explicitly mentioned in this rule, 'cannot be denied the opportunity of interview without good reasons.' So, there is no reason why media persons—in a sign of the times the judges used the term 'newspapermen' even though the principal petitioner was a woman—who 'could be termed' as 'friends of the society' be denied the right of interview. All they had to do was to follow security procedures of search and other related protocols of visit to a jail and interactions with prisoners.

More justification followed: 'Rule 559 A also provides that all reasonable indulgence should be allowed to a condemned prisoner in the matter of interviews with relatives, friends, legal advisors.... Surprisingly, but we do not propose to dwell on that issue, this rule provides that no newspapers should be allowed. But it does not provide that no newspapermen will be allowed.'

That finessing done, the court addressed a final point—whether media persons ought to be permitted to be present to witness the executions was another matter altogether, and that depended entirely on the call taken by the superintendent of Tihar.

'We therefore direct that the Superintendent of the Tihar Jail shall allow the aforesaid persons, namely the representatives of the *Hindustan Times*, *Times of India*, *India Today*, the Press Trust of India and the United News of India to interview the aforesaid two prisoners, namely, Billa and Ranga, today,' the Supreme Court allowed. 'The interviews may be allowed at 4 o'clock in the evening. The representatives agree before us that all of them will interview the prisoners jointly and for not more than one hour on the whole.'

An hour with India's most talked about convicted killers. After weeks of pushing, for Dutt and her colleagues that would have to be enough.

And young Patra of *National Herald*, who was denied permission to be present at the hangings, was enabled by the Supreme Court's ruling to accompany Dutt, Rai, and others to visit Tihar for an interview with Billa and Ranga.

But they would have to wait for several weeks, because the date of the execution, set for the following day, had again been 'stayed' by the courts—in the judicial back and forth we read of earlier. As that process ran its course and clemency was finally denied Billa and Ranga, the opportunity for an interview arrived.

NINTH LIFE

'A cat, they say, has nine lives,' Prabha Dutt wrote in the weekend edition of the *Hindustan Times* on 31 January 1982, a Sunday. 'Billa—or the one with the cat's eyes—having given the hangman's noose a slip half a dozen times, will finally be hanged "till he dies" at the "phansi kothi" in Tihar jail tomorrow morning. So will Ranga, his partner in crime.'

Dutt's article was datelined the 30th, the day earlier, in the usual newspaper format. It ran on the front page in column eight—the column on the extreme right—by a large four-column photo of Ranga's relatives huddled outside the gates of Tihar.

As with this newspaper, the convicts made front page news with every paper of note across the country. As they had always done. Every twist and turn of their fate, the same as the horrific fate of their victims, kept pace with the both the mundane and remarkable. What many had termed the crime of a generation surreally kept pace with politics and diplomacy. For instance, the ongoing saga of Billa and Ranga shared media space with the visit of King Juan Carlos and Queen Sophia of Spain, who had just provided a glamour quotient to India's annual celebration of itself as a republic on the 26th of the month: Juan Carlos was guest of honour at the Republic Day parade. The royal couple were received at Palam and then fêted by Indira Gandhi. That splashy whirl of diplomacy between constitutional monarch and re-elected monarch was attended by India's foreign minister, P. V. Narasimha Rao, a linguist who counted Spanish as one of several Indian and global languages he spoke fluently.

Rao, of course, had more hard-nosed duties. The foreign minister of Pakistan, Agha Shahi, arrived just days later, on 29 January for talks with his Indian counterpart. Delhi's political and media circles were abuzz with suggestions of an imminent non-aggression pact between the two long-time foes who were attempting to move beyond the penumbra of 1971, which brought the war in Bangladesh—the war for Bangladesh. There was no need for India to fear anything in terms of escalation or a regional arms race, Shahi maintained—to outright disbelief from the Indian side, which had recently inked a deal for the acquisition of Jaguar close air support and strike fighters with the potential threat from Pakistan in mind. Shahi was all silk. Any Indian concern about Pakistan inking a large deal with the United States for forty state-of-the-art F-16 fighter aircraft were based on 'exaggerated reports'.

Back at the ground zero of Tihar, there was less sophistry. Indeed, there was a sense of finality. Much as it seemed to be a surprise that, with the notoriety attached to the murders people had actually arrived and claimed Ranga as family, nobody showed for Billa.

And here were Dutt, Rai, Patra, and their colleagues, for a thirty-minute hard won chat with Billa at the phansi-kothi, the so-called hanging house to which he and Ranga had been shifted a week or so earlier. The scaffold from which they would drop to their deaths was in the same complex.

Thirty minutes with Billa, because Ranga wasn't interested in spending thirty minutes with journalists; he had conveyed this through his jailers—and the jail authorities had conveyed this to the small group of media persons.

The journalists trooped into Tihar for their interaction with Billa.

Billa was all jittery bravado, and Dutt caught the mood that *HT* announced with a headline: 'Trembling legs betray Billa on death's eve'.

That mood was diluted with an opposite tone in a secondary headline that carried the story to the back page—Page 16: 'Billa laughs on death's eve'.

As it happened, both moods were true. Here was a twitchy convict with a last throw at showing off, and nervous about the noose that would kill him in some hours.

The hanging of Billa was scheduled for 8 a.m. on 31 January. Ranga's execution was scheduled for an hour later.

Tihar had one scaffold. There would have to be a queue.

■

Years later, at her home in a quiet, leafy enclave in Gurgaon just across the border from New Delhi, Usha Rai would recall that exchange. It was an October morning in 2019, more than forty years after Geeta and Sanjay were abducted and killed. We were taking tea at her dining table, a young German Shepherd restlessly circling us, protective of Rai, as she collected her thoughts about all those many years ago. And, specifically, about the impression of bravado versus the physicality that Billa presented.

'Billa was not a big man,' Rai seemed surprised by the fact, even decades later, of a person so slight and yet, capable of containing such abundant violence. 'He was a tiny, puny man.'

Billa was jittery and that eclipsed the bonhomie with which he greeted Dutt and her colleagues. He had even written letters to some, including Dutt.

Billa led with a ready confession of having killed 'five or six times'—all committed on 'impulse', he shared with some nonchalance, except for the killing of his 'friend Sudhir'.

That was premeditated, he clarified. He thought Sudhir would snitch to the police, so Sudhir had to be killed.

Five or six murders. Dutt attempted to corroborate it with whatever chatter Billa had shared with jail attendants. They said he had admitted to having committed 'six or seven' murders. Maybe more, he had suggested.

'What about the murder of Sanjay and Geeta?' asked Dutt.

'I will take the truth with me.'

'Why are your legs trembling?' Rai asked.

'Not at all,' Billa shot back. But he couldn't mask the nervous laughter that escaped the protestation.

■

Patra, who later held leadership positions with major mainstream dailies, would in a conversation with me back up Dutt and Rai's recall of Billa's nerves. He remembered Billa as being both nervous and bombastic during the brief interaction, for which Tihar's death row star was separated from the journalists by the bars of his cell.

Billa stood about a foot away from the bars.

'He was very nervous,' Patra went back to that time. 'His voice was shaky, his eyes were shifty—even over bright. He would look at us, and then his eyes would look away—fall away. His hands trembled, as did his feet, which he kept shuffling.'

Billa employed bravado to paper over these death row tics, Patra recalls. 'He was bombastic—and speaking about himself in the third person.'

'Billa kisi se darta nahin.' Billa is not afraid of anyone.

'Billa ko kisi se parwa nahin—sirf Rab ke siwaye.' Billa doesn't give a damn about anyone except God.

'One look at him and you just knew he was the killer, that he had committed the murders,' Patra recalled with a psychographic certainty. But even Patra had doubts in the beginning.

Unlike some of his colleagues who tracked the sordid crime from late-August 1978, Patra is candid about that overlay of fact and feeling that characterized interpretations of the brutal killings and the bizarre capture of Billa and Ranga. One version was the portrayal of the duo as sophisticated killers with convoluted motives—this was based on information put about by the police in the immediate aftermath of the discovery of Geeta's and Sanjay's corpses. The opposite impression came later, created by the haphazard, clumsy abduction and panicky murder of the victims, and the manner of the near-incredible flight and eventual capture of the killers.

'In the beginning, even I wrote articles that were sceptical of Billa and Ranga being the killers,' he told me, 'But as the investigation progressed there was no doubt. By then the forensics had added up.'

■

Billa riffed off his isolation in Bollywood-style asides during his death row chat with the visiting journalists.

‘Even the theft of straw is a crime, so is the theft of crores,’ he told Dutt and her colleagues.

Dutt interpreted his mood by enhancing drama: ‘He speaks in a roundabout manner,’ she wrote in her signature style, ‘but his eyes with a curious gleam about them said it for him—“There are bigger fish than me that they could fry”.’

She pushed him for a legacy message—would he like to offer a final advice to other criminals?

‘I would say they should go ahead and commit bigger crimes.’

This melodramatic tone persisted throughout the interview, his words and occasionally his eyes and twitchy hands doing the talking, but his face remained emotionless, pushing back against the probing the same as he had for several years consistently pushed back against any accusations and evidence of his hand in the murders.

He had spoken of his imminent death as an inevitability lived several times over, including earlier in the month. He had known on 21 January, a Thursday, when he learnt of his clemency petition at the Supreme Court being turned down. He fully expected to be hanged the following Sunday, the 24th, and, as he revealed during his interaction with the small group of journalists, he was surprised by a week’s postponement.

This time around there would be no more surprises.

▪

Even as Ranga remained reticent and removed from any public or media interaction, Billa appeared ready to publicly confront his execution.

It was no matter, Billa claimed. He slept and ate ‘normally’—‘four hours of sound sleep every night.’ He had eaten a snack and taken tea just before meeting the journalists. He would be hanged the following morning.

That wouldn’t dampen his appetite. ‘I will eat at night also.’

The journalists asked some anodyne questions and received interesting answers somewhat boosted in translation.

Why did you take to a life of crime?

Wealth. 'Instead of wealth I got death.' Cynical laughter.

Do you have any money in the bank?

'I spent it all on myself—and there was the Bombay CID.'

Cannily, Billa let that discomfort hang. After all, Billa had twice escaped from custody.

Before, and after, he had travelled to several places until the police caught him for the final time. More accurately, he had blundered into a group of 'unsuspecting' soldiers. With that capture, his life had come a full, violent circle from the time Billa claimed to have run away from home as a teenager when his parents had threatened to break his legs. They had been upset with his 'ways'.

■

The theatrics weren't done.

Billa's statement carried his last words. And Ranga, even though he refused to meet the media, like Billa had handed over a final statement to the press.

Billa gave over his statement personally, to the visiting journalists.

Ranga's was delivered by his brother, who also ended speculation about the possibility of publishing Ranga's autobiography; Ranga had put together about a hundred pages of handwritten text. His brother said he didn't wish to make money from it.

Statements by both Billa and Ranga maintained their innocence—individually, following a pattern from the earliest days of investigation and their prosecution—for the crime for which they were to be hanged—the brutal deaths of Geeta and Sanjay. Both claimed 'injustice'. Both projected themselves as 'martyrs'.

Billa wrote so in a Q & A format in spiky, closely written Hindi. Ranga wrote his disclaimer in Hindi using the Gurmukhi script.

And his statement was relatively more substantive than Billa's. Through an affidavit, Ranga willed his eyes, kidney, heart, blood 'and any other part of my body to the needy'. The twenty-six-year-old left it to the doctors who would supervise his hanging to decide the circle of distribution.

There would be no takers.

In his statement, Ranga persisted with his innocence, pinning on Billa all blame and only admitting to his crime of having been with Billa on 26 August 1978; he was unmindful too of the default culpability of aiding and abetting in murder. There was self-pity too, unlike Billa's ready self-aggrandisement.

'A wall of contempt has been built around me,' he wrote.

Billa's statement ended with 'JB', his signature. And a descriptor that acknowledged inevitability with a twisted dig at the world:

'Whatever you may consider me to be.'

'There was no remorse at all in them,' Usha Rai would revisit the attitudes of Billa and Ranga, whom she had tracked in courtrooms and jail, in her conversation with me. 'No remorse at all.'

Nearly fifty of Ranga's relatives had come down from Panipat on 29 January, took up residence on the sidewalk near Tihar, forming a remarkable bastion of support for their reviled kin.

Nobody would come for Billa.

EXECUTION

Hangmen had been summoned by Tihar officials. Two had already arrived, carrying coils of stout manila rope with them. Fakira and Kallu Singh. Kallu's name evidently arrived at on account of his being very dark—a cloak of a bizarre, amiable racism common in northern India. Fakira, fond of jokes, was darker; some called him bhoot. Ghost. Unkind as that was, it carried a ghoulish familiarity with his vocation.

Media gossip credited Kallu, quieter of the team, with carrying serious pedigree; it was said a forebear had hanged pre-Independence rebel icon, Bhagat Singh.

(In a future Delhi couldn't yet imagine, Kallu would hang a bodyguard and a co-conspirator convicted of assassinating Prime Minister Indira Gandhi; the general desecration of politics and the specific desecration of the Golden Temple that would trigger that horror upon horror was still a lifetime and over two years into a future as yet known hazily only to political analysts and practitioners of security affairs. Kallu's son Mammu would hang several convicts across jails in Patiala, Meerut, Jaipur, and Allahabad. Kallu's grandson Pawan would hang in 2014 a person who would come to be known as the killer of Nithari: the remains of nineteen children and women would be found in the sewer by a house in a locality of Noida. Bustling, burgeoning Noida, not the residential and corporate backwater of 1982, just six years into its formal existence. But that would be far into the future of a frenetic new millennium with new ills and evils.)

■

The indictment of a court beyond the courts would accompany these two occupants of Ward No. 16, Billa in Cell No. 4, and Ranga in Cell

No. 6, to an uneasy afterlife of public record and public memory.

Nobody had been hanged at Tihar's phansi-kothi since 1978—that was A. B. Gupta, for burning alive his children and his wife.

Three would remain on death row after Billa and Ranga.

The Kashmiri militant Maqbool Butt was on death row for killings and sabotage—and he was also tied to the hijacking of an Indian Airlines F-27 Fokker Friendship aircraft, 'Ganga' in January 1971; he was at Lahore airport to greet the hijackers, two members of the National Liberation Front, who forced the flight from Srinagar to Jammu to divert to Lahore. Before his execution in 1984, Butt would read Salman Rushdie's epic *Midnight's Children*, cherishing, among other things, its description of pre-Partition Kashmir.

A couple of hired killers remained too. Ujagar Singh and Kartar Singh were hired by a well-known eye surgeon. N. S. Jain, to kill his wife, Vidya—she had stood in the way of Jain's affair with his paramour. The two killed Vidya Jain in late 1973. Dr Jain, who had been a personal eye specialist to the president of India at the time, V. V. Giri, until his Gordian plot of convoluted planning and red herrings collapsed around him, had received a life sentence for his part in the crime. The contract killers he had hired to murder his wife now waited their turn at the gallows in Delhi's central jail.

But their time was yet to be, several years after their crimes, arrest and sentencing. Billa and Ranga were fast-tracked to death by India's notoriously overloaded and tortoise-like justice system.

■

When they were awakened after dawn, around 5 a.m., Billa and Ranga were each offered a cup of tea. They were then asked, recalls Sunil Gupta, who was a young jailer in Tihar at the time, if they wished to record their wills with a magistrate. Both declined.

Except for the interaction with the journalists, they had largely remained quiet and withdrawn. Phansi-kothi, the terminal station where only a last-minute commutation was the way out alive, had that effect. They were essentially on suicide watch. Gupta mentions two-hour shifts by guards drawn from the Tamil Nadu Special Police—

brought in after a jailbreak in 1976 in a desperate attempt to curb collusion and corruption; the outcome is another story.

Phansi-kothi prisoners were denied personal belongings. Their clothes were designed to be suicide proof: pyjamas without strings, for instance. They were not permitted visitors beyond one meeting with family and friends—a meeting the prisoner was allowed to decline. Recording of a will was a part of this death watch protocol. A death row inmate was permitted a thirty-minute walk a day within the phansi-kothi complex. 'The rest of the time,' as Gupta put it, 'he is meant to mentally prepare himself to die.'

In all this funerary quiet, Ranga hadn't been able to resist a dig at his former partner-in-crime as they were led to their executions. The nervously loquacious Billa, who had spoken to the journalists as Ranga kept to himself, had a meltdown.

Billa was in tears.

Ranga saw that and mocked him. 'Dekho, mard ho ke ro raha hai!' See, he is a man and he cries.

This snide remark didn't come as much of a surprise to Gupta. 'All our psychological profiling on Billa and Ranga led us to one conclusion,' he would write of this incident and their general demeanour towards each other, 'they could not stand each other and leaving them together in close proximity was dangerous as they would attack each other physically.'

Gupta recalls that, even as a young jailer, he attempted to 'counsel them' against 'aggressive behaviour'. But in some ways, they were beyond counsel. People who have received the inevitability of the black warrant, their passport to execution, aren't model citizens of temperament, not when one or the other's defence has been to place the primary blame for a crime on the other.

Gupta shares the final steps in the ritual of execution—bathe, dress in loose black kurta and pyjamas, and head to the phansi kothi. It was a plain room, with the hanging platform and its 15-foot well the main exhibit.

Kallu and Fakira waited. They worked as a team, for efficiency as well as to step in and pull the lever that would open the trapdoor if one or the other got a case of nerves. Even though, following a loose hangman's protocol, they had each been given a bottle of Old Monk Rum the evening before—it wasn't in the rulebook but it was the way of this select world—to calm such nerves as might have manifested themselves before the taking of a life for the fee of 150 rupees per person per hanging, with food, board, and transportation provided for.

■

The roads leading to Tihar were shut down. The media weren't allowed in; they would have to wait for the aftermath, the same as family members of Ranga and onlookers.

There would be few to witness the hangings.

Gupta and his colleagues watched as nooses were placed around the necks of Billa, and later, Ranga.

Billa sobbed as his face was covered.

When his turn came, Ranga remained defiant, ironically shouting the cry of the Sikh pious as they seek eternal blessings by acclaiming God, the timeless being: Jo Bole So Nihaal, Sat Sri Akal.

Tihar's superintendent at the time, A. B. Shukla, waved a red handkerchief (that he habitually carried) for both the hangings. The waves were a signal to the executioner to pull the lever that opened the trapdoor. In turn Billa and Ranga disappeared into the well of the platform, the knot around their necks and drop expected to work in tandem to break the vertebrae and bring near-instantaneous death.

As it happened, when the prison doctor checked Billa he was found to be dead.

Ranga, on the other hand, remained alive. Gupta claims Ranga still had a pulse.

'So, one jail staff was given the task to jump into the well beneath his hanging body and pull his legs.'

That snuffed out whatever life remained in Ranga.

■

By the time the city and the country awoke to the various interviews and accounts of the journalists' interactions and impressions in the newspapers the following morning, 31 January 1982, Billa and his partner in crime, Ranga, were dead and, as nobody claimed their bodies, not even Ranga's relatives, they were cremated in Tihar.

For their part, Roma and Madan Chopra would learn of the death of the killers of their children from a distance.

They had left India. They would return after a long sojourn but with little closure.

Geeta and Sanjay were always with them.

LOVE–HATE CITY

The story that began with the killing of Geeta and Sanjay and ended with the execution of their convicted killers carried with it the times of turbulence and trial for Delhi, for India.

Of course, the darkness in Delhi wouldn't end with Billa and Ranga.

How could it? Delhi's soul was lost long ago in the hall of smoke and mirrors of mythology, and ancient, medieval, and modern histories, from the disrobing of Draupadi of the Pandavas of mythical Indraprastha that presaged decades of political restlessness and culminated in a war of annihilation with their cousins, the Kauravas of Hastinapur, to being the way station to centuries of invasions and wars amid grand empires of stupendous wealth and culture and equally stupendous hubris, to literally its Nadir—its sacking for an insult to Nadir Shah, to the horrors of the 1857 revolt, and after, the great horrors of Imperial durbars celebrating Victoria and Edward and Alexandra and George and Mary as hundreds of Hindustan's 'nobles' lined up to pay homage to distant-yet-near empresses and emperors even as Hindustan bled and starved, a way station that sanctified loot from Bengal to Bombay, and then bathed New India in its own blood as the partition of the subcontinent acquired a capital P in posthumous infamy.

Delhi remained visceral; sometimes it seemed as if the city was strained by all that was good and joyful, and yearned to be gutted by its own worst instincts. This carried over into politics as in life. In several ways, the 1970s and 1980s presaged a hardening of politics, of engineered hatreds that remain with us to this day.

The city's underbelly offered a smorgasbord of rage and chaos. Indeed, even as Billa and Ranga lived in limbo between their incarceration and delayed execution, darkness was never far.

On 27 January 1982, just days before the execution of Billa and Ranga, police arrested a twenty-two-year-old part-time taxi driver, Avinash. His alias was Kalé. Dark. The slur for the colour of his skin held a numbing story of sex crimes. Kalé was charged with the killing of two children in the Paharganj area. It wasn't far from where he lived in a tenement in Bagichi Allauddin, which some newspapers would call Bagichi Alladin—the garden of Alladin.

There was no djinn to protect young Sarita, all of ten. She lay naked with a massive head wound near a public urinal in the Motia Kalan neighbourhood not far from the little garden-only-in-name. Kalé was seen that evening, running away in bloodstained clothes—so said Assistant Commissioner of Police Anil Sinha.

The confession had evidently come from Kalé himself, who seemed to be infused with the guiding spirits of Billa and Ranga. He had tricked Sarita into coming to the public lavatory on the pretext of giving her money for her father. He had attempted to rape her. When she resisted, he smashed her head against the fixtures.

The police officer spoke of other confessions. During his interrogation, Kalé told the police that he had killed two boys in June and August of 1981, after attempting to sodomize them. In June that year, Kale's victim was Prem Lal, an eight-year-old from Chuna Mandi in Paharganj. He took Prem to nearby Panchkuin Road to a house that was under construction. It is where he killed the boy. In August his victim was Pyare Lal, from the neighbourhood of Multani Dhanda. Kalé took him to Aram Bagh in the vicinity, to a housing complex being built. The nine-year-old's head was smashed in with a brick. Like young Sarita, the boys too had been poor. They too were lured by the promise of money to be paid to their fathers.

Horror followed horror. Kalé's confession brought forth a past in which he had himself been sodomized, at knifepoint, when he was a student of class seven in a neighbourhood school. He quit school. A life of alcoholism, vagrancy, and sexual crime followed not long after. He was impotent, the police claimed. Impotency as he assaulted the children drove him to a killing frenzy.

Kalé's arrest made front page news, but the outrage and relief seemed to die more quickly than the children had, and as brutally. There was more front-page crime to be had.

Two days after Kale's arrest arrived news of a sort of closure for another atrocity exhibition, yet more indication that it wasn't just Delhi over which Delhi had lost its grip, as it were. It was as if the misgovernance and rot across India had set in with Delhi's administrative eyes wide shut since the days of the Emergency, a Capital out of touch with the country in its care.

The government of Bihar prosecuted 38 police personnel—officers and from junior ranks—and two medical officers. The Central Bureau of Investigation had found them guilty in the so-called Bhagalpur Blinding Case from 1980. Seventy-six officials were charged on various counts and held guilty by the Bureau, whose report had been formally submitted earlier in the week. 'Bhagalpur', which had become a one-word geographical indicator of atrocity, was heading to ragged closure, shepherded by a landmark Supreme Court judgement that ordered compensation for human rights violations.

It put a lid on things with pay-offs, not prevention. Human rights as an ipso facto palliative, not a right.

It was all so very Delhi.

Not long after, India watched, aghast, as an incendiary mix of political manipulation and ethno-religious resentment exploded into chaos that, in 1983, led to the butchering of over 2,100 Bengali Muslim men, women and children in what came to be known as the Nellie Massacre, after the eponymous village due east of Guwahati, the largest city of Assam. It was only the first of several firestorms that followed in the name of preserving nationhood, identity and a costly, hyper-inflationary pride.

Outrage quickly settled into the numbness of perfunctory statements and recording of statistics.

Call it the Delhi Syndrome.

■

For me Delhi has always been a love-hate city, a place of emotion, of life, and home for nearly twenty-five years through university, work, the usual highs, lows, love, and heartbreak, an altogether visceral time that mixed a sense of belonging with a sense of dislocation—often at the same time. I no longer live there, but it has remained a place of frequent visits for work and, sometimes, to simply be in Delhi. When I lived and worked there, I couldn't wait to leave. After I moved away, I couldn't wait to return for a Delhi fix, besotted by all its charms even after being buffeted by its many storms.

It was easy to identify with what Khushwant Singh wrote in *Delhi*, one of his more evocative and, perhaps, misunderstood books.

'I return to Delhi as I return to my mistress Bhagmati when I have had my fill of whoring in foreign lands,' wrote this pre-eminent balladeer of the capital. 'Delhi and Bhagmati have a lot in common. Having been long misused by rough people they have learnt to conceal their seductive charms under a mask of repulsive ugliness. It is only to their lovers, among whom I count myself, that they reveal their true selves.'

Perhaps that is as it should be. Delhi has known love and heartbreak and horrors through more than a millennia—close to two if one considers mythology—wielding influence far beyond its borders, deciding the futures of billions through its many avatars. And now it is in its ninth life, as it were, as the core of the National Capital Region.

Love–hate city.

■

Delhi would do what it always did. Move on. Layer trauma with trauma, add PTSD over PTSD, as if the fashionable diminution of a gargantuan unresolved madness would address that sickness, the same as it had done for millennia. It's what Dr Sanjeev Jain told me when I talked to him about those times—and the times since.

Jain has co-edited an excellent book on the shattering mental health aspects of the Indian Mutiny of 1857—also the so-called Sepoy Mutiny or the so-called First War of Independence depending on who is doing the calling—and the Partition that followed nine decades later, swamping British India's grand new capital given over to an independent India riven with rioting and its after effects. He was a third-year student at Delhi's Maulana Azad Medical College in 1978. Jain was as shocked by the brutality and reality of Geeta's and Sanjay's killings as any other 'Dilliwala'. It grew into a fascination that led to him studying Delhi's collective trauma, and touchpoints marking Delhi's descent into chaos. Every so often, engineered chaos.

'If order could create disorder,' Jain mused, 'imagine what disorder could do?'

It wasn't difficult to imagine even in soothing winter sunshine as we sat around a wrought iron table in the lawns of his compact and comfortable home in Saket—decades after the 1970s—amidst the trauma of brazenly engineered communal violence in Delhi over the winter of 2019–20; and just weeks before a surprise, brutal lockdown and staggering governmental mismanagement over the Covid-19 pandemic would lead to the death of hundreds of thousands in India—some credible estimates placed deaths in the millions—and the displacement and destitution of tens of millions. We spoke of the generational horrors that accompanied Delhi in an arc that began hundreds of years before Partition—that in several ways paved new Delhi—and the several decades since Partition.

Perhaps such bad blood was implicit in this capital of kingdoms and empires. In an easily navigable radius drawn from where we conversed lay the major monuments of Delhi, from remnants of the earliest forts to awe-inspiring bastions of the Mughals, imposing minars, grand tombs beyond counting, opulent viceregal homes now occupied by free India's figureheads, a parliament for servants of an empire transformed into an edifice for those who would make servants of the people. All are variously celebrated by architects, historians, and awestruck tourists. All were conceived as passive-aggressive masterpieces created as much by artistry as by strategy, arrogance, self-importance or hubris; as markers of a race or a victory, a staggering superiority that has always presumed the dark matter of command-and-control and any collateral damage it precipitated in lives lost and lives destroyed as the necessary physics of what is sometimes called total politics.

Everyone played total politics. Warrior clans and kings and queens and mercantile empires that followed, the Chauhans, early Islamic invaders, the Surs and the Mughals, the Marathas who attempted to topple the Mughals and the British who tripped them both, latter-day moguls and power mongers who ruled over populations that, in sheer numbers, were collectively more than that dominated by all the padishahs in the past.

As ever, power remained a bloody business.

Jain, at the time of our conversation a professor of psychiatry at the National Institute of Mental Health and Neuro Sciences (NIMHANS) in Bangalore, spoke of how Delhi has had a long relationship with matters of a mind gone astray or become diminished. Of how the Tughlaqs recognized it, in particular the sultan Firuz Shah Tughlaq, who established institutions for the study and treatment of dementia. Jain spoke of the madness related to the Mutiny, and madness related to Partition, when the nights were longer than days, that found expression in curious ways. He spoke of hospitals in North Delhi aborting 'Partition foetuses'—a euphemism for the result of religion-driven hatred and rape. Much like other horrors, Delhi—the individual and the collective—buried it.

'Delhi has for long moved on,' Jain said, 'by burying, not confronting or dealing with trauma.'

Geeta and Sanjay offered yet another opportunity to confront trauma, deal with it, and find restitution with an outpouring of emotion. And then quietly bury it to be able to move on to ever newer traumas. Disquiet upon disquiet. Trauma upon trauma.

■

Like 1984.

I had to go to work on 1 November, the day after Indira Gandhi was assassinated by two of her Sikh bodyguards for her perceived sin of clearing Operation Bluestar, the assault that June on the Golden Temple complex; it mattered little what the cause was, it mattered little that Bhindranwale and his band had turned the complex into a kingdom of their mercy and that their desecration came before the one by India's army answering to Indira's orders. Mark Tully, the BBC's iconic South Asia chief who was expelled for several months for his reportage during the Emergency, would later speak of Indira's insistence on keeping Sikh bodyguards despite knowing the risks after Bluestar as her 'desperately wanting to show that she was not an enemy of the Sikh community' and to do whatever she could to 'calm things down after Operation Bluestar'.

At best, an uneasy calm. At worst, a storm warning.

It was a bit of a trek, as it turned out, from my student digs in Hauz Khas to the sprawling trade fair grounds in Pragati Maidan—the field of progress. There was an international mining machinery exhibition scheduled in a fortnight. Various exhibitions at the trade fair grounds brought the opportunity of 'work experience' and handy income to so many students. The exhibition would be showcased at three towering, ziggurat-shaped structures which included the cavernous Hall of Nations complex at the northeastern edge of the grounds. I had seen these as a child travelling by train from Calcutta to school in Rajasthan—tracks reaching from the east, and the west and south of India converged near Pragati Maidan to continue to the transit hub of New Delhi Railway Station. And there I was, working as a gofer for a major chamber of commerce that was hosting the exhibition.

The day began with a sky so blue it seemed like a palette of ordered childhood, neat and seemingly innocent, had been emptied to paint it. The streets were empty of transport. Despairing of ever finding a bus or the opportunity to thumbing a lift, I began to walk north from Hauz Khas, taking the road past the Asian Games Village. At the beginning of the Defence Colony overpass—some called it 'Def Col flyover'—I noticed a vegetable vendor driving a battery-powered rickshaw cart. He agreed to take me a few kilometres north, to the location of the zoo. It was a short walk from there to Pragati Maidan. I hopped onto the cart and sat by the vegetables. When we reached the top of the flyover the vendor just stopped. If he hadn't, I would have asked him to.

The sky had changed. Delhi was burning.

It looked as if snakes were holding up the sky. That was my first impression of the numerous columns of smoke we saw around us, near and far. Thin, urgent viper-twisters and lazy, fat pythons. Some bent further into the sky where a gust of wind had elbowed them in passing.

We mapped the location of the columns of smoke. Green Park, Masjid Moth, Greater Kailash, further south, further east across the Yamuna in east Delhi.

Not too far from us, by a tidy park in the Jangpura Extension locality, a mob chased down a young Sikh man, beat him as he shouted for help, and then set him on fire. The young man screamed as he ran for a few metres. Then he stilled.

We saw it from the flyover. The vendor let loose a string of expletives. He then looked around, as if to see if anyone had heard him. I was numb with horror. No stranger to displacement on account of politics and religion, and political strife and death from a childhood spent in the urban battlefield of early 1970s Calcutta, it broke something in me.

Work was called off that day, I discovered after the kindly vendor reached me to Pragati Maidan. My boss, usually a work-demon, generously drove me home to Hauz Khas.

Not far from where I lived was a gurdwara. It was set on fire. Sikhs were attacked and killed. In the clusters of apartment blocks where I had my tiny one-room home, we formed vigilante groups to prevent hate-filled hoodlums from entering the complex and harming Sikh families.

On 3 November, Delhi and India watched Indira's stately funeral cortège and images of her funeral with the country's leaders and several of the world's leaders gathered around the pyre—on 'colour TVs' that Indira had cleared with the arrival of colour broadcasting in 1982 before the Asian Games in Delhi.

In some ways, the games were proof of the organizational triumph of her elder son Rajiv, who left his job as a pilot with Indian Airlines to fill the vacuum left by her first political heir Sanjay. And now Rajiv stood, bereaved son by his dead mother; and as the new prime minister who qualified the mayhem of the anti-Sikh pogrom as the effect of a great tree falling.

Meanwhile, several thousand Sikhs, mostly men and boys, across Delhi and northern India would be butchered, maimed, burnt alive, and several women and girls raped. The stereotype of the hard-working, often-loud, garrulous, warm-hearted Sikh who lived and died by bonhomie and brotherhood was transformed by design almost overnight into the stereotype of an emotion-driven terrorist and killers of a prime minister, into people who had to collectively pay a blood price for that transgression.

A template of hate that Delhi, and the country it played puppeteer to, knew so well that it sometimes appeared it could be done blindfolded, was now updated:

If one of yours committed a crime in the eyes of another community, all of you were culpable. You would be dragged through the expedient conscience of the country, cursed and butchered with those of your kind, appreciable numbers chalked up as blood price before the masters decided enough rage had been leached from the system, and stepped in to control the chaos they had helped to germinate months or years earlier.

There would be ever newer partitions.

AFTERWORD

As much as it is about the darkness of those times, and the darkness that fell over Delhi, this book is about the darkness that enshrouded a family that were four. And then, quite suddenly, two.

Roma, Madan, Geeta, and Sanjay in the span of a few hours became just Roma and Madan.

It was second nature for me to trace Geeta and Sanjay's parents, to try and reach them, to try and talk to them. I found out where they live, and what they do; knew of their friends and professional and personal affiliations. I had phone numbers and emails with which to reach them. But I did not wish to intrude into their lives and their tragedy with a cold call. It would be better if someone who knew them first spoke to them of my purpose. I had heard that the journalist Usha Rai remained in touch with them, and also found out about a few other people who could reach the Chopras.

I took my dilemma to Rai, and told her that every instinct urged me to call them, even walk up to their door and announce my intent, but it would not be the right thing to do. I had found out that the couple was fiercely protective of their privacy, and how fiercely they guarded the memory of their children. Rai offered to reach Roma and Madan Chopra after hearing me out.

The mother has remained high-strung, the father more controlled, visibly more even-tempered, she told me by way of background. I had heard the same from others I spoke to. The deaths of their children broke Roma Chopra. Her husband, shattered but seemingly inured against every odd, carried on with the persona of an officer and a gentleman.

Rai dialled the number as I sat across from her in her comfortable living room in Gurugram. Roma Chopra took the call. For several minutes Rai explained on my behalf.

'No *way*,' I heard Roma Chopra's emphatic negation of anyone asking her to again revisit this greatest trauma and tragedy of their lives. 'And Madan won't talk, either.'

'I can understand,' Rai sombrely told me when she disconnected the call after some pleasantries and words of care. 'They want to put it behind them.'

My hope is for Roma and Madan Chopra to not see this book as disrespectful or intrusive, but as a memorialization of a time of tumult and fracture, and yet, a strangely resolute time, from a person of their children's generation who came of age in the same city that took Geeta and Sanjay away.

Roma and Madan Chopra know the story of Geeta and Sanjay better than anyone else. They have lived with it for a lifetime.

Somewhere along the way, their story and the story of their children became the story of Delhi, of India, of our times.

Of us all.

■

There remains an irony. The names of Geeta and Sanjay Chopra have largely faded for all except those who called them family and friend, and those of a generation from their time and place still living, and enshrined in educational and empowering institutions created in the memory of the children and lovingly nurtured by Roma and Madan Chopra and their family and friends. Awards for bravery instituted in 1978, one named after Sanjay—and awarded to boys—and the other named after Geeta and awarded to girls, preserve the memory of the siblings' truncated lives and sudden death.

Billa-Ranga, stumbling, bungling, and vicious, remain as symbols of criminality several decades into an uneasy afterlife.

That is the nature of evil. It remains long after hope lives and dies.

ACKNOWLEDGEMENTS

David Davidar, the publisher of Aleph and I discussed aspects of *Fallen City* back in pre-Covid days—a lifetime ago considering the mayhem that infection and its mismanagement wreaked on so many lives. I had just finished fieldwork and several months of archival research for this book when 'lockdown' was imposed upon Delhi and India. It is good to have survived that state of limbo. And it is good to have resumed work with David and Aleph's publishing director, Aienla Ozukum, my partners in the progress of three previous books with Aleph.

Fallen City would also not have happened without Aslam Qadar Khan, a friend since our schooldays. Aslam opened his home to me for four months over the winter of 2019 and early 2020. His generosity enabled me to take up residence in Delhi—a city that I once called home for nearly twenty-five years—and relive the 1970s and 1980s in a most visceral manner.

Uttam Kumar Sinha enabled a membership at the Nehru Memorial Museum and Library.

My thanks to the team at this remarkable library, especially the ladies and gentlemen who supervised digital archives and who were there whenever I requested their help. They offered priceless advice as to how I could maximize my time at the library.

Usha Rai and Prakash Patra shared their memories of the times contained in this book's arc.

Dr Ambarish Satwik shared his medical expertise.

Dr Sanjeev Jain shared his mind map of Delhi alongside numerous cups of fine tea.

I stand on the shoulders of those who first chronicled so many of the events in the book, and recorded those fraught times. Especially, Rai and her colleagues like Prabha Dutt who resolutely pushed the enabling boundaries of journalistic practice. Sunil Sethi's deft sense of 'colour' adds to this book's palette. They and others are all acknowledged through the book and in the bibliography.

There are several books that I considered to be required reading to absorb various facets from history and politics to crime and ecology to be able to recreate an overall Delhiverse, as it were. Some of them did not contribute directly to this book as source material, but I acknowledge them in the bibliography for their equally welcome contribution in helping to broaden my knowledge and understanding in so many ways.

And here's to an indestructible pair of brown suede shoes I purchased for seven hundred rupees in the congested, charming and friendly by-lanes of Taj Ganj in Agra. These helped me to go walkabout in that city and several hundred kilometres in wintry, smoggy Delhi to rekindle sense-memories, and to retrace the geography of the death and afterlife of Geeta and Sanjay Chopra, and the criminal and judicial travels of their convicted killers.

Dhaka / Goa
June 2024

BIBLIOGRAPHY

BOOKS

Alexander, Michael (ed.), *Delhi & Agra: A Traveller's Reader*, London: Constable & Robinson, 1987.

Ali, Ahmed, *Twilight in Delhi* (with an introduction by the author), New Delhi: Rupa Publications India Pvt. Ltd, 2007 (first published London: Hogarth Press, 1940).

Chakravarti, Sudeep, *The Avenue of Kings*, New Delhi: HarperCollins India, 2010.

——— *Tin Fish*, New Delhi: Penguin Books India, 2005; (republished) New Delhi: HarperCollins India, 2011.

Choudhury, Sunetra, *Behind Bars: Prison Tales of India's Most Famous*, New Delhi: The Lotus Collection (an imprint of Roli Books), 2017.

Dalrymple, William, *The Last Mughal: The Fall of a Dynasty, Delhi, 1857*, New Delhi: Penguin Random House India, 2006, 2013.

Dhondy, Farrukh, *The Bikini Murders*, Noida: HarperCollins Publishers India, 2008.

Farooqi, Mahmood [compiled and translated by], *Besieged: Voices from Delhi 1857*, New Delhi: Viking (Penguin Books India), 2010.

Gupta, Sunil, Choudhury, Sunetra, *Black Warrant: Confessions of a Tihar Jailer*, New Delhi: The Lotus Collection (an imprint of Roli Books Pvt Ltd), 2019.

Jain, Sanjeev, Sarin, Alok (Eds.), *The Psychological Impact of the Partition of India*, New Delhi, SAGE Publications India Pvt. Ltd, 2018.

Kapoor, Coomi, *The Emergency: A Personal History*, Gurgaon: Penguin Random House India, 2015.

Krishen, Pradip, *Trees of Delhi: A Field Guide*, New Delhi: Dorling Kindersley (India) Pvt. Ltd, 2006.

Liddle, Swapna, *Connaught Place and the Making of New Delhi*, New Delhi: Speaking Tiger Publishing, 2018.

Mehta, Vinod, *The Sanjay Story*, Mumbai: Jaico Publishing House, 1978; Noida: HarperCollins Publishers India, 2012.

Mitta, Manoj and Phoolka, H. S., *When a Tree Shook Delhi: The 1984 Carnage and its Aftermath*, New Delhi: The Lotus Collection (an imprint of Roli Books Pvt. Ltd), 2007.

Pereira, Maxwell, *The Tandoor Murder: The Crime that Shook the Nation and Brought a Government to its Knees*, Chennai: Context (an imprint of Westland Publications Private Limited), 2018.

Safvi, Rana, *The Forgotten Cities of Delhi*, Noida: HarperCollins Publishers India, 2018.

Sen, Avirook, *Aarushi*, Gurgaon: Penguin Books India, 2015.

Singh, Khushwant, *Delhi*, New Delhi: Penguin Books India, 1990.

Singh, Malavika, *Perpetual City: A Short Biography of Delhi*, New Delhi: Aleph Book Company, 2013.

Smith, Ronald Vivian, *Delhi: Unknown Tales of a City* (a collection of columns in *The Statesman* and *The Hindu*), New Delhi: The Lotus Collection, an imprint of Roli Books, 2015.

——— *Lingering Charm of Delhi: Myth, Lore and History*, New Delhi: Niyogi Books, 2016 (reprint 2018).

Spear, Percival, *Delhi: Its Monuments and History*, (Third edition, updated and annotated by Gupta, Narayani and Sykes, Laura), New Delhi: Oxford University Press, 2008.

Tully, Mark and Jacob, Satish, *Amritsar: Mrs Gandhi's Last Battle*, New Delhi: Rupa Publications India Pvt. Ltd, 1985, 2011.

ARTICLES, ESSAYS, & OTHER SOURCES

'A close look at Billa connection', Express News Service, *Sunday Standard*, New Delhi, 3 September 1978.

'A reminder of Noah's times', Express News Service, *Indian Express*, New Delhi, 6 September 1978.

Anand, Jatin, 'Ranga-Billa redux: How rapists were sent to gallows', *Hindustan Times*, New Delhi, 9 January 2013.

'Anti-RSS memo presented to PM', Express News Service, *Indian Express*, New Delhi, 4 September 1978.

'Army moves into riot-hit Delhi', Hindustan Times Correspondent, *Hindustan Times*, New Delhi, 1 November 1984.

'A stranger in the street', Hindustan Times Correspondent, *Hindustan Times*, New Delhi, 1 September 1978.

Ashraf, Ajaz, 'First person: The story behind how Sanjay Gandhi slapped Indira six times at a dinner party,' *Scroll.in*, 26 June 2015.

Auerbach, Stuart, 'Sanjay Gandhi is Cremated in Ancient Hindu Rites,' *Washington Post*, 25 June 1980.

Badhwar, Inderjit, 'Pitts S-2A aircraft is considered to be among the most sturdy, aerobatic biplane', *India Today*, 15 July 1980.

Baviskar, Amita, 'What the Eye Does Not See: The Yamuna in the Imagination of Delhi', *Economic and Political Weekly*, Vol. 46, No. 50 (December 10, 2011), pp. 45–53. (Accessed 23 June 2019)

'Better ties India's aim, PM tells Zia', Hindustan Times Correspondent, *Hindustan Times*, New Delhi, 2 September 1978.

Bhatia, Ravi, 'The "legitimate" claimant of reward', *Indian Express*, New Delhi, 12 September 1978.

'Billa and Ranga arrested', Express News Service, *Sunday Standard*, New Delhi, 10 September 1978.

'Billa and Ranga given death sentences; plea for life term rejected', Express News Service, *Sunday Standard*, New Delhi, 8 April 1979.

'Billa finger-prints on car confirmed', Express News Service, *Indian Express*, New Delhi, 5 September 1978.

'Billa given 14-day judicial remand', Express News Service, *Indian Express*, New Delhi, 24 September 1978.

'Billa got sword for "butcher" shop', Express News Service, *Indian Express*, New Delhi, 17 September 1978.

'Billa's hand in murder confirmed', Express News Service, *Indian Express*, New Delhi, 7 September 1978.

'Billa may have wanted ransom', Express News Service, *Indian Express*, 1 New Delhi, September 1978.

'Billa offers to make a confession', Express News Service, *Indian Express*, New Delhi, 18 October 1978.

'Billa, Ranga had hired room in Majlis Park', United News of India, New Delhi, 8 September 1978.

'Billa, Ranga taken around crime spot', Express News Service, *Indian Express*, New Delhi, 11 September 1978.

'Billa remand extended till September 23', Express News Service, *Indian Express*, New Delhi, 20 September 1978.

'Billa wanted to settle down in Anand Parbat', United News of India, New

Delhi, 9 September 1978.

Bindusar, 'Delhi', *Indian Literature*, Vol. 17, No. 1/2 (January-June 1974), pp. 95–103, Sahitya Akademi. (Accessed 2 May 2019)

'Bhindranwale and his gangs were not religious men, and they are not martyrs', Editor's Note, *India Today*, 15 December 1984.

Bobb, Dilip, 'Geeta and Sanjay Chopra murder case takes a dramatic twist', *India Today*, 15 October 1978.

Bobb, Dilip, Raina, Ashok, 'Geeta and Sanjay Chopra murder case: Killers Ranga and Billa arrested', *India Today*, 30 September 1978.

——— 'Charles Sobhraj: "One of the most accomplished murderers in the annals of modern crime"', *India Today*, 15 October 1978.

Breese, Gerald, 'Delhi-New Delhi: Capital for conquerors and country,' *Ekistics*, Vol. 39, No. 232, March 1975), pp. 181–84. (Accessed 23 June 2019)

Brown, Carolyn Henning, 'The Forced Sterilization Program Under the Indian Emergency: Results in One Settlement,' *Human Organization*, Vol. 43, No. 1 (Spring 1984), pp. 49-54, Society for Applied Anthropology. (Accessed 28 July 2019)

'Charles Sobhraj v The Superintendent, Central Jail, Tihar, New Delhi, Supreme Court of India (Date of judgement: 7 April 1978; Date of document: 31 August 1978).

Chawla, Prabhu, 'Crime Clock', *India Today*, 30 September 1978.

——— 'Reconstruction: Tryst with destiny', *India Today*, 30 September 1978.

'Children's murder shocks MPs', United News of India, New Delhi, 29 August 1978.

'Chopra friend rules out vendetta', Express News Service, *Indian Express*, New Delhi, 1 September 1978.

Chopra, Surabhi, 'Archives of Violence: Seeking and Preserving Records on Mass Sectarian Attacks in India', *National Law School of India Review*, Vol. 28, No. 1 (2016), pp. 61–73, Student Advocate Committee. (Accessed 23 June 2019)

'College girl escapes abduction bid', Express News Service, *Indian Express*, New Delhi, 1 September 1978.

'College mates wait in vain', Hindustan Times Correspondent, *Hindustan Times*, New Delhi, 30 August 1978.

'Delhi burns as mobs rule streets', Hindustan Times Correspondent, *Hindustan*

Times, New Delhi, 2 November 1984.

'Delhi development since 1957', Delhi Development Authority special feature, *Indian Express*, 5 September 1978.

'Delhi flood situation grave: Four Jamuna bridges closed', Express News Service, *Indian Express*, New Delhi, 5 September 1978.

'Delhi murders that remain unsolved', Express News Service, *Sunday Standard*, New Delhi, 3 September 1978.

Deshmukh, Rajguru, 'Billa: The stars in his eyes', *Sunday Standard*, New Delhi, 1 October 1978.

'Detectives question estate agents', Express News Service, *Indian Express*, New Delhi, 6 September 1978.

'Doctor's not sure either way', Express News Service, *Indian Express*, New Delhi, 5 September 1978.

'Double murder culprits are still at large', Hindustan Times Correspondent, *Hindustan Times*, New Delhi, 31 August 1978.

Dutt, Prabha, 'A pair of hands waving, then vanishing', *Hindustan Times*, New Delhi, 31 August 1978.

'Ex-Navy officer interrogated', Express News Service, *Indian Express*, New Delhi, 5 September 1978.

'Fresh carnage in Delhi pockets', Hindustan Times Correspondent, *Hindustan Times*, New Delhi, 3 November 1984.

'Fresh clashes in Hyderabad', Press Trust of India/ United News of India, Hyderabad, 3 September 1978.

'Gallantry award for Sanjay Chopra', United News of India, New Delhi, 10 September 1978.

Ghosh, Arun, 'Delhi, the imperial city', *Economic and Political Weekly*, 12 August, 1989.

Gill, Raj, 'Callous cops give a rude shock', Delhi Affairs, *Hindustan Times*, New Delhi, 4 September 1978.

'Girls join in protest', Hindustan Times Correspondent, *Hindustan Times*, New Delhi, 1 September 1978.

'Grandmother of Chopra kids dead', Express News Service, Chandigarh, *Indian Express*, New Delhi, 9 September 1978.

Gupta, Shekhar; Kapoor, Coomi; Santhanam, Raju; Sethi, Sunil, 'Indira Gandhi's assassination triggers off unprecedented backlash of violence', *India Today*, 30 November 1984.

‘Hitch-hiking among college girls decreases’, Express News Service, *Indian Express*, New Delhi, 1 September 1978.

‘Hunt for a crucial witness’, Hindustan Times Correspondent, *Hindustan Times*, New Delhi, 31 August 1978.

Illustrated Weekly of India, Issues dated 5-12 November 1978; 12-19 November 1978; 19-26 November 1978; 10-17 December 1978.

‘Jamuna may cross red mark’, Express News Service, *Indian Express*, New Delhi, 2 September 1978.

Jategaonkar, Arun Vinayak, and Jategaonkar, Vasaisti Arun, ‘Did Duḥśāsana Ever Drag Draupadī to the Assembly Hall?’, *Annals of the Bhandarkar Oriental Research Institute*, Vol. 92 (2011), pp. 103–22, Bhandarkar Oriental Research Institute. (Accessed 28 July 2019)

Jerath, Arati R., ‘The Parents: Shattered dreams’, *India Today*, 30 September 1978.

Joshi, Chand, ‘Death, death and death’, *Hindustan Times*, 3 November 1984.

‘JP’s message to Vajpayee, Chopra’, Express News Service, Patna, *Indian Express*, New Delhi, 2 September 1978.

‘Justice Nanavati Commission of Inquiry (1984 Anti-Sikh Riots) Report’, Vol. 1.

Kalbag, Chaitanya, ‘Ranga-Billa case: Supreme Court mysteriously flip-flops’, *India Today*, 15 February 1982.

Kamath, M. V., ‘Is it Time for a Third Party?’, *Illutsrtated Weekly of India*, Issue dated 5-12 November 1978.

Khansili, Garima, ‘Palaeolithic locality near Delhi (Gurgaon, NCR): Preliminary observations’, *Bulletin of the Deccan College Research Institute*, Vol. 74, Deccan College Post-Graduate Research Institute (Deemed University), Pune, 2014.

‘Kanti will shift to Bombay’, Press Trust of India, New Delhi, 3 September 1978.

Karlekar, Hiranmay, ‘In Shock and Anger’, *Hindustan Times*, New Delhi, 30 August 1978.

‘Kidnap car found in Adarsh Nagar’, Express News Service, *Indian Express*, New Delhi, 1 September 1978.

‘“Killers” car found in North Delhi’, Hindustan Times Correspondent, *Hindustan Times*, 1 September 1978.

‘Kuljeet Singh @ Ranga vs Union Of India & Anr’, Supreme Court of India, Date of Judgement 21 April 1981, indiankanoon.org. (Accessed 20 August 2019)

‘Kuljit Singh alias Ranga Vs Lt. Governor Of Delhi & Ors.’, Supreme Court of

India, Date of Judgment 20/01/1982, http://judis.nic.in. (Accessed 20 August 2019)

Lahiri, Nayanjot, 'Commemorating and Remembering 1857: The Revolt in Delhi and Its Afterlife', *World Archaeology*, Vol. 35, No. 1, The Social Commemoration of Warfare (Jun., 2003), pp. 35-60, Taylor & Francis, Ltd. (Accessed 23 June 2019)

Lakhani, Somya, 'The legacy of Firoz Shah, 14th-century ruler who built Kotla in Delhi', *Indian Express*, New Delhi, 2 September 2019.

'Lok Sabha stunned', Press Trust of India, 1 September 1978.

'Majlis Park house of Billa, Ranga searched', Express News Service, *Indian Express*, New Delhi, 12 September 1978.

'Making the police accountable', Letters, *Indian Express*, New Delhi, 4 September 1978.

'Many Billas but not the one police want,' Express News Service, *Indian Express*, New Delhi, 8 September 1978.

'Missing boy, girl found murdered on Upper Ridge,' Hindustan Times Correspondent, *Hindustan Times*, New Delhi, 30 August 1978.

Nath, V., 'Planning for Delhi', *GeoJournal*, Vol. 29, No. 2, Urban Issues and Urbanization Characteristics of Asia (February 1993), pp. 171–80, Springer. (Accessed 2 May 2019)

'Negligent policemen will be punished: PM', Hindustan Times Correspondent, *Hindustan Times*, New Delhi, 31 August 1978.

'No consolation for Chopra', Express New Service, Chandigarh, *Sunday Standard*, New Delhi, 10 September 1978.

'No cremations at Nigambodh Ghat', Express News Service, *Indian Express*, New Delhi, 6 September 1978.

Noorani, A. G., 'The State as Law-Breaker', *Economic and Political Weekly*, Vol. 20, No. 9 (Mar. 2, 1985), p. 340. (Accessed 23 June 2019)

'Orgy reminiscent of Partition days', Hindustan Times Correspondent, *Hindustan Times*, New Delhi, 4 November 1984.

Pandey, Gyanendra, 'Partition and Independence in Delhi: 1947-48', *Economic and Political Weekly*, Vol. 32, No. 36 (Sep. 6-12, 1997), pp. 2261–72. (Accessed 23 June 2019)

'Parents are dazed', Hindustan Times Correspondent, *Hindustan Times*, New Delhi, 30 August 1978.

'Parhé ruh kanpā déné wāli murder mystery kā sach, jisné karōrō lōgōn ké

urāyé thé hōsh,' *Dainik Jagran*, 29 August 2018.
Patra, Prakash, 'With Billa, hours before the hanging', *The Telegraph*, 9 March 2015.
'PM renews invitation to Zia at Nairobi', Express News Service, *Indian Express*, New Delhi, 2 September 1978.
'PM surveys flood-hit areas', Express News Service, *Indian Express*, New Delhi, 6 September 1978.
'PM to attend Kenyatta's funeral', Press Trust of India, New Delhi, 29 August 1978.
'Police are not so optimistic', Express News Service, *Sunday Standard*, New Delhi, 3 September 1978.
'Police baulk at naming Billa murderer', Hindustan Times Correspondent, *Hindustan Times*, New Delhi, 3 September 1978.
'Police get definite clue to identity of Chopra children's murderers', Express News Service, *Indian Express*, New Delhi, 2 September 1978.
'Police whistle in the dark for killers', Hindustan Times Correspondent, *Hindustan Times*, New Delhi, 4 September 1978.
'Posh Delhi colonies in North deluged', Express News Service, *Indian Express*, New Delhi, 6 September 1978.
'Prabha Dutt vs Union Of India & Ors', Supreme Court of India, Date of Judgement 7 November 1981, *indiankanoon.org.* (Accessed 25 August 2019)
'Rains, floods affect movement of trains', Express News Service, *Indian Express*, New Delhi, 6 September 1978.
'Rajya Sabha pays silent homage to brave kids', Hindustan Times Correspondent, *Hindustan Times*, New Delhi, 31 August 1978.
'Ranga held in Ludhiana, being brought [to Delhi]', United News of India, Ludhiana, 6 September 1978.
'Ranga makes 83-page statement in camera', Express News Service, *Indian Express*, New Delhi, 22 September 1978.
'Ranga's version of children's murder', Express News Service, *Indian Express*, New Delhi, 26 September 1978.
'Ranga to be produced in court today', Express News Service, *Indian Express*, New Delhi, 3 October 1978.
Roy, Radhika, 'Indira Gandhi had died by the time she reached AIIMS', *India Today*, 30 November 1984.
'Regularisation of unauthorised colonies', Delhi Development Authority special

feature, *Indian Express*, New Delhi, 5 September 1978.

'Reluctant sepoys' account', Express News Service, *Sunday Standard*, New Delhi, 10 September 1978.

'Revamping of police force demanded', Hindustan Times Correspondent, *Hindustan Times*, New Delhi, 2 September 1978.

'Rs 20,000 for killers' arrest', Hindustan Times Correspondent, *Hindustan Times Weekly*, 3 September 1978.

'Rs 5000 reward for arrest of Billa', Express News Service, *Indian Express*, Bombay, 2 September 1978.

Santhanam, Raju, 'Beant told me if I lose my guts he will fire at me: Satwant Singh', *India Today*, 15 December 1984.

'Saved from being lynched', Express News Service, *Sunday Standard*, New Delhi, 10 September 1978.

'Scathing attack on police by leaders', Express News Service, *Sunday Standard*, New Delhi, 3 September 1978.

'Schoolboy missing since September 1', Express News Service, *Indian Express*, New Delhi, 5 September 1978.

Sen, Anikendra Nath, 'Delhi's "Keystone Cops"', *Illustrated Weekly of India*, 19-26 November, 1978.

Sen, Vikramajit, 'Law: Life or death?', *India Today*, 30 September 1978.

Sethi, Sunil, 'Sanjay Gandhi dies in a dramatic plane crash, his passing to leave a political vacuum', *India Today*, 15 July 1980.

———'Tihar Jail: A dangerous underworld of lethal weapons, violence, homosexual assault, drug addiction', *India Today*, 31 May 1980.

Sethi, Sunil; Purie, Mandira, 'I have never stood for any forcible sterilisations: Sanjay Gandhi', *India Today*, 15 April 1977.

Shafi, Syed S., 'Delhi: Many Windows in Time and Space', *India International Centre Quarterly*, Vol. 29, No. 1 (Summer 2002), pp. 127–35, India International Centre. (Accessed 2 May 2019)

Sharma, Anupam, 'Police in Ancient India', *Indian Journal of Political Science*, Vol. 65, No. 1 (Jan.-March, 2004), pp. 101- 110, Indian Political Science Association. (Accessed: 28 July 2019)

Sharp, Henry, 'Delhi: A Story in Stone', *Journal of the Royal Society of Arts*, Vol. 86, No. 4448 (18 February 1938), pp. 318–33, Royal Society for the Encouragement of Arts, Manufactures and Commerce Stable. (Accessed: 23 June 2019)

'Shocked Lok Sabha condemns attack', Express News Service, *Indian Express*, New Delhi, 1 September 1978.

Singh, Patwant, 'The Ninth Delhi', *Journal of the Royal Society of Arts*, Vol. 119, No. 5179 (June 1971), pp. 461–75, Royal Society for the Encouragement of Arts, Manufactures and Commerce Stable. (Accessed 23 June 2019)

Singh, S. P., 'Hanging is the blood', *The Pioneer*, New Delhi, 6 September 2014.

'Solemn farewell at Shantivana', Hindustan Times Correspondent, *Hindustan Times Weekly*, New Delhi, 4 November 1984.

'Spate of rallies by students', Express News Service, *Indian Express*, New Delhi, 1 September 1978.

'Special Shah report on family planning', Express News Service, *Indian Express*, New Delhi, 2 September 1978.

'State vs Jasbir Singh @ Billa and Kuljeet Singh @ Ranga', Delhi High Court, Date of Judgement 16 November 1979, indiankanoon.org. (Accessed 30 July 2019)

'States toll now 500', Press Trust of India, New Delhi, 2 November 1984.

'Summit begins with appeal for peace,' Associated Press, Camp David, 7 September 1978.

'Text of Nagarwala's confessional statement,' United News of India, New Delhi, 27 August 1978.

'The hide and seek before the remand,' Express News Service, *Sunday Standard*, New Delhi, 10 September 1978.

'The many faces of Billa', Hindustan Times Correspondent, Chandigarh, *Hindustan Times*, New Delhi, 1 September 1978.

'Threat to Calcutta, Delhi rail link', Express News Service, *Indian Express*, New Delhi, 9 September 1978.

'Troops evacuating Delhi villagers: Unprecedented flood threat as wave hurtles down Jamuna', Express News Service, *Indian Express*, New Delhi, 4 September 1978.

'Unanswered questions about kidnap car', Express News Service, *Indian Express*, New Delhi, 2 September 1978.

'Vajpayee admitted to AIIMS', Press Trust of India, New Delhi, 2 September 1978.

'Vajpayee hurt in stoning', Hindustan Times Correspondent, *Hindustan Times*, 1 September 1978.

'Vajpayee injured in stoning at rally', Express News Service, *Indian Express*, New Delhi, 1 September 1978.

'Violence erupts in many states', Hindustan Times Correspondent, *Hindustan Times*, 1 November 1984.

'Was Billa really behind murders?' Hindustan Times Correspondent, *Hindustan Times*, New Delhi, 2 September 1978.

'When they thought of blowing up bridge', Express News Service, *Indian Express*, New Delhi, 8 September 1978.

'25 Delhi villages, Jehangirpuri, face submersion,' Hindustan Times Correspondent, *Hindustan Times*, 4 September 1978.

'3 frequencies go off the air', Express News Service, *Indian Express*, New Delhi, 6 September 1978.

'100 killed in Teheran clashes, martial law imposed on 12 cities', Mohan, R., Teheran, *Indian Express*, New Delhi, 9 September 1978.

RESOURCES

Archaeological Survey of India, Delhi Circle
Asian Human Rights Commission (*humanrights.asia*)
Digital Library of India (*dli.ernet.in*)
Economic and Political Weekly
Encyclopaedia Britannica (& *britannica.com*)
Google Earth (*google.com/earth*)
Hindustan
Hindustan Times
Illustrated Weekly of India
India Today
Indian Express
indiankanoon.org
Jansatta
JSTOR (*jstor.org*)
National Herald
Project Gutenberg (*gutenberg.org*)
The Nehru Memorial Museum & Library, New Delhi
The Statesman
Times of India

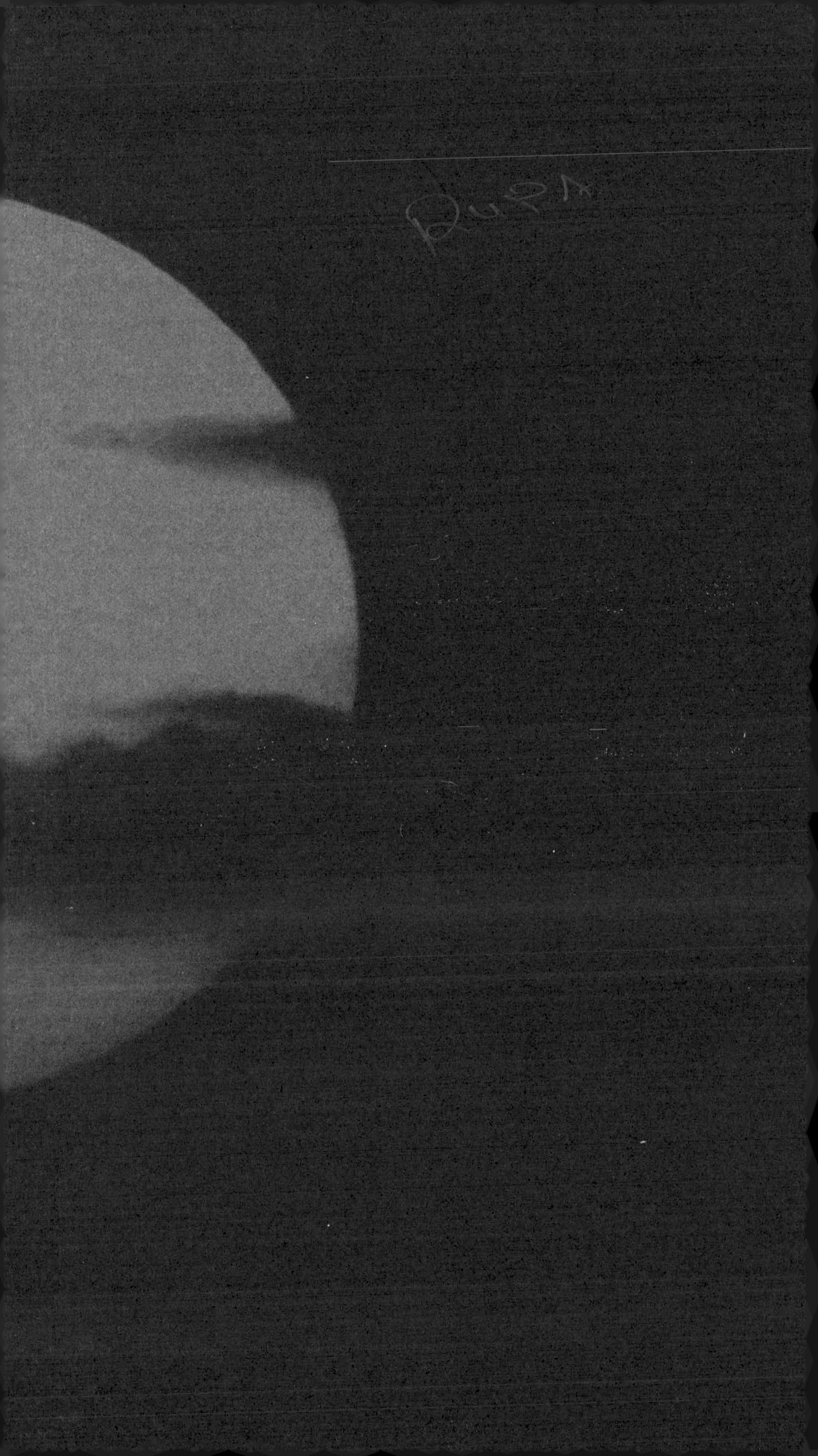